MARY-MARGARET
and the CASE of the
unfaithful
mechanic

MARY-MARGARET and the CASE of the UNFAITHFUL MECHANIC

A Pint of Trouble Mystery

DESMOND P. RYAN

To those who ask the right questions, trust their instincts, and never underestimate the power of a good cuppa (or a wee dram of whiskey).

Chapter One

"I'm off then, luv," Mary-Margaret O'Shea called up the stairs.

There was no response.

"Michael!" she hollered, with a hint of exasperation that only a mother could muster.

Still, there was no response.

Mary-Margaret noticed his black brogues by the front door—both tips gleaming—and the coat hanging on the hook, further confirming he was home. She glanced down at her own sensible shoes, then over at the faded floral runner on the stairs, which had clearly seen better days.

"'Tis ye who is not answerin', so 'tis ye who can clean up whatever mess shall follow," she said to herself as she climbed the stairs to the second floor of her son's three-storey Victorian house. With less care than usual, she proceeded to his closed bedroom door.

"Michael," she said softly yet pointedly as she pushed the door open. "I'm off to the church for the mornin'."

"Mmmph."

"Did ye hear me, me son?"

"Uhhh."

"Michael, I. Am. Off."

"I heard you, Mom," he responded, opening his eyes slightly.

"Well, ye could have saved us all a moment in time by respondin' accordingly."

"I was sleeping, Mom."

"So I see. Ye are not the only detective in this house, ye know."

"And I'd like to go back to sleep."

"Fine. Don't worry about me. I'll be at the church."

"Great."

"And Max is away to school."

"Uh-huh."

"And there's a pot of rollies on the stove for ye when ye get up," she added.

"Mmmph."

"Were ye working nights, lad?"

"Mmmm-mmmm. Evenings. Overtime."

"And no court this mornin'?"

"Uh-uh."

"Well, ye'd best be gettin' some sleep, then," Mary-Margaret said, turning back down the hallway as Wee Phil, Mary-next-door's Jack Russell, tore down the hall and bounced onto Michael's bed with the enthusiasm of a three-year-old entering a candy store.

"Jesus!" Mike called out.

"No, luv, 'tis only Wee Phil, but I'll be sure to put a word in for ye. Ye know, of course, it wouldn't hurt ye to darken the doors of St. Francis…"

She kept talking as she went down the stairs and out the front door.

* * *

While St. Francis of Assisi's, her parish church, was just around the corner from her own house, Mary-Margaret took public transit across the city from Michael's house to get there. She didn't mind. It was just one streetcar. And, since she was now retired as the church secretary, she didn't need to arrive exactly at 8:45 am every day to start her day at 9. And it was a lovely ride, especially when she didn't have to be squished in with the rush-hour rabble.

Not that it was her plan to retire and move in with Michael. Far from it. In fact, moving in with him had, if she was going to be honest, cramped her style. She had to drop one of her book clubs, and she couldn't remember the last time she had been to yoga. But duty called. Her son's life was going to hell in a handbasket after his second wife left him, and while she wasn't sure she could help him, Mary-Margaret knew she had to be the Voice of Reason for Max, her teenaged grandson. And the longer she stayed, the more she recognised that this, for now at least, was where she was meant to be–not because it suited her, but because it was required.

The only real fly in the ointment had been caring for Wee Phil, who wasn't her dog. He was Sally-next-door's dog. As the name would suggest, Sally-next-door lived next door to Mary-Margaret's own house. A flight attendant and a single woman, Sally-next-door often found herself laying over in another country for days on end and had mentioned to her neighbour a few years back that she might have to give her new pup up. Of course, Mary-Margaret immediately stepped in, but when Michael's life fell into the trash bin, there was a problem. And, to every problem, there is a solution, and this one was obvious: Wee Phil would come with her to Michael's for the duration. Aside from the commitment she'd made to Sally-next-door, Mary-Margaret's reasoning was that all boys, especially her grandson, should have a dog. Luckily for everyone, except Michael, Wee Phil's rightful owner had readily agreed.

And then there was another matter: where to park Michael's truck when she arrived with Daphne, her 1964 eggshell-blue Renault Dauphine. Naturally, Daphne would have to be parked in the space behind Michael's house. A car of such vintage couldn't possibly be left on the street.

Being forever resourceful, Mary-Margaret resolved the issue by applying for a city permit allowing him to park on the street in front of the house— provided he could find a space. When the permit arrived in the mail a week later, she even offered to affix it to his windshield as per the instructions, but Michael begrudgingly did that himself.

Given that she had a car at her disposal, more than a few people had asked Mary-Margaret why she took the streetcar from one end of the city to St. Francis' at the other, to which Mary-Margaret's stock response was that it was none of their business. If pressed, usually by Michael or Father Miguel— the latter of whom was also quick to suggest that she need not attend the church as often as she did—Mary-Margaret was quick to point out that travelling on public transit gave her that common touch. Curiously, as different as the two men were, they both uttered the same groan in response to her reasoning.

After an uneventful ride on this particular morning, Mary-Margaret got off at her stop, but not before giving the young driver a flirtatious wink.

One of the joys of maturing, she thought with a smile, thinking that she would never have been so bold in her younger days. And, even if she had been, her husband Jimmy, God rest his soul, would have been fit to be tied, had he been alive. *Yes*, she thought, turning back to wave as the streetcar lumbered away, *there are some advantages to aging.*

***

"And who might ye be?" Mary-Margaret said, stopping in her tracks as she stepped into the church office.

"Lola," the young woman replied, popping the gum in her mouth. "The new girl."

Mary-Margaret's brow furrowed. "What happened to Ashleigh? I thought she was the New Girl."

"She was, but now she's on mat leave…" Lola replied indifferently.

"I knew she was expecting, but—"

"Yeah. I dunno. Complications," Lola said, blowing a bubble with the gum.

"Well, this is news to me!"

"Uh-huh," Lola said, returning to her computer screen.

"Did Father Miguel call ye in?"

"The main guy? Yeah. I guess it was him. Got a call from the agency this morning—"

"Agency? You mean you're not even a member of the church?"

"No," she laughed. "I'm a Methodist."

"Jesus, Mary, and Joseph," Mary-Margaret gasped, her hand covering her mouth as she hurried down the hall to Father Miguel's office, coming as close to running as she could manage.

"Father," Mary-Margaret said, disregarding the closed door as she burst in.

"Mary-Margaret," the young priest said with a sigh, glancing apologetically across his desk at the woman who was seated before him.

"Father," she almost pleaded, "ye know I'm but a phone call away."

"I do."

"And that I'm more than able—" Mary-Margaret began, but stopped when the woman seated before the priest turned to face her. "I'm sorry. I see that yer in a meetin'. Perhaps I can wait outside, and we can have a word when yer done."

"That won't be necessary," Father Miguel said, his voice steady.

"Ach. Good. Yer done then. In which case—"

"No," Father Miguel said, taking a deep breath and letting it slowly out. "*We're* done. The woman the agency sent over is fine and will be with us until Ashleigh returns from her maternity leave. Now, if you'll excuse us, we have a funeral to plan."

"My deepest condolences, luv," Mary-Margaret said, finally noticing the puffy red eyes of the middle-aged woman looking back at her. "I'm a widow meself, and I know—"

"Thank you, Mary-Margaret," Father Miguel said in a tone that signaled the conversation was over. "I'm sure we'll see you at the funeral mass, and you can extend your condolences then."

Mary-Margaret looked at the woman and then at Father Miguel before stepping back and beginning to close the door.

"Wait," the woman said. "Are you Mary-Margaret O'Shea?"

"I am," Mary-Margaret answered, wasting no time stepping back into the office.

"The woman who solved the murder...?"

"I hardly think," Father Miguel cut in, "that Mary-Margaret *solved* it."

"Indeed," Mary-Margaret replied to the woman, ignoring Father Miguel's comment.

"Can I speak to you? After...?" the new widow said, looking back at the priest.

"Annette," Father Miguel said patronizingly, "sadly—unspeakably so—your husband's death was an accident. The police have already told you—"

"Of course ye can, luv. I'll be waiting in me… I mean the new New Girl's off—"

"No," Father Miguel interrupted. "Ashleigh has left a lot of time-sensitive things for Lola to catch up on, and I don't want her—"

"Which is to say the old New Girl wasn't doin' her job, which we all knew she wasn't. Beyond her scope, I'm thinkin'. I should know—I did that job for thirty-five years. So, am I right, or am I right?" Mary-Margaret said smugly and then looked at her watch before turning her attention to Annette. "Ye look like ye could use a bite to eat. How about I meet ye at O'Leary's Pub just around the corner when yer done?"

"I don't know if I can eat, but—"

"Whether good times or bad, luv, we need to eat. I'll see you at O'Leary's."

Chapter Two

O'Leary's Pub had been a staple of the neighbourhood for as long as anyone could remember. John and Maureen O'Leary had the clever idea to open a pub on the main floor of their home, with their family occupying the upper floors, back when the neighbourhood was still largely made up of Irish immigrants. As the pub grew in popularity, a second kitchen was added upstairs, with the stairway behind the bar remaining the only access to the family's living quarters. Over the years, all of the O'Leary children worked in the pub, serving drinks and meals originally cooked by Maureen but later prepared by professional chefs.

After Maureen passed and John's knees gave out, the pub was handed down to his son, Johnny, who first took six months off to travel Ireland. He returned with Maeve, a feisty woman who helped him run the pub and was known to threaten to ban patrons for life if she felt they had slighted her or her family. John became known as Big John–so named not because of his size, but because he hated being called Old John and continued to work behind the bar for more hours than a man his age should, as well as pitch in to care for his grandson, Nolan.

And now, Mary-Margaret stood outside of O'Leary's, the morning sun never having fully appeared, and pulled on the door. It was locked. She looked at her watch and noticed that it was just going on 10:00. The sign on the door said they weren't open until 11:30.

Mary-Margaret rapped on the door.

No answer.

She reached into her purse and pulled out her keys and rapped again, this time using their metal.

Still no answer.

Mary-Margaret pounded on the door with her fists.

A light came on inside from behind the bar. Knowing the pub as she did, Mary-Margaret knew that meant someone was coming down from upstairs. She stood back and put on her brightest smile.

"Fancy seein' you in here at this hour of the day," Maeve O'Leary stated after unlocking the door and pushing it open a few inches, her unruly red hair still unpinned in a ponytail, her makeup not yet applied. "I'm not openin' for another—"

"I know," Mary-Margaret said apologetically. "I can see the sign here says that yer not—"

"So ye did see the sign. Well, that's somethin', isn't it?" Maeve said, crossing her arms across her chest. "And so…?"

"Well, you see, I need a favour…" Mary-Margaret persisted, coming as close to looking desperate as she felt she could while not giving in to the likes of Maeve O'Leary.

Maeve hesitated before poking her head out of the doorway and looking up and down the empty street. She considered a moment more before opening the door and quickly ushering Mary-Margaret inside.

"Just this once," she said, locking the door behind Mary-Margaret. "And don't ye be tellin' yer Michael—"

"As if I want me Michael knowing that I'm darkening the insides of a pub at ten o'clock in the morning!"

"Oh, aye. Ye've got a point. So, shall I pour ye yer usual, then?"

"A cuppa would do me," Mary-Margaret said. Maeve arched her eyebrows. "I'm here on business."

"What do ye mean?" Maeve said, her eyes narrowing.

"Oh, me own business. I've a lady coming by in a few minutes to—"

"I'm not runnin' a community centre, luv. And ye know as well as I that there's a coffee shop just down the way."

"—discuss murder," Mary-Margaret concluded.

"Ohhh," Maeve said with a slow nod. "I see."

"I can't be flappin' me gums just anywhere, as I'm sure ye can appreciate."

"Of course ye can't," Maeve replied, her tone softening as she recalled how Mary-Margaret had solved the murder of their barmaid—thieving gobshite that she was—just a few months back. "I've just got a kettle on in the kitchen upstairs for meself. Barry's okay?"

"Grand. And do ye happen to have a few McVitie's lying about up there as well?"

"Now yer really pushin' yer luck," Maeve said with a smirk. "Go on over to yer usual table, and I'll bring a cuppa and a plate. And yer friend? She'll have a cuppa as well?"

"Ach, I don't know about that, luv. Looks like a coffee drinker to me," Mary-Margaret said disapprovingly. "What time do ye plan on having yer kitchen open?"

"Ye don't ask fer much now, do ye?" Maeve said with a laugh.

"Well, it's only because I've had to coax the widow to come here to tell me about the—"

"Oooo, the widow. So her husband is the one who got murdered. This is gettin' juicy. I was goin' to spend the mornin' upstairs workin' on the books, but I think I'll bring me papers down and plop meself right over there," Maeve said, pointing to a table not too far from Mary-Margaret's.

"I'd prefer ye not," Mary-Margaret stated, all business now. "On account of this being confidential. At the moment."

Maeve cocked her head to one side.

"Ach, the groundwork of an investigation is too complex for me mind to be explainin' to ye at the moment, so perhaps, instead of overtly eavesdroppin', ye could make up a sandwich for us."

Maeve was about to respond in a manner that might have soured the entire interaction when the door to the pub slowly opened.

"Oh, I'm—" the woman said quietly.

"Come in, luv, come in," Mary-Margaret said, getting up from her seat.

"I saw the sign on the door, but then I saw you—"

"'Tis just a formality, is the sign. Come in. Maeve, the landlady here, was just goin' to get us some biscuits and tea. Or coffee. And make us a sandwich.

They do a lovely club here. I'll have half on brown with a wee pickle on the side, luv. And ye?"

"I'll just have a cup of coffee," she said. "If that's okay?"

"Fine by me," Maeve said with a huff, giving Mary-Margaret a dirty look before turning to head up the stairs to the second floor.

The two women stood facing one another for a moment.

"Ach, we've not properly met, have we?" she said, thrusting out her hand. "Mary-Margaret O'Shea."

"Annette," the woman said, timidly extending her hand. "Annette Giancola."

"Pleased to meet ye," Mary-Margaret said, grabbing the woman's hand in both of hers and holding it for a moment before sitting down. She motioned for Annette to sit as well. "'Tis a terrible spot ye've found yerself in, luv, but—take it from one who's been there—it does get better. Have ye any smallies?"

"Pardon?" Annette asked, lowering herself into the seat as though the slightest movement might send her shattering into pieces.

"Children. Ye know. Wee ones."

"Oh. Yes. Well, No. Well, three. But they're hardly—"

"'Tis them ye need to be puttin' yer mind to, then. I should know. I buried me grief until me children were—"

"—children. They're all in their twenties now," she said.

"Oh," Mary-Margaret exclaimed. She looked closely at Annette. "I just…ye look…I didn't think—"

"They're not mine," she clarified. "I'm Marco's second wife."

"Oh. I see," Mary-Margaret said with a knowing nod. "That makes a bit more sense."

"I've yer sandwich here," Maeve called from behind the bar. "And yer tea and coffee."

"And the biscuits?" Mary-Margaret called back.

Maeve didn't respond.

"Well, that's grand, then. And are ye—" Mary-Margaret began, noticing that Maeve was making no attempt to deliver them to the table.

"No," Maeve shot back. "Ye best come pick them up. As me sign on the door says, O'Leary's is closed until 11:30, so I'm not to be servin' ye. Against yer country's liquor laws, the likes of which are…too complex for me to explain to ye."

Annette Giancola looked from one woman to the other, her eyes as wide as those of a deer caught in the headlights of an oncoming truck.

"Never mind her, luv," Mary-Margaret said in a hushed tone, patting her hand. "Our Maeve gets like that every once in a while. She's from County Kerry. Not her fault."

Mary-Margaret took a deep breath as she got up to retrieve the food and drinks from the bar.

"I'll be just upstairs if ye need anythin'," Maeve said, heading up before Mary-Margaret could get to the bar. "Holler up when yer leavin' so's I can lock up behind yiz."

Mary-Margaret stuck her tongue out before turning back to face the new widow, tray of food and drinks in hand.

"Now," she said after getting everything organized and taking a sip of her tea. "Tell me what happened."

"They say my husband just died, but I think he was murdered," Annette Giancola said flatly.

"Why?"

"Because Marco could be a difficult man," Annette said, looking down at her coffee, "and I'm sure he stood in the way of a few people who wouldn't think twice about killing him."

"Difficult how?"

"I don't know how the police wouldn't have checked them out before closing the case," Annette continued, ignoring Mary-Margaret's question.""Depends on who's in charge of the investigation," Mary-Margaret said. "Ye don't happen to know the name of the detective, do ye?"

"Detective Sergeant Gill."

Mary-Margaret fought the urge to spit out her tea.

Chapter Three

Mary-Margaret barely recalled the streetcar ride back to Michael's, her mind replaying everything she'd just heard. It wasn't until she put the key in the lock and opened the front door that a shrill scream pierced the air, snapping her back to reality.

Instinctively, she jumped back and quickly pulled the door shut again. *Think, me girl, think.*

Before she could come up with a plan, Arthur Lukowitz casually opened the door she had just closed. He was the house cleaner who the agency had sent over a few years back when Mary-Margaret was dealing with gallstones, and Michael thought a bit of help around the house might be in order. The gallstones had passed, but Arthur had remained—not because he was any good at cleaning, but because Mary-Margaret had taken quite a liking to him. And, just like Sally-next-door's dog, Arthur had migrated with her to Michael's house.

"Oh, me stars!" Mary-Margaret said, her hand on her chest. "Was that ye screaming like a banshee?"

"Was that you trying to break in?"

"Ye gave me quite a start, lad."

"You almost made me wet my…never mind," Arthur replied, his shoulders slumping as he looked down at the very tight overalls he was wearing. "Given your age, I suppose I should be more concerned about you having been startled than my—"

"Given me *age*?" Mary-Margaret squawked, but, sensing something was off with her friend, let it go. Wee Phil shot down the stairs towards her.

"Has he been out to the jacks?"

"Many times," Arthur said as he followed them both into the kitchen. "You know, I think that dog's playing me. Either that, or he's got the bladder the size of a small…well, I suppose he does. Do you want a cup of tea?"

"Ye've read me mind, lad. And since when do ye come by on a Tuesday? No mind. Shall I bring out the biscuits?"

"Might as well," Arthur said, turning on the burner under the kettle. He let out a long sigh that Mary-Margaret knew all too well. "And I came by today because I wasn't here yesterday, which you obviously didn't notice."

He let out another long sigh.

"In fact," she said gently, "I did notice, luv, but didn't want to ask. What's got ye so in the dumps this time?"

"Ugh, I don't know," he began, pulling down a couple of mugs from the cupboard. "The usual, I guess."

"Still at that place ye rent by the week?" she asked as she got the box of biscuits.

"Yep."

"And have ye any more clients?"

"Nope."

"But yer still working at the church, aren't ye?" she asked, referring to the cleaning job she had managed to get him a while back at St. Francis of Assisi's through something just shy of trickery. "And still getting the five hundred a week for it, aren't ye?"

"Well, that's another thing…" he said with a huff.

"Oh?" she asked sharply, turning to face him.

"Yeah, well, it's not really…working out."

"Says who?"

"Father Miguel. He suggested I—"

"And Father Miguel knows what about what?" she almost spat, turning back to the counter to fill a plate with biscuits. "Honestly, if he would just mind his own altar… What did he say, luv?"

"He said," Arthur began, taking another big sigh, "that I wasn't a fit for the church, or the job. Mostly the job, to be fair."

"Meaning…?"

"I don't know. Maybe it was…I don't know."

"And ye didn't ask for clarification?" she asked, not looking at him as she pushed past to put the now-empty McVitie's box in the trash. "Remind me to pick up another box next time I'm out at the shops. In the meantime, a person—priest or otherwise—can't just go about making such statements for no reason, so what was he on about?"

"I honestly don't know, MM," Arthur replied, watching the steam rise from the kettle, the whistle just starting to sound.

"Does the New Girl have…and that's another thing: did ye know there was a *new* New Girl? Not even Catholic, so she tells me. And from an agency—one that Father Miguel likely engaged. So what does he know about anything, never mind mopping and dusting?"

"Well, it's not just mopping and dusting," Arthur replied, turning off the flame underneath the boiled kettle before cautiously removing it from the stove. "He seems to think that I'm a terrible cleaner in general."

"Well, I can't argue that," she said and then passed him the box of Barry's tea. "But he, of all people, should know that we can't be good at everything. And it's clear that yer a good soul, so that should count for something."

"Apparently not," Arthur said, making the tea.

"Come on, luv," his friend said softly. "Let's go into the living room and have it out over a cuppa."

Arthur looked towards the corner of the room.

"Ach, just leave it," she said, glancing at the pail of soapy water he was looking at. "No point trying to push through when yer heart isn't in it. And it's not like me Michael's going to notice if his kitchen's in a tip anyway."

Arthur followed her into the living room, where they both sat in one of the two wingback chairs by the front window. Wee Phil hopped onto Mary-Margaret's lap as soon as she sat down.

"Away with ye," Mary-Margaret directed, and, when the runty Jack Russell terrier showed no signs of moving, gently shoved him off of her. "And that'll be enough of that chatter about whether or not some muppet who thinks he should be Pope likes yer cleaning. The main thing is: ye've got a job that pays. Now, I've something to tell ye that might be of interest."

"I could use a distraction," Arthur said as he shoved a couple of the McVitie's biscuits into his mouth.

"Well, there I was at the church this morning…did I tell ye they've got a new New Girl? Yes. I did. Well, as anyone could imagine, I was incensed by the whole affair and marched meself down the hall to speak to Father Miguel."

"Did he say anything about my cleaning?"

"No, luv, he didn't."

"Good."

"But that might have been because he had a woman whom I don't recall as being from the parish sitting in his office."

"An outsider?"

"Indeed. But, poor wee thing, she was there to sort out a funeral mass for her husband."

"Oh."

"Oh indeed, but it gets worse," Mary-Margaret said and then, without waiting for Arthur to comment, continued. "Seems her husband was murdered, but the police think otherwise."

"Oh no!" Arthur exclaimed. "Who's—

"Detective Sergeant Billy Gilly, no less. He seems to think the lad died of…what do they call it…? Misadventure."

"Wait. Did you just say Billy Gilly?"

"I did. Which is why I've offered to take on the case."

"So she thinks…?"

"Not a doubt in her mind, and I'd have to say I agree with her, with or without that incompetent eejit's involvement."

"And she's paying you?"

"No, although they do pay Billy Gilly, don't they, so perhaps I should consider going pro. But no. Having one professional detective in the family is enough, although God knows me Michael struggles to connect the dots more often than not these days, doesn't he?" Mary-Margaret said as she briefly considered what it would be like to be a professional private eye.

"Ach, no. I'm doing this out of the goodness of me heart. And I'm hoping ye can help me."

"You know it!" Arthur exclaimed, leaning towards her. "Give me the deets."

"Well," Mary-Margaret began, then, seeing the empty plate in front of her, paused and added, "Could ye not have saved one for me, luv?"

"Sorry. I didn't have breakfast."

"Fair ball. And clearly," she said, looking down at her ample body, "I've not missed a meal recently. So, getting back to me story. Our girl–Annette Giancola is her name—"

"That's a great name."

"'Tis, now," Mary-Margaret said and then continued. "Our girl tells me that her husband didn't come home from work one night—"

"An affair?"

"No. Now, if ye'll let me finish—"

"Sorry, MM. I think it's all the sugar from the cookies. My body metabolizes sugar differently from the average—"

"I'm sure it does, luv," she cut in, "but I'm thinking ye'd like to hear what we know so far, so, if it's all the same with ye...?"

"Right. Sorry. Go on."

"So, our girl, Annette Giancola, calls the police to report her husband missing. Not that they had a happy marriage, mind."

"So she's our number one suspect?"

"No, just likely no more lonely now than she was while he was alive is all," Mary-Margaret replied, looking at the empty plate and wishing there was at least one biscuit left for her.

"Children?"

"Grown and flown. But his, not theirs."

"So...?"

"Well, she tells the police that the last place she knew him to be was at the garage that he owned. Her man was a mechanic, ye see. So they send a car around to have a wee look, and the lads see nothing, so she gets a call telling her as much and advising her to tuck in for the night. They tell her that he'll probably be home in the morning."

"But he doesn't come home, does he?"

"No, he does not. So, our girl decides to drop by the shop and, lo and behold, finds him dead in the back, his head bashed in."

"That's not good," Arthur said, his hand covering his mouth as a wave of shock washed over him.

"Not at all. So, she calls the police from inside the shop to tell them what she's found, reminding them, of course, that they should have found him the night before instead of dropping the ball with a resounding thud. After a bit of hemming and hawing—and likely cleaning the yokes from their cheeks—the police decide to send out someone from Homicide. Why they didn't send our Mandy, I don't know."

Mandy, or Detective Sergeant Amanda Black, was arguably the hardest-working investigator in the Homicide Squad. Known as the 'Pitbull in Stilettos' by her peers and subordinates—thanks in part to her outrageously high-heeled shoes and exemplary conviction rate—she had known Michael for most of his career and had, quite recently, become a close friend of Mary-Margaret's.

"But why...him?"

"God only knows, luv. God only knows. But ye can bet I'll be making a phone call or two to find out," Mary-Margaret replied, shaking her head slowly. "As useful as a chocolate teapot, that one is."

"And I'm taking it that Billy Gilly didn't think the dead guy had been murdered?"

"Not even close to it. Said he was drunk, likely stumbled, and bashed his own head on the cement floor."

"How likely is that?"

"Well, according to our girl, his being drunk wasn't a long shot, but honestly from what she says about the state he was in when she found him, there's no way his head would look like that from just a fall. I'll have me Francis give me his two cents worth on it, but from what the new widow is saying, our mechanic friend was beaten to death."

"Ew," Arthur said with a nod. "Speaking of Frank, how is he? I haven't heard you talk about him lately. Are you two still a thing?"

"Ye haven't heard me talk about him lately because there's been nothing to say. And we're not *still* a thing because we never *were* a thing to begin with. Just good pals is all," Mary-Margaret advised matter-of-factly, slightly exasperated that Arthur would even suggest what everyone else knew to be true. "And none of that has anything to do with this. Are ye keen on what I'm telling ye, or are ye more interested in concocting a tale about me and some morgue technician?"

"I'm sorry, MM. And yes, I'm interested. Go on."

"Good," Mary-Margaret said with a sniff before continuing. "Our girl tells me that her husband was a mechanic. Worked his way up from the bottom and, until he was bashed mercilessly about the head and left to bleed to death, owned a shop that catered to high-end cars. A chain of shops, if I understand correctly, although he continued to work at the one where he was murdered."

"If I owned a chain of shops and was a multi-millionaire, I sure wouldn't be working as a mechanic. Or cleaning anyone's house. Or church—though not that I'm not grateful for you getting me that gig."

"'Twas the least I could do, luv," she said, tempted to point out that he didn't exactly clean now, so what would be different—but thought better of it, especially given his recent tendency to spiral into depression. "So, next steps."

"Hmm," said Arthur. "Have you told Michael yet?"

"Ach, no. The poor lamb is run ragged as it is these days. And is it any wonder when he's forced to work with the likes of Billy Gilly? Likely has to run five to the four just to keep the city safe with that eejit outranking him and likely ordering him to do all sorts of foolish things, does me Michael."

"But he doesn't actually *work* with Bi—"

"And it matters how? Incompetence is like a cancer, spreading itself around until it brings the whole organization down. It's a miracle me Michael gets on as well as he does."

"What about Mandy? Have you spoken to her yet?"

"I don't imagine she's in any better a spot than me Michael. Worse, in fact, considering she and that muppet *do* both work together. Well, out of the same office anyway—though she's out there solving murders like it's a walk in the park, while Himself is just writing them off as…misadventures. Like it's all a bit of bad luck, so says he. I don't envy our Mandy, that's for certain. Working alongside a gobshite like that, it's a wonder she keeps her sanity!"

"So what are we going to do?"

"If I knew that, I'd be doing it right now instead of sitting here wagging me chin, would I?" she snapped. Arthur looked away. "Sorry, luv. Just wondering why a wastrel like that gets into Homicide while me Michael can't even get that Police Officer of the Year award."

"Well," Arthur began slowly, his eyes narrowing, "maybe this case will be the one that'll do it for him."

"Now yer firing on all cylinders, luv," Mary-Margaret said with a smile. "Perhaps I should just give him a ring now."

"And, while you're doing that, I'll start washing the floors," Arthur said, picking up the empty plate and the two mugs before he headed into the kitchen.

Chapter Four

"Detective O'Shea, Six District."

"Michael, 'tis yer mother."

"Oh."

"I've a homicide on the go for ye."

"Uh-huh."

"Indeed. A lad's had his head bashed in and his case needs investigating. Likely get ye yer Police Officer of the Year Award."

"I'm sure."

There was a pause.

"What are ye waiting for, lad?"

"For you to hang up so that I can get back to work."

"Michael, did ye not hear me?"

"I'm afraid I did."

"And…? A lad's been murdered, me son."

"And I'm sure Homicide has it well in hand."

"Are ye now? And what makes ye so sure, then?"

"Mom, I have to go."

"Ye've not even let me tell ye what's happened."

"No, I haven't. Does Wee Phil have to go out?"

"Ach, yer right. It's been ages. Listen, Michael, I'll call ye right back, okay?"

"Sure, Mom."

"Bye-bye bye bye-bye bye."

"Well?" Arthur asked when Mary-Margaret came into the kitchen.

"Where's Wee Phil?"

"He's just out the back—"

"Oh. Luv," Mary-Margaret said slowly. "The penny has just dropped. Me Michael was trying to get me off the line, he was."

"What do you mean?"

"Telling me to…ach, never mind. Point being: he doesn't believe me. Likely thinks I'm daft."

"What did you tell him?"

"Just that a lad's had his head bashed in."

"And he didn't believe you?"

"Well, I might not have been that explicit, but nonetheless…"

"Hmm," Arthur said, and then looked at his watch. "Listen, I hate to leave you high and dry like this, but I've got to—"

"Give us another minute," Mary-Margaret said, getting her cell phone. She pressed redial as she walked back to her chair in the living room.

No answer.

Mary-Margaret called the front desk of Six District Station and advised the Station Duty Officer who answered the phone, that she was Detective Michael O'Shea's mother and had to speak to him immediately regarding an urgent family matter.

"Mom…" he began when he picked up the line.

"Michael, 'tis yer mother."

"Yes. I know. Everyone in the station knows. Listen, you can't—"

"I can, and I did. Now, I need you to pull up a file for me," she ordered.

"This isn't TV, Mom," Michael said. "And you're not—"

"I know exactly who I am and am not, Michael, and I'm telling ye to pull up a file. Now, here's the name."

Mary-Margaret proceeded to give Michael the name of the deceased. Michael proceeded to listen to her tell him.

They both waited.

"Well?" Mary-Margaret finally demanded.

"Well, what?"

"What have ye got for me?"

"I don't know what episode of *CSI-Nutterville* you're watching, Mom, but here in the real world, police don't share confidential information with civilians."

"I'm *not* a civilian. I'm yer mother," she stated. "So, what does yer report say?"

"It says I have to hang up the phone."

"Do ye want me to pop by the station then? Perhaps bake a cake for the lads? Bring a pillow to sit on, and a thermos of tea just in case yer too busy to talk to yer old mam straight away, and I have to wait? Sit on that board ye have over the radiator in the front there that yiz call a bench? Would that be better for ye, Michael?"

There was a long pause.

"What's his name?" Michael said with a sigh.

"Marco Giancola," she said, not missing a beat. "Likely around yer age, Michael. Shame really, isn't it? Someone so young, murdered like that. Had quite a life, though. Built an empire, he did. Fat lot of good it's doing him now, though, isn't it? Reminds me of what Father Brian used to say. Money can't buy happiness. Can't even keep ye from getting yer head bashed in. Well, Father Brian never said that part. That's me thinkin'—"

"I found the Sudden Death Report, Mom," Michael cut in.

"Grand, luv. And what does it say?"

"That he died."

"And…?"

"I can't—"

"Do ye have the autopsy photos there, Michael?"

"I don't even know if they did an—"

"Ach, never mind. I'll ask Fra—-I mean, I'll sort it out on me own. In the meantime, what does the report say?"

"I've told you—"

"Ye've told me nothing. Now, was our lad drunk when he died?"

"How would you know about that?"

"Ach, Michael. Because the Murder Fairies visit me in me sleep. What do you think, lad?"

"I do wonder."

"I spoke to his wife…widow. Annette. Lovely girl. Ye know, Michael, once this all gets sorted, ye might want to—"

"You're kidding me, right?"

"Just trying to help, me son. A man on his own is a danger to himself. Now, about our victim. Was he drunk?"

"Yes."

"And the injuries to his head. Do ye have any pictures at all?"

"No."

"But photos were taken?"

"I'm sure."

"Grand. So, can ye get them for me and bring them home with ye after work? And, while yer at it, can ye pick up some bread? Not that flimsy, cheap stuff ye've got lurking in the fridge. A good sourdough—"

"No, Mom. I'm not going to bring home photos from a crime—"

"So it was a crime. I knew it!"

"Mom—"

"And the garage. What's the address of it?"

"I'm not going to—"

"Michael, I could find it out meself, but I'm no spring chick anymore, and I wouldn't want to spend the precious time I've got left on God's green earth looking up addresses."

"I can't—"

"Me life clock is ticking, Michael, and I can't say when the alarm is going to sound."

"The place is called Marco's Motors."

"Yes, I know that. Not the most imaginative lad on the block, was he? Never mind. And this would be the one located where…?"

Having been completely worn down, Michael provided his mother with the address of the shop before hanging up the phone. She thought she heard what sounded like a sob before the line was disconnected, but couldn't be sure.

Chapter Five

"Drop the mop," Mary-Margaret ordered.

"Do we have an address?" Arthur asked as he set the mop back in the pail of mucky water, his eyes sparkling like a dog spotting a ball.

"We do, so get the kettle going again and let's see what we can find."

"Why don't you let me do a little checking," Arthur said, pulling out his iPhone, "and you make the tea?"

"Good plan, lad," Mary-Margaret replied.

Just over five minutes later, the two of them were seated at the dining room table, mugs of tea set in front of them, a strong sense of purpose filling the air.

"Here," Arthur said, holding up his phone for her to see.

"What is it yer showing me, lad?" Mary-Margaret said, squinting her eyes.

"It might be time for you to get some reading gla—"

"It might be time for ye to get a larger font on yer phone."

"Never mind. I'll read it to you."

"A summary will do."

"Okay. So, says here that Marco's Motors was started in 2007 by Marco Giancola."

"Yes, we know that," she said, her pride still stinging.

"And that Giancola partnered with a Robert Jensen in 2016."

"And what did this Bobby Jensen bring to the table?"

"Money."

"It says that there, on yer wee screen?"

"No, I just figured that was it, given that…Bobby..Jensen owns…owned a few other businesses at that time."

"And yer getting this all off of that, are ye?"

"Yep."

"Can anyone—"

"No," Arthur said, shaking his head condescendingly. "I go where very few people can go on here."

"I don't doubt that," Mary-Margaret replied. "So, this Bobby lad. What happened to him?"

"Hang on a sec, MM," Arthur said, scrolling through his screen. "Says here that, after Jensen partnered with Giancola, they opened fifteen other Marco's Motors throughout the province."

"She'll not be hurting for money now, the widow Giancola, will she?"

"Well, she might," Arthur said absently, still scrolling. "Depending on how well the business was run."

"Well, ye'd think they would know what they were doing, given the size—"

"Size doesn't always matter, MM," Arthur said, looking up from his screen.

"So what happened next?"

"I don't know."

"What do ye mean? Doesn't yer magic little phone tell ye?"

"Let me check the address."

Mary-Margaret sipped her tea as Arthur fidgeted with it.

"Here," he said, reaching out to hand her the phone but then pulling it back. "I'll give you a summary."

"If ye had a reasonable sized font…"

"They don't own the building."

"Which has what to do with what?"

"They own all the other Marco's Motors buildings," Arthur stated.

"And so…?"

"And so I'm wondering why. That property must be worth a fortune."

"I'm sure it is, but—"

"If I owned a property with a garage on it that had been there for years and was probably being rented out at way under current market value anyway,

I'd be wanting that tenant out so that I could sell it for a bazillion dollars to a condo developer."

"But why would they build a condo—"

"Here," Arthur said, unable to stop himself from handing her the phone. "This is a street view of the area. Notice anything?"

"That there isn't any parkland to be seen?"

"Right. And why?"

"Because the garage is surrounded by tall buildings?"

"Exactly. Condos. And it looks like the site of Marco's Motors is ripe for redevelopment."

Mary-Margaret put her hand on Arthur's arm.

"But Marco *loved* working at the garage," she said with a wistful sigh, as if she had known the man in life.

"So?" Arthur said, checking out other websites.

"So there's no way he'd want to leave, but what if—what if he had some mad long lease, like twenty years or more, and the owner was pressuring him to vacate? And what if this owner lad just…snapped? Got all worked up and—killed—"

"You know," Arthur said, looking her straight in the eye. "I think this calls for some undercover recon."

Mary-Margaret's cell phone rang.

Unknown Number.

"Hang on, luv," she said, picking up her phone. "Likely me Michael calling me back."

"Is this Mary-Margaret O'Shea?" a male voice asked.

"'Tis."

"This is Detective Sergeant Gill from Homicide," he said.

"'Tis Billy Gilly," Mary-Margaret whispered to Arthur, her hand over the receiver. "Likely wanting us to help—"

"I'm calling to formally caution you about getting involved in my investigation."

Arthur waited for Mary-Margaret to convey the message with both thumbs up.

"I'm sorry...?" Mary-Margaret said, the scowl on her face alerting Arthur to the fact they were not, in fact, likely being invited to join the team.

"The Giancola case," D/S Gill said.

"And just how—"

"Every document linked to a suspicious death investigation is tracked—"

"So 'tis a suspicious death. Not a death by foolish—"

"And I just received a notification that the original report had been accessed. By your son."

"And since when does what me son does at work have anything to do with me?"

"I phoned your son, Mrs. O'Shea, to find out why he accessed the report."

There was a pause.

"Mrs. O'Shea, Marco Giancola was a heavy drinker. He was known to drink in his shop in the evenings after it closed. On the particular evening of his death, he was doing just that. Unlike other evenings, Mrs. O'Shea, Mr. Giancola slipped and cracked his head open on the cement floor. No one murdered him. He died alone. Marco Giancola's death is no longer suspicious. Just unfortunate."

"And ye know all of this how?"

"Mrs. O'Shea, I am a trained homicide investigator. It is my job to investigate unnatural deaths. As a result of my investigation, which was quite comprehensive and exceeded our already high investigative standards, I have concluded that Marco Giancola died as a result of a massive trauma to the head brought on by a fall from no more than five feet onto a cement floor. Simply put, Mr. Giancola was drunk, fell down, hit his head, and died."

There was a pause.

"Are you still there, Mrs. O'Shea?" D/S Gill asked.

"So, what yer saying is our man was a drun—"

"What I'm saying, Mrs. O'Shea, is that, if I find out that you or anyone you know or might know or even consider knowing gets involved in any of my case—"

"So it's not closed?"

"Involved in any of my cases," he continued. "Past, present, or future, open or closed, then I will have you criminally ch—"

"Hello? Hello?" she said, pulling the phone away from her ear and smacking it with her hand. "Have we lost connection? Hello?"

Mary-Margaret held the phone out and looked at it. She then looked over at Arthur and shrugged before disconnecting the call.

"'Twas the oddest thing, Arthur," she said sweetly. "Billy Gilly was just sharing some inside info with me when the phone started acting up."

The phone rang. Mary-Margaret looked at it before swiping the call away.

"Likely a spam call. I've been getting so many of them lately. Ach, I wouldn't be surprised if the new New Girl at the church is selling our phone numbers to those companies as a side hustle. It's an utter annoyance, it is. Almost criminal, in fact."

Chapter Six

Mary-Margaret was not having a good night's sleep. Given the traffic in the hallway outside her door, she assumed no one else in that house was, either. Between Michael's getting up to go to work or coming in from work or whatever was causing his wandering about, along with Max needing the bathroom a couple of times, it was like she had set her bed down in the middle of Pearse Station. Rather than fight it, she decided to start her day early with a good cuppa and a poached egg on toast, even though her clock said half four.

She stood over the stove in the kitchen, her bathrobe wrapped tightly around her, waiting for just the right moment to scoop the egg out of the gently boiling water in the pan. She felt a twinge in her neck and was glad that she was going for a massage at eleven that morning. A smile crept across her face as she then remembered that she was meeting her new friend for dinner that evening. When they'd met at Max's school, where her new friend worked as the secretary, she'd advised Mary-Margaret that everyone called her 'The Old Bird'. Given that she was of similar age to herself, Mary-Margaret found it a bit hard to consider but, if she could call Arthur Sister Augustine, or Lucille, or…then why not?

Should I be tellin' her about this? Mary-Margaret wondered as she lifted the perfectly poached egg and plopped it down onto a piece of toasted rye bread. It hadn't been her idea to use rye, but it was what was in the freezer, so she made do. This was unlike the time she found only some off-brand tea in the house and immediately chucked it out, replacing it with Barry's. At least rye bread was digestible, not like that off-brand tea Michael had picked up from God knows where.

"And I'm seeing someone's finally up," she said aloud, as Wee Phil bounced into the kitchen, sliding to a stop just before hitting the back door. "Is half four too early for ye, then, pup?"

She opened the door and uncharacteristically let the tiny dog out into the laneway on his own. Having noticed the frost on Daphne's windshield, Mary-Margaret had no intention of stepping out into the pre-dawn chill. Wee Phil must have found the air particularly nippy as well because he came bounding back up the couple of stairs within a minute of being let out.

"I'm not looking forward to scraping the car," she said to the little dog, his tail wagging madly in anticipation of a treat. "Remind me to talk to me Michael about building a carport if he expects me to be staying on, not that he does, but that's not our worry, is it, Wee Phil."

Once she'd had her breakfast and gotten dressed, Mary-Margaret discovered that scraping the frost was the least of her concerns. When she turned the key over in the ignition and pressed the Start button—a design that was common for cars of Daphne's era—the headlights dimmed, but nothing else happened. Mary-Margaret tried again, but to no avail. She looked at her watch and saw that it was just after five. If he was working day shift, Michael would already be up. If he was not...?

Mary-Margaret leaned on the horn. To her surprise, Michael was not the first person to come into the laneway to help her.

"What the h—" Johnny, the first of Michael's neighbours to approach the car, began, fully clothed with a can of beer in his hand, obviously not having gone to bed from the night before yet.

"Are you okay, Mary-Margaret?" Doug, another neighbour, called as he rushed out of his back door into the laneway, his hair askew, pulling his bathrobe around him.

"I'm calling the police," Brian stated firmly from inside his back door.

"Mom?" Michael said from the kitchen back door.

"Who else were ye expecting?" she said, looking back at the house, her head stuck out her side window.

"What's happened?" Doug asked, the first to approach the car.

"Ach, 'tis the battery, I'm thinking," she replied. "Likely dead."

"My god!" Brian called out. "Here I was, thinking someone was trying to steal your car. Not like we haven't had enough cars stolen from this laneway over the years. If that's all it is, I'm going back to b—"

"Cars stolen from the laneway?" Mary-Margaret exclaimed. "Ye never told me that, Michael. Well, that's another reason why ye should build something secure back here."

"Sorry, everyone," Michael called out, still not leaving the warmth of his kitchen.

"Do you have CAA?" Doug asked. "They can boost—"

"I've no time for that, but I'm seeing three strong lads—"

"Four," Doug corrected.

"Three," Brian called before turning back and closing his door.

"Three strong lads is all I need. Yiz can come on out and give me car a push. Don't take too long or ye'll catch yer death in this cold air."

"What?" Michael exclaimed with a wince.

"Ye heard me. I'll put Daphne in neutral, and ye lads can push me out of the parking spot here—if ye can even call this slip a parking spot—and then I'll steer us towards the street, there, and ye keep pushing until the motor kicks in."

"Are you insa—" Michael began.

"Or ye can drive me over to me old neighbourhood straight away yerself, me son."

He took a deep breath and stepped out towards the car.

"Do you mind?" he asked Johnny and Doug.

"No problem," Johnny said with a shrug, shoving his beer can into the back pocket of his worn jeans.

"Well, it's going to take more than just the two of you, I suppose," Doug said, tightening his bathrobe while directing his dog back into the house.

"I owe you one, guys," Michael said as the three men pushed the car into the laneway, relocated to the back of the car, and pushed it towards the street.

"A bit more, lads," Mary-Margaret directed. "Come on now. Maybe just down the street a bit, then."

She wrenched the steering wheel to the right as the three men continued pushing, now at a quick trot, until the engine caught.

"Thanks, lads!" Mary-Margaret called out, waving out her open window as she drove through the red light at the main intersection.

"She's quite a corker," Doug said with a laugh.

"She's something," Johnny said, pulling the beer can from his back pocket and taking a sip. "Oh. Shit. I guess I shouldn't be doing this in front of a cop, huh?"

"I think we're well past that point," Michael grumbled, not making eye contact with his neighbours as they all retreated in silence into their respective homes.

* * *

As expected, Daphne was just fine by the time Mary-Margaret drove by the front of Marco's Motors. That she had not stopped, even when the traffic lights and better judgement indicated that she should have, didn't hurt any. Regardless, Mary-Margaret was where she wanted to be, seeing what she expected to see: a single marked police car parked in front of the garage, engine running, the lone officer's head bobbing to one side.

Mary-Margaret drove a little further before coming to two conclusions. First, if an officer was detailed to the front of the building, there would have to be one parked at the back. Second, if the officer at the front had nodded off, then the officer at the back would most certainly be out cold.

Mary-Margaret pulled her car over on a side street less than a block away from the building and then checked her watch.

Almost 5:40.

She glanced up and saw that the street was permit-only parking from 10 pm – 6 am, but decided to take her chances. Or, more truthfully, said a quick prayer to Saint Rita before quietly getting out of her car.

Under the cover of the dim streetlights, Mary-Margaret snuck onto the main street past the dozing officer, hurried around the corner, and poked her head into the laneway. As expected, she saw the back of an idling police car parked just behind the rear entrance of the garage, headlights lighting up a doorway and, beyond it, a tempered-glass garage door not unlike the one at the front of the shop, both of which she assumed rolled up to bring the cars in and out.

As she approached the police car, choosing to walk down the middle of the laneway rather than keeping close to the wall, she noticed the officer's head was down. Instead of the interior of the car being dark, however, Mary-Margaret noticed a bright light reflecting off the officer's face. As she got within poking distance of the car, she could see that he had earbuds in and was watching something on his iPhone.

Even better, she thought as she crouched down slightly to pass his door before rising up to all of her five-foot-two frame and walking towards the back doors with the confidence of one who owned the place. She paused before lifting the yellow police tape that spanned the width of the back of the property, suddenly aware that she was less than fifteen feet from the front of the police car. She was also aware that she was lit up as bright as could be by the car's headlights. When she saw the officer didn't look up, however, she quickly lifted the yellow tape, then noticed a regular-sized door beside the garage door. She stepped closer to it, lowered the tape behind her, and twisted the handle. The door opened, so she stepped inside and quickly closed it behind her, only to find herself in a near pitch-dark garage.

Chapter Seven

Much to her surprise—and growing annoyance, because she should have known such would be the case—Mary-Margaret stood inside the garage, the murder scene, enveloped in darkness. She dared not move for fear of tripping over a tire or wrench or some other tool of the trade she suspected would be lying around. Or worse, slipping in Marco Giancola's blood. The faint glow from the tempered-glass doors at the front and back created more shadows than light, concealing, Mary-Margaret was sure, clues that Billy Gilly had missed.

I've no choice, do I? she reasoned as she pulled her iPhone from her purse and clicked on the flashlight app.

The entire garage lit up. As she quickly put her finger over the light, Mary-Margaret was surprised at how neat the place was. There were no tires or wrenches or miscellaneous tools lying about. Rather than stained with oil—or blood—these floors put those in Michael's kitchen to shame. She momentarily thought about heeding Michael's words and getting rid of Arthur and hiring a competent cleaner instead before pushing the thought from her mind and clicking off the flashlight app on her phone.

It's murder we're here for, me girl. Keep yer focus.

She gave her eyes a moment to adjust, relying on the bit of light that came through the doors on either end of the garage to guide her. Looking up, she could see the overhead lights and imagined that they outshone the sun when they were turned on. Again, she was drawn to the polished concrete floor and how, even with the sparse illumination, it gleamed. Given the outside chill, it was surprisingly hot and stuffy in the garage, and the air hung heavily, smelling of motor oil and something else. Blood? Latent fear? Mary-Margaret inhaled deeply and then recognized the odor. She turned and noticed a door she assumed led to the washroom. Three well-used coveralls hung from hooks beside it, radiating the unmistakable scent of sweat, grease, and what she knew to be many men's failure to notice their own stink.

Mystery solved.

She pulled out her iPhone and activated the flashlight app again, this time being careful to keep the device pointed down with her finger covering most of the light. Because the building was narrow, the three bays ran one after the other, although all of the lifts were empty now. Had the cars been removed by the murderer, or was it the practice of the shop to finish all of the jobs before closing?

I wouldn't be wanting Daphne dangling on a hoist overnight, her underside exposed like that to anyone inclined to take a peek.

As she made her way to the front of the garage, she noticed tools hanging from the walls on either side of the building in a manner that suggested the mechanics—or was it only Marco who worked here?—were very well-organized. She saw a door to her right with a sign that said OFFICE overhead. She was just about to check it out when she saw a bright light moving around on the other side of the tempered glass behind her.

Jesus, Mary, and Joseph! Inside with ye, me girl!

Before she could take more than a couple of steps, the back door was open, and the light of a flashlight was on her.

"Stop where you are!" a male voice commanded.

Mary-Margaret froze.

"Put your hands up where I can see them!"

Mary-Margaret thought about complying, but changed her mind, turning instead to face the dark silhouette behind the flashlight full-on. It was at this point that she realized that he was also pointing his gun at her. But it was too late. She had already come up with a plan.

"I said—"

"I know what ye said, luv," she replied calmly. "And I would do as ye ask except that me shoulder's been acting up as of late. A bit of arthritis, I'm thinking, but Louise, she's me massage therapist whom I'll be seeing later this morn—"

"Put. Your. Hands. Up!" another male voice coming from the front door demanded.

"And do ye have yer gun out, too, then, lad? That's grand, isn't it? The two of ye'll end up shooting each other. Ye know, I've got to tell me Michael about this. The way yiz are carrying on. Someone's likely to get killed."

"Put. Your—" he repeated.

"Did ye not hear me, luv?" Mary-Margaret said, turning to face the officer behind her. "Me shoulder…ach, never mind. And how was yer nap? Are ye rested, or are ye still just waking up? Me Michael is a wee bit cranky when he wakes up, too, so yer not alone, lad."

The two officers looked past Mary-Margaret at each other, their flashlights shining right through the garage, with their guns, as Mary-Margaret had noted, pointing more at each other than at her.

"Let's put those things away, shall we?" Mary-Margaret suggested in a tone she'd perfected after decades of parenting. "It's all fun and games until someone accidentally shoots someone else, and no one wants that, do they?"

The two uniformed officers sheepishly re-holstered their guns.

"Grand. Now, since we all know we're here, why don't ye," she continued, turning to the officer at the front of the garage, "turn on the big lights there, and yiz can both put yer flashlights away as well."

The officer at the back of the garage nodded to the officer at the front, who then turned on the overhead light. They all squinted for a moment, including Mary-Margaret, because, as she had initially suspected, the lights were brighter than any sun anyone had ever seen. Once their eyes had adjusted, the officers turned off their flashlights and slid them back into the pouches on their duty belts.

"I'm Mary-Margaret O'Shea," she began, looking at one and then the other. "Me son is Michael O'Shea. Detective Michael O'Shea. Do ye know him?"

Both officers shook their heads.

"Not surprised," she said. "No ill will meant, but the lot of ye don't seem to know much nowadays. Regardless—"

The officer at the front, who was closer to her, stepped towards Mary-Margaret.

"Stay where ye are, luv," she said to him. "No need crowding anyone and making it more uncomfortable in here than it already is. Do ye think ye could press that button there and open up the big doors? Let in a wee bit of fresh air? They must have the thermostat set at broil. And ye," she said, turning to the officer at the back, "would ye mind doing the same? A good cross-breeze wouldn't hurt, would it? Give the place a good burping, it would."

The officer at the front looked at the officer at the back. They both shook their heads.

"Well then," Mary-Margaret said, "There's nothing for it but for me to step outside. It's smoldering in here, and I'm feeling that I might melt."

"Stay where you—"

"Or ye'll do what? Wrestle me to the ground? Oh, that'll be grand, won't it? Imagine the write-up: the two of yiz are detailed to guard a crime scene—a murder scene, no less—and a woman—a pensioner, the mother of a police detective—lets herself in while yiz are what…sleeping? Watching videos? Sure and all. And then, after the old girl wakes yiz up herself, ye decide to— what do yiz call it—ground her? A pensioner. A retired church secretary, no less. With an arthritic shoulder. Can yiz see it, lads?"

The two officers looked at her, speechless.

"When I tell me son, the police detective, about what's happened here—"

"Would you like to step outside where it's cooler, ma'am?" the officer at the front of the garage said, his voice cracking.

"Indeed. But, before that, I'd like ye to point out the spot where yer lads left our victim to bleed to death while they hurried off to get themselves a coffee. That's what yiz drink, isn't it?"

"I'm more of a chai tea—" the back door officer began.

"We don't know, ma'am," the front door officer interrupted. "We were just detailed to

watch the shop."

"And a bang-up job yiz did at that, didn't ye?" Mary-Margaret said with a sigh, looking him up and down. "And yiz wonder why we don't trust the—"

"We'd appreciate it if you wouldn't say anything—" he continued.

"I'm sure yiz would," Mary-Margaret cut in, her mildly Machiavellian brain now on high gear. "So perhaps yiz can do me a favour."

"The *favour* we're doing is not arresting you for—"

"Let's rewind for a minute, lads, and consider one of ye was getting some kip while the other was watching God knows what on his phone. Do ye remember that part? Ye know, me friend Mandy—maybe ye know her. She calls herself Detective Sergeant Amanda Black when she's at work…"

Mary-Margaret let the words hang in the air as she looked from one officer to the other, watching them both squirm.

"Anyway, me friend tells me that, when she gets evidence, it can take months before it gets returned. I'm thinking that yer phone, luv, would be evidence if it was to become common knowledge that an old woman got into the crime scene right in front of ye—headlights shining on her, truth to be told—while ye were watching yer show. Or was it something else ye were looking at?"

"N-no. It was—" he stammered.

"I'm sure, luv," Mary-Margaret said with a knowing smile. "I've raised four children. Two of them boys. I'm sure ye were just watching the football on yer little screen there."

"No. I was—"

Before he could finish, an F-150 pickup truck pulled up right in front of the closed glass door. A short, plump man leaped out and ran into the garage.

"What the—" he began.

"You can't come in here, sir," the front door officer stated.

"Who's she?" he demanded, his dark jacket sleeve barely exposing the chubby finger he pointed at Mary-Margaret.

"I'm Mary-Margaret O'Shea. And who might ye be?"

"I'm the owner of the building," the short, plump man said, not making any attempt to remove the black pork-pie hat from his head.

"Are ye now?" she said, stepping past the front door officer towards him. "Just the lad I wanted to talk to."

Chapter Eight

Mary-Margaret held out her hand, the two uniformed officers standing with their mouths hanging open behind her.

"Danny," he said, warily taking her hand.

"Danny...?" she asked, letting the word linger as she shook his hand. *Clammy. Can't be trusted.*

"Just...Danny," he said, shoving his hand into his pants pocket once the interaction was over.

"Well then, Just Danny," Mary-Margaret said with her warmest smile, "Is there a place where we can go and have a wee chat, then?"

"Why?"

"What do you mean, *why*?" she demanded. "Because I'm asking is why."

"Are you the police?"

"Ach, do I look like the police, lad? Tara Rafferty, yes—or so I've been told—but she's a lawyer, not a police officer. At least on the telly. Have ye ever seen her shows? She's a real cracker, that one."

Danny looked at Mary-Margaret, his unibrow furrowed. He then looked over at the front door officer, who shrugged.

"We can go across the street to the coffee shop over there," he grumbled, pointing to the Tim Hortons.

"Can we get yiz anything on our way back?" Mary-Margaret said over her shoulder as she followed the short man across the street.

Both officers shook their heads sheepishly, their mouths still agape.

* * *

"So, Just Danny," Mary-Margaret said, sitting down with the small tea and chocolate dip donut she had got her reluctant companion to purchase for her—she could have murdered a medium, but that, she had thought, would just be taking advantage of him.

"Danny," he corrected, sitting across from her with his large double-double coffee. He had yet to make any attempt to remove his hat, which, in Mary-Margaret's opinion, was not at all flattering on him. *Could use something with a bit of height, this one. And clothes that fit. Looks more like a ragamuffin than a landowner.*

"Danny," she said with a smile, refocusing on the real reason she was sitting across from him. "Is there any reason someone would want to murder yer tenant?"

"You don't waste time, do you?" he said, cracking the plastic lid open before taking a sip of his coffee. He pulled his mouth away quickly, looking angrily at the cup.

"While I may look it, I'm not young, and I've not got a lot of time to spend on natterin'," she said, snapping the lid off of her tea. "Did ye burn yer lip, then?"

"No," he said, pushing the cup away from him.

"No, ye didn't burn yer lip, or no, ye don't know who'd want to kill yer tenant?"

"Both."

"But ye don't seem too sad that he's gone," she said, taking a bite of her donut.

"Of course I'm sad. It's just that, well, he was my tenant, not my friend."

"And a very good tenant at that, I'd imagine."

"I suppose."

"Paid every month?"

"Yep."

"And I'm sure the rent wasn't cheap?"

"I don't think—" Danny began, his chair making an awful scraping sound as he pushed it away from the table.

"What I'm trying to say here is that yer tenant likely paid off yer building over the years, didn't he?"

"I have no idea," he said, looking down at his surprisingly well-manicured fingernails.

"And now that he's dead…well, even if the rent was a pretty penny, that'd be nothing compared to what ye'd be getting if ye sold it outright and invested the money, assuming that's what ye'd be doing with the cash."

Danny looked up at her but didn't respond.

"Am I right," Mary-Margaret asked as she picked up her cup, "or am I right? I didn't raise four smallies on me own without learning a thing or two about managing money, luv."

He still didn't respond.

"So?"

"Who are you?" Danny asked, looking a little more closely at her as he pulled his chair back in.

"Ach, I told ye, lad. I'm Mary-Margar—"

"Yes, but who *are* you?" he said, leaning across the table, narrowing the distance between them more than she'd have liked.

"Me name is Mary-Margaret O'Sh—"

"I don't care what your name is, lady. I'm wondering who the heck you are to be wandering around my building with uniformed officers standing by after it's been sealed off as a crime scene," he pressed, leaning in even closer, such that his face was inches from hers.

"Just a concerned citizen is all," she said as brightly as she could, sensing that he might go off on her. She snapped the lid back on her cup and shoved what remained of her donut into its little bag. "Thanks for the tea and the wee nibble. And I'll be seeing ye at Marco's funeral, then, yeah?"

Before he could answer, Mary-Margaret was up and out the door, hustling down the street toward her car as fast as her legs could carry her. With every step, a growing feeling of unease settled in as she started to wonder if the man she had just left behind was capable of more than just profiting from the sale of the building where Marco's Motors had operated—and if their little talk had, perhaps, put her in a bit of danger.

* * *

"Are you back at St. Francis?" Louise asked, noting the tightness of Mary-Margaret's shoulders as she began massaging her long-time client.

"Ach, no. They've got a new New Girl there now. Not even Catholic. Can ye imagine such a thing?" Mary-Margaret replied, looking at the tiled floor through the face cradle.

"Hmmm."

"None of this would ever have happened if Father Brian was still around. Do ye know, I went to see Father Miguel about it and he all but shoved me to the curb."

"Huh."

"He was just finishing up funeral arrangements with the poor widow. Husband was a mechanic. Marco Giancola. Have ye heard of him?"

"The name sounds familiar," Louise said as she leaned into Mary-Margaret's back.

"He owns—owned—a chain of garages. Marco's Motors."

"That's the name of the place just around the corner, isn't it. I used to go there years ago. Surprised you never went there."

"Can't take Daphne to just any mechanic. She's an import, which is another reason why my Jimmy, God rest his soul, shouldn't have bought that car in the first place. I miss him like a limb, I do, but my God, he made some horrible decisions."

"Well, he was a fine man regardless."

"That he was, God rest his soul. That he was."

Louise continued massaging Mary-Margaret's body in silence for a few minutes.

"Terrible time for Marco to die," Louise said with a sigh. "Not that there's ever a good time, I suppose, but still…"

"What's so terrible about now, then?"

"They're talking about tearing that building down and putting up a luxury condo. I'm sure Marco'd get a good dollar on the place."

"He didn't own it," Mary-Margaret said.

"Hmm. That's too bad. I'm sure whoever does will be glad he's dead."

"Why's that, then?"

"Nothing holding them back from selling the building if the occupant's gone, is there?"

"But it's part of a chain. I'm sure—"

"And, with one of the partners dead… If I was the surviving partner, I'd be selling up while the selling was good."

"And ye think this partner lad mightn't be able to run the business on his own now that it's going gangbusters?"

"Who can say, but," Louise said, "Marco's Motors was all about Marco. His name, his picture. All of the branding was around him."

"I'm sure they can run the Marco's Motors chain just fine without Marco," Mary-Margaret said, thinking back to her visit to the coffee shop earlier and how it still built its brand around the legacy of the long-deceased original owner.

"Perhaps but, if I was the business partner," Louise said, lifting up the sheet as Mary-Margaret awkwardly maneuvered herself over onto her back, "I'd sell while the company was on top."

Chapter Nine

Even though it was only a few kilometers from Mary-Margaret's own house, she was unfamiliar with this part of the city. She had parked Daphne and was now scanning the street for the restaurant whose name she'd written down on a scrap of paper. She couldn't help but notice that everyone on the crowded sidewalk seemed…young.

The businesses along the street bore that out, with curbside patios, blaring music, and an overall energy that made the whole area buzz. As she wove through the crowd, she was glad that she'd find a familiar face once she reached her destination.

Finally, she matched the name on the scrap of paper to the sign above a door and stepped inside. She was immediately hit by a wave of sound—loud music thumping and the high-pitched squeals and laughter of young people filled the air. The voices overlapped in a blur of excited chatter, making it hard to focus on anything but the buzz of energy. The room was alive with noise, each sound sharp and fast, adding to the overwhelming chaos.

"Mary-Margaret! Over here!" she thought she heard a voice squawking out from beyond the crowded bar.

While she wouldn't have considered herself set in her ways before, Mary-Margaret had to admit, in that moment, she felt very much like yesterday's poured cement. The lighting was dim enough to make it hard to see where she was going. The music was loud enough to drown out the young, tattooed server rushing past her. And even though she was still near the doorway, the air in the place was already stale enough for her to know that this wouldn't be a place she'd frequent.

"Over here!" she heard again.

Mary-Margaret glanced over and spotted Sue Bird—The Old Bird—waving at her, the many silver bangles on her arm likely jingling. With the bass thumping through the speaker mounted on the wall above the tables, however, there was no way Mary-Margaret could be certain.

She took a deep breath, arched her back so that she stood her full height, and smiled warmly as she approached the table.

"Did you have any trouble finding the place? I hope you like spicy food. Their enchiladas are terrific," The Old Bird said, her voice barely audible above the music.

Mary-Margaret cautiously sat down across from her friend, noticing that her chair wobbled. Before she could look around for a replacement, the tattooed server was standing over her.

"What can I getcha?" she asked, pad in hand.

"I'll have another margarita," The Old Bird said to the server before Mary-Margaret had a chance to respond. "I'd highly recommend them, Mary-Margaret."

"Sure, and you?" the server said, looking expectantly at Mary-Margaret.

"I don't suppose yer barman knows how to make a crown float, does he?" she hollered.

"I don't think so," the server said, glancing over at the blue-haired young man behind the bar.

"Ach, well then...have ye got any whiskey?"

"Yep. Straight up or...?"

"Yes. That'll do just fine, thank ye," Mary-Margaret said with a polite smile.

"Look at you!" The Old Bird said as the server strode over to the bar. "I never figured you to be a hard liquor kinda gal."

"Well, whiskey is practically our national drink, isn't it?"

Anyone looking at the two women would think they were as different as chalk and cheese. Mary-Margaret, dressed simply in a nondescript blouse that covered her ample torso, pants, and comfortable shoes, with a conservative haircut and moderate makeup on a face marked by a few wrinkles—testament to both her regular moisturizing routine and a full life.

In sharp contrast, The Old Bird wore a tight, sequined denim jacket over a faded men's tank top that barely covered her flat chest, paired with a flowing yellow skirt and red vintage lace-up heeled oxfords. Her frizzy white hair—likely permanently damaged from too many cheap dye jobs—cascaded halfway down her back, the bangs framing a face that spoke of both too many late nights in smoky bars and too many bottles of hard liquor.

And yet, there they were, sitting across from each other in this noisy bar, already setting the stage to, perhaps, become the best of friends.

"Here," the server said, reaching over Mary-Margaret to pass The Old Bird her drink before slapping Mary-Margaret's tumbler of whiskey down in front of her. She disappeared as quickly as she had appeared.

"Cheers!" The Old Bird said, raising her glass.

"Sláinte," Mary-Margaret said. She took a sip of the whiskey and was pleasantly surprised by the quality of it. She had assumed that a place like this would not stock anything as smooth as what she was drinking now. Another, albeit after dinner, might be in order. She was already wondering if Arthur had his driver's licence yet so that she could call him to come get her and Daphne later.

"So this is where I hang out," The Old Bird said. "Prices are great, food is good, and you get used to the music."

"The music?"

"It seems a bit loud when you first come in, but—"

"Ach, right. Grand. I mean, of course."

"So," The Old Bird said after coughing into her arm, "what's happening with you these days, amigo?"

"Well," Mary-Margaret began, and then proceeded to tell her new friend about her latest adventure while their dinners were served.

As predicted, the food was good.

"You sure don't mess around, do you?" The Old Bird said as the server cleared away their plates. "I know you probably have it all figured out, but—"

"Hardly, luv," Mary-Margaret said, catching the server's eye for another whiskey. "If ye've got any ideas, I'm all ears."

"Well, since you're asking, I'm not liking this Annette chick. Seems too… polished."

"Ach, perhaps I've not portrayed her properly. If ye'd seen her at O'Leary's, which, by the way, I'll be takin' ye to next time, ye'd have seen she was in floods. And, if she had killed her husband, why wouldn't she just let the eejit Billy Gilly close the case as…what was it again…Misadventure?"

The server set a tumbler with a liberal pour of whiskey in it in front of Mary-Margaret.

"I'll have another as well," The Old Bird said, finishing up what remained in her glass before passing it to the server and watching the young woman walk back to the bar. "I don't know. Maybe a guilty conscience? Trying to spin the story her way? Don't know, but I still don't trust her. I mean, she goes on about the business, about how she and her old man weren't getting along too well, but she never says anything about a business partner? Come on. There's something going on between the two of them."

The server returned with the drinks.

"Could have been an oversight," Mary-Margaret said, raising her glass. "Sláinte."

"Cheers," The Old Bird said, raising her glass. "An oversight my rumpus. Last time I heard of an "oversight" like that," she said, making air quotes, "was when Sid the Rat kinda forgot to mention he had a piece on the side. I found that out for myself a few days after he dumped me at a Bowie concert. You know, I still get friggin' weepy every time I hear *Modern Love*. I can't believe I was that blind."

The Old Bird took a long sip of her drink.

"Ye might be right," Mary-Margaret considered. "I've not had much experience in the likes of that, although me son, Michael, the police detective, has been tripped up before. And ye'd think, being a detective and all, that he'd be the last to be fooled. Love is blind, I suppose."

"Love is stupid," The Old Bird stated with a laugh that sounded like a crow's cackle. "So what's next? You gonna confront her?"

"Well, the funeral's tomorrow, so I hardly think that's the time or place."

"Agreed. But I'd bet my last dime that that guy'll be right up front with the new widow. She'll likely be hanging off of him."

"Well, ye might be right," Mary-Margaret said, taking a sip of her whiskey.

"Might be? Ha!" The Old Bird cawed. "I *am* right. Too bad the funeral's tomorrow or I'd go with you, just to prove it to myself."

"I'll let ye know, if—"

"Speaking of which," The Old Bird said as she looked at her watch. "I gotta go. It's a school night. When did it get so late? I've got this one. You get the next."

Before Mary-Margaret could say anything, The Old Bird was up at the bar paying the bill.

Chapter Ten

Even the brilliant afternoon sunshine and fresh air couldn't brighten the mood at Marco Giancola's funeral. Attendees were dressed in solemn black. The organ echoed ominously throughout the chapel, and, just as The Old Bird had predicted, the widow Giancola made that slow walk down the aisle behind her husband's casket, supported by a strikingly handsome man whom Mary-Margaret soon discovered was the business partner.

"Dear friends and family," Father Miguel began, "we gather here today to celebrate the life of Marco Giancola and to commend him to God's mercy. In our grief, we seek comfort in our faith and in one another. Let us begin this Mass by recalling the promise of eternal life and the hope we have in Christ. Let us pray."

Suddenly, the doors into the narthex burst open. Father Miguel looked up and saw Sister Augustine–in full nun's habit, as always–come rushing in.

"Pardon me for interrupting, Father," she called out softly. "Just running a little late. Sorry."

Mary-Margaret had recognized the voice even before she looked back over her shoulder.

For the love of God...

"Don't mind me," Sister Augustine said, looking from side to side as she rushed up the aisle. "I'll just find a seat...ah, here we are! Excuse me, pardon me."

The nun pushed herself past several people until she was standing beside Mary-Margaret.

"Carry on," Sister Augustine said with a wave.

Father Miguel cleared his throat.

"As I was saying," Father Miguel continued. "Let us pray. Lord, our God, the death of your…"

"Jesus, Mary, and Joseph, Arthur," Mary-Margaret hissed as those around her prayed. "What in God's name are ye thinking?"

"It's *Sister Augustine* MM. Don't burn my cover," she hissed back.

"Ach, ye've lost the plot, lad."

"No, MM. I'm here to make sure *you* don't lose the plot," Sister Augustine said, lowering her voice as she pointed to a small device on her wimple. "Video camera."

"I know what 'tis, luv. Ye've used it before."

"To brilliant success, I might add," Sister Augustine whispered, nodding to the people around them as the prayer continued.

"And?" Mary-Margaret whispered back.

"I've captured the faces of everyone here," she whispered, glancing around with a small, satisfied smile.

"Grand," Mary-Margaret said out loud, rolling her eyes.

Father Miguel looked up from the pulpit and fixed his gaze on Mary-Margaret. Someone coughed awkwardly. Father Miguel then glanced back down with a sigh, although whether it was irritation or resignation was up for debate.

"We ask this through Christ our Lord. Amen," he concluded. "You may be seated."

"Oh, you roll your eyes now, MM," Sister Augustine whispered with a knowing smile, "but you'll thank me later."

The two sat silently beside each other for no more than a moment before Mary-Margaret leaned over toward her friend.

"By the way…I already know everyone who's here," she whispered.

"Do you?" Sister Augustine whispered back without looking over at Mary-Margaret. "I think not, because, if you did, you'd know there was a murderer amongst us."

"I didn't say I knew their *business*," Mary-Margaret whispered louder than she'd intended, her annoyance finally getting the better of her. "I just said I *know* everyone—"

"Shhh," came a whisper so loaded with judgment it could have been printed in the missalette.

Father Miguel pursed his lips but did not look up. More than one person glared at them.

"Let's just get through this, and we'll talk later, shall we?" Mary-Margaret whispered.

"I will call upon," Father Miguel stated, "Irene Ashford for the first reading, *The Book of Wisdom*, chapter three, verses one through nine."

Irene Ashford made her way to the ambo and cleared her throat before nervously looking out at the mourners.

"And she's wearing something cut *that* low to a funeral mass, no less?" Mary-Margaret commented. The woman seated to her left gave her a dirty look.

"'Tis a wonder everything stayed in place," Mary-Margaret mumbled once Irene had finished the reading.

"I will now call upon," Father Miguel announced after the response, "Laura-Jean McQueen for our second reading, taken from 1 Corinthians, chapter fifteen, verses fifty-one through fifty-seven."

"I hope she's taken her medication," Mary-Margaret muttered as she watched one of the few people she truly disliked prepare to do her piece.

As everyone but Mary-Margaret had anticipated, the reading went off without a hitch, as did the remainder of the mass.

"I expect ye'll be wanting to ride with me to the gravesite?" Mary-Margaret said, following Sister Augustine out of the nave along with the others.

"You bet," she said, her voice dropping into its more familiar, natural pitch. "I want to see if the widow Giancola is a grave-jumper."

"A what?"

"Grave jumper. Someone who jumps into the grave after the coffin is lowered. Did you see how upset she was?"

"I think shocked is more what she was, luv. From what I've got, there wasn't a lot of love lost between them. Forgive me, Father," she said, looking up, "if I'm speaking out of turn at a time like this."

As they stepped outside of the church, Mary-Margaret spotted Detective Sergeant Gill. And he spotted her. And gave Sister Augustine a very close look.

"Good afternoon, Mrs. O'Shea," he said as he approached them both.

"Indeed," she said, chin up.

"A friend of Marco Giancola's, were you?"

"A supportive member of the parish."

"Of course," he said with a condescending smile. "You do recall, of course, previous encounters we've had with one another?"

"Hard not to."

"And you do recall my most recent phone call with you? Where I explicitly stated that you're not to get involved in any homicide investigations, past, present, or future...?"

"I more clearly recall that it was I and me friends who solved the last two cases ye lads were floundering around with."

"Be that as it may—" the detective sergeant sputtered.

"Hardly," Mary-Margaret cut in. "But for the work of meself, ye'd probably still be trying to figure out who murdered Jane Ann Hill, never mind solving Cassandra Lewis' murder."

"That's debatable," he replied.

"Debatable whether ye'd still be in homicide but for me, is what I'm thinking," Mary-Margaret added, giving him a curt look up and down.

"Mrs. O'Shea," Detective Sergeant Gill said, snapping a piece of gum from the wrapper and popping it into his mouth, "what I am here to tell you very clearly is—"

"Sorry, lad," Mary-Margaret said, stepping around him. "If I'm going to be in the procession, I've got to get to me car now. Sister Augustine, are ye ready, luv?"

* * *

The roadway inside the cemetery was mucky and already lined with cars by the time Mary-Margaret and Sister Augustine arrived, forcing them to walk a great distance to the gravesite. Mary-Margaret glanced down and immediately realized that her boots would be ruined by the excessive salt Umberto had once again dumped everywhere—entirely unnecessary, as usual, since there wasn't a patch of ice on the roadway.

"There they are," Sister Augustine said, pointing towards the crowd.

"Not much gets by you, does it?" Mary-Margaret commented. Her step faltered slightly as they veered off the roadway onto the uneven, partially frozen ground, but she quickly regained her balance without a second thought.

"No, I mean there," Sister Augustine repeated, pointing to the man supporting Annette Giancola.

"Do you think she needs all of that?" Mary-Margaret asked, noticing how tightly he was holding the new widow.

"Not unless he's holding her back," Sister Augustine replied.

"If that's the case, I don't see how that back rubbing he's doing now is helping."

"Should we get a bit closer?"

"No. Let's just stand back and see what happens."

What happened was what one might expect at a graveside: a few words were spoken, the coffin was lowered, a few more words were exchanged, and then Annette Giancola took some freshly dug soil and tossed it onto the ornate box that held her dead husband's body.

"I should have worn boots," Sister Augustine grumbled, pulling up her habit to show a ratty old pair of runners.

"We'll just be a minute more. Think of something warm, luv."

While Sister Augustine closed her eyes, Mary-Margaret couldn't help but notice Annette Giancola step back into the arms of the handsome man.

"Something's not right there," Mary-Margaret said, her eyebrow raised.

"What?" Sister Augustine said, opening her eyes.

"There. The way he's holding her," she said, looking disapprovingly at the couple. "When I was standing with me four smallies—three of them hanging off of me—at me Jimmy's graveside, God rest his soul, Angus and

Eleanor stood by. There was nothing like what I'm seeing here going on there."

"You had the children, MM."

"Francis doesn't even hug me like that," Mary-Margaret countered before turning back to the car. "Come on, luv. Let's get you warmed up."

"I *knew* you two were an item," Sister Augustine said with a laugh.

The two friends sat in the car, the engine running and the heat blasting as they watched the mourners return to their cars.

"Here, MM," Sister Augustine said, pulling a pair of small binoculars out of her habit pocket and passing them over.

"I would say something, except I'm glad you've brought them. Ta, luv," Mary-Margaret said, bringing them up to her eyes just in time to see Annette Giancola and the handsome man get into the funeral car.

"That's odd," Mary-Margaret commented, scanning the the roadway with the binoculars. "She mentioned that he had grown children. Why aren't they getting into the car with her?"

"Maybe they drove themselves?"

"To their da's funeral?" Mary-Margaret scoffed. "Not at all likely. In fact, I didn't recall seeing anyone resembling his children at the graveside."

"How would you know what they look like?"

"A mother knows," Mary-Margaret stated. "They must be estranged."

"Maybe they live out of town and couldn't get a flight in on time," Sister Augustine suggested.

"Lad, when it's yer da's funeral, the airlines make space for ye. If ye want them to." Mary-Margaret stared at the funeral car through the binoculars as it drove right past them. "No, there's something not right going on there."

"What are you thinking?"

"Do I have to spell it out for ye? For someone as—*in the know*—as ye. Ach. Those two in the car, there, are having an affair, is what I'm thinking."

"Well, that would give us another suspect, wouldn't it?"

"Or maybe two. As odd as it sounds, perhaps the widow Giancola *is* involved," Mary-Margaret said, passing the binoculars back to Sister Augustine before putting the car in gear. "Best get back to the church for the repast before all of Monique Prudhomme's pinwheel sandwiches are gone."

Chapter Eleven

"Sister Augustine," Father Miguel said as she and Mary-Margaret walked down the hall towards the gymnasium. "A word?"

"I'll meet ye inside," Mary-Margaret said as she carried on into the packed gymnasium.

"Since when do you travel with nuns, Mary? Trying to earn your way into Heaven?" Eric Switzer asked, his voice cutting through the hum of the room.

"Meaning?" she retorted.

"He doesn't mean anything by it," Monique Prudhomme said, taking Mary-Margaret's arm. "You know Eric…he's just a busybody."

"And I don't recall ever seeing your car at Marco's Motors, so what's your connection to the deceased?" Eric continued, following the two women towards the refreshment table.

"If she's involved, you can bet there's a murder," Laura-Jean McQueen remarked, handing Mary-Margaret a cup of lukewarm tea from behind the serving table. Her sing-song tone grated on Mary-Margaret's ears like nails on a chalkboard.

"Me car's an import," Mary-Margaret replied, taking the Styrofoam cup without making eye contact.

"So it *was* murder," Laura-Jean declared, her voice cutting through all the others in the room. The people around the table shifted uncomfortably, but still leaned in, eager to hear Mary-Margaret's response.

"I *knew* it!" Eric exclaimed in a stage-whispered

"Don't you take your car to Marco's Motors, Eric?" Irene Ashford said, gently steering him away from the table by the elbow. "It's a standard, if I recall correctly, and I'm sure you do know that I can drive a stick, don't you?" She glanced quickly at Mary-Margaret and added with a playful wink, "Run while you can."

"Would ye mind holding me tea?" Mary-Margaret said, passing the cup to Monique. "I'm just off to the jacks. And would ye mind snapping up a couple of yer pinwheel sandwiches for me and Sister Augustine?"

Before Monique could respond, Mary-Margaret had passed off her cup and was in the hallway outside of the gymnasium heading towards Father Miguel's office. The door was slightly ajar, and she could hear weeping from inside.

"I'm very sorry, Sister," Father Miguel said in a tone that suggested anything but. "I'm sure you'll find another—

"Excuse me, Fa—" Mary-Margaret said, pushing the door open. "Oh, I'm sorry. Am I interrupting?"

"In fact, you are," Father Miguel advised.

"Oh, me stars!" she exclaimed, looking at her friend in tears. "What is it, luv?"

"Nothing you need to—" Father Miguel began.

"This isn't about Sister Augustine accompanying me to the cemetery, is it?"

"No, not that it's any of your concern."

"Good, because if it wasn't for her, I don't know how I would have managed. A godsend, if ye don't mind me saying, is this one. Really ought to be more involved in the church than just as a cleaner."

"I don't think—"

"Ach, it's just come to me, hasn't it?" Mary-Margaret said, looking up to the ceiling. "And to think, being the humble servant she is, Sister Augustine didn't think to mention it to ye, Father Miguel. She should be the new new New Girl!"

"I have no idea what you're talking about," Father Miguel said.

"It's as clear as the light that shines in the darkness and would bring ye one step closer to the Vatican, Father."

Both Father Miguel and Sister Augustine stared at her.

"Ach, did ye not see it, Father? Having this new New Girl here—not even a Catholic—being the forward face of yer parish, is nothing short of a slap in the face to the Vatican and to the Pope Himself. Not an endearing act, to say the least. No, what ye need is someone as your first point of contact who embodies all that it means to be Catholic. And who better to do that than a nun? This nun?"

"Mary-Mar—" Father Miguel began.

"Well, I am good with computers," Sister Augustine said, brushing the tears off of her face. "And I do enjoy a good Gregorian Chant as much as the next person."

"And ye don't get any more authentically Catholic than by being a nun," Mary-Margaret added, nodding convincingly at Father Miguel.

"I'm not looking to replace my administrative—"

"No, yer not," Mary-Margaret agreed. "Yer looking to improve the experience of anyone wishing to be a part of this congregation."

"No, I'm looking to—"

"And to be moved along to a better parish that would put ye in the sightlines of His Holiness," Mary-Margaret said, looking the young priest right in the eye.

"Well," he said with a sigh. "I can't argue that."

"And what better way to show how competent ye are than to have yer first line out there representing all that we hold sacred here at St. Francis of Assisi's?"

"She's a terrible cleaner," Father Miguel said, wiping some dust off of his desk.

"She's a grand secretary," Mary-Margaret countered.

"Executive assistant," Sister Augustine said. "They call us 'executive assistants' now."

"Even better. And, I'm sure, she'll work for half of what yer paying that new New Girl out there, which is a blessing in and of itself, considering how much this parish is costing the dioceses."

"I can have that front desk running like clockwork," Sister Augustine said enthusiastically. "I can upgrade all of your operating systems, sync your sermons, integrate your itinerary, and keep the chaos in check."

Father Miguel glanced down at Sister Augustine and then looked up at Mary-Margaret.

"Does that mean managing how the more…challenging individuals within my congregation try to access me?" he said to Sister Augustine.

"No one gets past Sister Augustine," she replied with a nod befitting a front-line soldier.

"Well," Father Miguel said. "I'm not promising anything permanent, and I'll have to give her notice, but, if you can only keep…everyone…from wandering into my office, then you can stay."

"Oh, thanks be to—" Mary-Margaret began,

"But only until Ashleigh gets back from maternity leave."

"That's fine, Father," Sister Augustine said, beaming from behind her wimple.

"And you will relinquish your cleaning duties immediately."

"Most certainly!" Sister Augustine said, thrusting out her manly hand.

"Well, let's celebrate with…a cup of tea, shall we?" Mary-Margaret said, motioning for Sister Augustine to get out of the office before Father Miguel could change his mind.

"Excellent idea," Father Miguel said. "Please close the door behind you."

"Sqwee!" Sister Augustine exclaimed as soon as they were in the hallway.

"There she is," Monique said, directing Annette Giancola towards Mary-Margaret.

"Thank you so much…for everything," the widow said. "The repast was lovely. Marco would have…"

She broke off into sobs.

"Me thinks she doth weep too greatly," Sister Augustine whispered to Mary-Margaret.

"Mind yerself," Mary-Margaret remonstrated. "The woman has just buried her husband."

"I'm sorry," Annette said, wiping her nose. "It's just…a lot."

"Ach, of that I'm sure," Mary-Margaret replied, giving her a hug. "And it doesn't get easier. Just different. Here. Why don't we go have a wee sit somewhere?"

"No, Robert is waiting for me. I just wanted to thank you for…this."

"Robert, is it?" Mary-Margaret said, trying not to sound too judgy.

"Marco's business partner. Robert Jensen. He's been such a rock through all of this. Why don't you drop by his house—I'm staying there for a bit. Robert's idea. Just for a few days until I can get my thoughts together. Why don't you drop by, and I'll introduce you properly. And you can update us both on what you've found out about Marco's…death."

"Indeed," Mary-Margaret replied, casting a brief look at Sister Augustine. Neither needed to voice their thoughts—it struck them both as strange that, just an hour after burying her husband, the widow Giancola was asking for an update on Mary-Margaret's findings, never mind that she was staying at his business partner's house.

"Let me just ditch this habit," Sister Augustine said, knowing exactly what their next steps would be.

Chapter Twelve

Mary-Margaret drove past a Range Rover and a BMW Z4 as they made their way up the circular driveway to the address Annette Giancola had given her. They stopped near the stone steps leading to the front door and Mary-Margaret pulled up Daphne's parking brake.

Arthur whistled softly. "You don't see too many of these old houses around anymore."

"*We* don't see too many of these old houses around anymore," Mary-Margaret corrected, her eyes trying to take it all in.

"Who knew there was that much money in fixing cars."

"Me Michael risks his life, night and day, and yet…" She let the words trail off.

"Mob money," Arthur stated. "I bet this came from organized crime."

"I wouldn't put it past him," Mary-Margaret said, finally getting out of the car. "And him having the vulnerable widow stay here for a few days. The gall."

Arthur followed Mary-Margaret up the stairs. The two of them stood, dwarfed by the size of the double doors in front of them. Mary-Margaret grasped the knocker on the door to her right and gave it a good pounding.

"Geez, MM, you don't have to break the door down," Arthur said quietly.

"Just getting my anger out is all," she replied before flashing a smile as the door opened.

"Oh," the handsome man Mary-Margaret recognized from the cemetery said. "May I help you?"

"Is that you, Mary-Margaret?" Annette Giancola's voice could be heard from somewhere behind the man. "Robert, it's that woman from the church I was telling you about. Let her in, please."

"But who is this?" Robert asked, giving the doughy man beside the rather plain-looking woman standing in front of him a once-over—too young to be her son, towering over her like a misplaced lamppost, but definitely not someone he would have thought this woman would be coupled with.

"Arthur Lukowitz. EA to Father Miguel," Arthur said with a polite nod.

Mary-Margaret gave him the side-eye.

"I mean…Arthur Lukowitz. No job description added."

"Oh," the man said, disinterestedly. "Come on in, then. Annette…?"

"I'm just pouring myself a drink. Ask our guests if they'd like one while I'm at it, will you?"

"Would you like a drink?" he repeated, barely allowing them into the house.

"No, thank ye," Mary-Margaret said. "We're fine, aren't we, Arthur?"

"Huh?" Arthur replied, looking around the grand entrance. "Yeah. Sure. Do you actually *live* here?"

"Yes. I…actually live here," the man replied with a yawn. "Annette?"

"I take it you've met Robert," Annette said, appearing behind him, a full glass of wine in her hand. "Oh. And you must be…?"

"We've met," Robert said, cutting Annette off before she could introduce Arthur. "Now, if you don't mind, I've got some paperwork to do in my office. Are you sure you're okay to be seeing guests now?"

"Absolutely, Robert. Thank you," she said with a familiarity basked in warmth that Mary-Margaret thought inappropriate, particularly given the circumstances. "Come in. Let's go into the solarium. It's so pretty in there when there's frost on the ground."

The two followed the widow down the hall into a large glass-walled room with a fireplace blazing in the corner.

"Sit," she motioned.

They sat.

"Are you sure I can't get you anything?" Annette asked. "Tea? Coffee? Soft drink?"

"We're fine, luv," Mary-Margaret said as she sank into what might have been the most comfortable chair she'd ever sat in.

"I'll have a glass of water," Arthur said, sitting in a less comfortable chair.

"Where are yer manners?" Mary-Margaret demanded as soon as Annette had left the room.

"MM, I don't like this at all," he whispered loudly, ignoring her comment. "Did you see how eager that Robert guy was to get away from us? And how smoothly this woman led us into the room, as if she owned the place? I think you're right."

"Of course I'm right. About what?"

"Those two are lovers."

Before she could respond, Annette was back.

"It's stunning in here, isn't it?" she said, passing Arthur a glass of water. "Robert is so lucky to have this house on the ravine. The sun sets just over there."

"Ye seem quite comfortable here," Mary-Margaret said. "Not that ye shouldn't be, of course, but it just seems that yer very familiar—"

"Yes, I am," she said, taking more of a gulp than a large sip of what Mary-Margaret suspected was a top-up of her wine. "I spent a lot of time here a few months ago after Robert had a stroke."

"Oh?"

"It was only a minor one, thank goodness, and he's fully recovered, but it took a while for him to get back on his feet."

"And where was yer husband during this time?"

"Marco? Doing what Marco does, I suppose," she said, taking another mouthful of wine.

"Which is…?"

"Mary-Margaret, I know I've just buried my husband, but that doesn't change the fact that he was a ladies' man and a nasty drunk. And, if I'm going to be completely honest, not beyond being both verbally and physically abusive."

"Oh," Mary-Margaret said, her body shooting up in the chair.

"Why do you think his children aren't here?" she continued. Not waiting for a response, Annette continued. "Marco was a mean man when he was drunk, and he was drunk a lot. Wait. Let me correct that. Marco was a mean man to me and his children when he was drunk. I've been told that he could be a real charmer after a few drinks, just not to us, apparently."

"I'm sorry, luv," Mary-Margaret began.

"Robert?" Annette said before anyone else heard his footsteps in the hallway.

"Yes," he said, striding into the room. "I'm sorry for running off on you like that. In the middle of something. I don't think I properly introduced myself. I'm Robert Jensen, Marco's partn—owner now, I suppose, of the Marco's Motors chain."

He thrust out his hand. Mary-Margaret remained seated as she shook it, while Arthur merely nodded.

"Are ye a mechanic yerself, then?" Mary-Margaret asked, knowing the answer.

"Me? A mechanic?" Robert said with a laugh. "No. I wouldn't know one end of a wrench from the other. I'm in the business side of things."

"I see," she said, furrowing her brow. "Well, with yer partner gone, and him being the brains behind the operation, will ye be selling up or—"

"I think that's a rather inappropriate question, don't you?" Robert said, his tone unexpectedly sharp. "Especially considering the day. More wine, Annette?"

"Ach, where are me manners?" Mary-Margaret said with an apologetic smile.

"Yes, please," Annette said, upending her glass before passing it to him.

"Are you sure you wouldn't like anything…?"

"Mary-Margaret. Mary-Margaret O'Shea. And no, thank ye. I'm fine," she replied, noting that his hand seemed to linger on Annette's for a bit too long as he took the glass from her.

"Suit yourself," he said, striding out of the room with Annette's empty wine glass.

"Don't mind him," Annette said. "He's just being protective of the business.

If word gets out that he's selling right now, it'll seem like the business is in trouble, and he won't be able to get top dollar for it. Between the three of us, the plan is to sell the business sooner than later."

"And then what?" Mary-Margaret asked.

"And then…I don't know. We all sail off into the sunset?" Annette said, smiling warmly as Robert came back carrying two glasses.

"Sip that slowly, Annette," Robert said as he handed her the glass. "I've put a sedative in the wine so that you'll be able to sleep later. If you gulp it down all at once, you're liable to pass out while our guests are here."

Mary-Margaret and Arthur looked at one another. Again, words were not necessary.

"Annette tells me ye had a wee stroke a while back. That must have been something for ye, no?" Mary-Margaret said.

"Oh, did she now? Well, I guess there's no harm in mentioning it since I'm back to full strength again," he said, smiling warmly at Annette.

"It's okay, Robert," she said, taking a sip of wine. "They're on our side."

"I don't understand," Mary-Margaret said, looking at one and then the other.

"Robert's always thinking of the business. Not wanting it to look as if it could be vulnerable. And, as the partner—I mean owner–the last thing we want is for word to get out that he could be pressured to sell under value."

"She's right," he said, puffing his chest out. "If I'm going to get top dollar when I sell—"

"If *we're* going to get top dollar," Annette corrected, her voice beginning to slur. "What sort of sedative did you put in this drink? I can already feel it."

"Nothing special," he said. "It's probably just the culmination of Marco's death, followed by such an emotionally draining day. Perhaps it's time to say goodbye to your friends and then head upstairs to bed."

"I suppose you're right," she said quietly, closing her eyes as she rolled her neck. "I'm sorry, Mary-Margaret. And…whatever your name is. I'm sorry. I've got to lie down for a while. Would you mind, Robert…?"

"Not at all. Would you follow me, please?" Robert said, leading Mary-Margaret and Arthur to the front door.

"Is she going to be okay?" Mary-Margaret asked.

"She'll be fine. Just needed a little something to calm her down, and that's exactly what I gave her. Once she has a good night's sleep, she'll be fine," he said with a condescending smile. He opened one of the huge front doors. "Drive safely."

Mary-Margaret and Arthur walked over to Daphne, neither of them saying a word.

"I don't like that one bit," Mary-Margaret said as soon as she got into the car.

"Ya think? Major creep factor going on there," Arthur replied.

Chapter Thirteen

"I'm on it, MM," Arthur said, filling the kettle with water as soon as they walked through the back door of Michael's house. "And I'll get some biscuits."

"Come on, Wee Phil," Mary-Margaret said as the Jack Russell came bounding towards her. "I'm sure Michael didn't think to take ye around back before he went to work. And they wonder why I never got them a pup when they were little. Let's go."

She clipped the leash on the dog and went back outside.

"You're all dolled up this afternoon, Mary-Margaret," Brian called from the laneway, a glass of wine in his hand.

"Indeed," she said, choosing not to say what she really wanted to say. *Grown men. Drinking in the laneway like this. It's a disgrace.* "Come on, Wee Phil. Let's get ye over to the bushes there for a piddle."

"Hot date tonight?" Johnny asked, raising a can of beer to his lips as she walked by him.

"Come on, fellas," Doug said. "Mary-Margaret always looks good."

"If ye must know," Mary-Margaret said, barely able to keep her disdain to herself, "I was just getting home from Marco Giancola's funeral."

Mary-Margaret stood by as Wee Phil began emptying his bladder.

"Oh, right," Doug said. "I read about that. Shame, really. I wonder what'll happen to his garage."

"Condos, baby," Johnny said with a belch. "And I wouldn't be surprised if his other shop by the lake gets knocked down, too."

"I didn't know that he had two shops in the city," Mary-Margaret said, waiting for the dog to finish.

"Oh, yes," Brian said. "Whoever was in charge of setting up the franchises was very strategic when they purchased the properties for the garages. They've got the two here, and a dozen or so just outside the city, all in prime redevelopment areas."

"Surely no one could have known that when they bought them," Mary-Margaret said as the dog, having finished his business and seeing a squirrel at the entrance to the laneway, began pulling on the leash.

"Well, if they didn't, they just got really lucky," Brian said.

"You mean his widow did," Johnny said, reaching down to pull another can of beer out of the box by his feet. "Want one?"

"No," Mary-Margaret stated as calmly as she could. "I've got a cuppa waiting for me inside."

Head held high, she walked past the three neighbours back into Michael's house.

"Ye'd think three grown men would have something better to do at the end of the day, then stand in the laneway drinking," she huffed to herself as she released the dog and took off her boots. "It's not like they don't have anywhere else to go. Ach. Never mind. Let's have that cuppa."

Mary-Margaret walked into the dining room, where Arthur was waiting, tea in mugs, McVitie's on a plate, steno pad in hand.

"What's with the steno, then?" Mary-Margaret said as she sat down in her usual spot.

"I thought we should start to keep track of what we know," Arthur said, jotting down a few things. "And I'm wondering if Father Miguel expects me to be dressed as Sister Augustine when I start my new job."

"What else did ye have in mind?" Mary-Margaret asked.

"I don't know. I was thinking something a bit more…Margot-Robbie-as-Barbie meets…you!"

"Me?" Mary-Margaret exclaimed. "Ach, well, if it's realism yer looking for, get rid of that Robbie girl. I'm sure she's lovely and all, but I'm the genuine article. And don't even try to compare yerself to Barbie. Never mind. I'll teach ye everything ye need to know. But, as far as what to wear…I'm thinking since the selling point was yer being a nun, then ye'd best stick to being a nun."

"Hmmm. Well, maybe I'll slowly move towards that Margot Robbie look."

"In the meantime," Mary-Margaret said, taking a sip of her tea, silently noting that she'd been cut from the role models completely, "What do we know?"

"Well," Arthur said. "We know that Marco Giancola was murdered. And we know that there are lots of people who'd probably want him dead."

"Do ye ever wonder how many people would want ye dead?" Mary-Margaret asked.

"No."

There was a brief pause.

"So," Mary-Margaret continued. "Who wants him dead and why?"

"The first on my list would be that Robert guy."

"Well, if that's the case, then he'll get a rude awakening when he finds that it was Annette that's the one pushing this to be looked at as a murder."

"I wouldn't be surprised if he kills her as well."

"That's a bit harsh, don't ye think?"

"Come on, MM. Who puts a sedative in someone's wine?"

"To his credit, not that I'm looking to credit the likes of him, but he did tell her that he was…"

"What? That he'd put enough in her drink to knock her old cold with just a couple of sips? And having her stay at his house? That guy has Serial Killer written all over him."

"What about Herself?"

"Annette? No. Why would she? And if she had, why would she want us to look into it? With our track record, there's no way an actual murderer would want us investigating."

"I can't answer that, luv, but we've got to keep an open mind," Mary-Margaret said, taking a biscuit from the plate. "But what if she called us in to get the investigation reopened, not because she's worried about Marco's death, but because she wants to frame Robert. Make him look guilty and shift the focus away from her. The lads out back were saying his chain of garages is sitting on some prime real estate, so maybe it's all about the money. Maybe Annette figured Robert was going to get the lot if Marco died, so she cozied up to him early, hoping he'd look after her once Marco was out of the way. But now? Well, now she's got to make sure she stays in his good books, just in case things don't work out like she planned. Who knows? If she can't frame him for the murder, maybe she'll end up killing him, too. Or, at the very least, land him in jail for Marco's murder—and then she gets the lot of it, doesn't she?"

"No, *that's* a bit harsh," Arthur murmured.

"No. That's life. Put her on the list."

"What if it was just some rando?" Arthur suggested. "What if Marco was in the shop having a few drinks and some guy just came in through the back and killed him. Or maybe didn't know he was there and just thought he'd steal some tools and stuff, but was confronted by Marco, panicked, and then killed him?"

"That's possible."

"And the guy might not even have known he'd killed Marco. Didn't he bleed out?"

"Ach, I'd hate to be the officers assigned to check the shop! Speaking of which, I think we can safely add the owner to the mix. He struck me as a bit of an odd one."

"Oh, right. Yes. He'd have something to gain if…but wait. If he killed Marco, there's nothing to say the business would get sold, which would mean he still couldn't sell the building if Marco's Motors was still leasing the place."

"Unless he and that Robert lad are in it together."

"Or he's willing to give Robert a ton of money to buy out the lease."

"Which he'd take, I'm sure," Mary-Margaret said. "Ye know, the more I think about him, the more me skin crawls. In fact, I'm beginning to wonder if we should have left Annette Giancola there."

"I wouldn't put it past him to…" Arthur said, making a slashing motion across his neck.

"Ach. Me either. And now that we're spelling it all out, I'm starting to wonder what's in Marco's will, and if it could override the business contract. What if Robert doesn't get the business and it goes to Annette? That would make things a lot cleaner for her if she did murder Marco. And maybe there's a clause, or whatever ye call it, that says if Annette dies within so many days, the business goes to Robert."

"Oh, you are starting to think dirty, aren't you, MM?" Arthur said with a wicked smile.

"Money changes everything."

"Or what if Robert *does* stand to get the whole company unless *he* dies within so many days, and then it goes to Annette, which is why she's shagging—"

"I can't imagine it with the likes of that man," Mary-Margaret stated with a shudder.

"Greed's not picky, so long as it gets its fill," Arthur said with a shrug.

"Yer right about that, luv," Mary-Margaret said with a sigh. "Money—or the prospect of it—changes a person, that's for sure."

"So it sounds like either one of them could kill the other one to end up with the jackpot."

"Indeed, although me bet's on Robert doing Annette in at the moment," Mary-Margaret said. "It's all about the money, isn't it?"

"I think we should call Michael."

"Why? He doesn't know anything about money."

"No, but he's a detective, MM. Maybe he can give us some ideas."

"Have ye been drinking, lad? Do ye honestly believe me Michael would be of any use to us? If he had ideas, he'd have been Police Officer of the Year a dozen times over by now."

"What about Mandy? Do you think she'd help?"

"Now yer spinning on all wheels," Mary-Margaret said, getting up and walking to the back door where she'd left her purse. "I think that's a brilliant idea."

Wee Phil ran after her, but his excitement waned when he saw that she was reaching for something inside of her purse rather than a treat for him.

Mary-Margaret tapped in the phone number.

"Detective Sergeant Amanda Black. Homicide."

"Well, don't you sound like all that and a bag of chips!" Mary-Margaret said. "Mandy, luv, it's me, Mary-Margaret. Mary-Margaret O'Sh—"

"You don't need to give me a last name, Mary-Margaret. There's only one of you. What's up?"

"I've got a bit of a…situation," she said hesitantly, as she walked back into the living room and looked towards Arthur. He motioned for her to keep talking. "Ye see, it's about a friend of mine. Yes, ye see, she's got herself in a bit of a bind, although she doesn't know it yet."

"I'm listening."

"Well, ye see, she's involved with this fella, maybe—"

"Wait. Maybe involved with him, or maybe he's a fella?"

"Maybe involved with him. Ye see, she's newly widowed, and he's kind of taken her in for the time being. Me and Arthur were just out to see her today. But here's the thing: he spiked her drink."

"Okay."

"With a sedative. She was in a heap in no time. He had to see us out."

"So he administered a noxious substance?"

"I suppose," Mary-Margaret said, shrugging at Arthur.

"And she knew nothing about it?"

"Well, he did say he'd put a sedative in her wine, but honestly, Mandy, she was flat out before ye could blink. Might as well have been a horse tranquilizer for all I know."

"Give me the address, and I'll have a car go by and check on her. Might be nothing. Might be something. What's her name?"

"Annette Giancola."

Chapter Fourteen

The back door had barely closed behind Arthur when Mary-Margaret's iPhone vibrated. Twice.

Hey Gran. Going to Kyle's for dinner. Luv ya.

OT. Be home when I get home.

Well, I guess that's that, then. No sense makin' anything if it's just going to be me. Let's get ye out for another piddle.

Wee Phil waited as patiently as he was capable of while Mary-Margaret clipped on his leash. She held the dog behind her as she peered outside, hoping Michael's neighbours had gone in. When she saw the coast was clear, she headed down the laneway and then out onto the street towards the park.

"Mrs. O'Shea," a voice she recognized called out.

Mary-Margaret stopped and turned around. Much to her horror, she saw Detective Sergeant Gill.

"Mr. Gill," she replied. "To what do I owe the honours?"

"That's Detective Sergeant Gill, but never mind," he grumbled, walking towards her. "I just got off the phone with Detective Sergeant Bl—"

"Mandy? Oh, grand. Lovely girl, is our Mandy."

"I've been very clear with you," D/S Gill continued, "and now I'm inches away from arresting you for interfering with a criminal matter, Mrs. O'Shea."

"Interfering?" Mary-Margaret said indignantly. "I believe I may be preventing a criminal matter from going unnoticed—unlike yourself, whom I very much wish I hadn't noticed at all—if I recall the conversation I just had with me Mandy correctly." She carried on before D/S Gill could get a word in. "But now that me attention has been dragged over to ye, why are ye here? Why aren't ye checking on the widow Giancola?"

"We've got a uniformed car heading over, not that it's any of your business, and I'm here to talk to you."

"And so ye have. Out on the street like this, no less. Now, I should think a person of reasonable intelligence would wonder why a grown man wouldn't just pick up the phone, if that was yer intention, rather than rush after me on a public street like this."

"I hardly think—"

"That's quite obvious, Mr. Gill. In the meantime, I see no reason why ye'd be lurking behind bushes and such—practically lying in wait, no doubt— when ye've got a phone in yer pocket if all ye wanted was a wee chat. Or were your intentions more nefarious, Mr. Gill?"

"My *intentions* were *not*—" the detective sergeant began, his face reddening.

"Ye've no lawful reason to be stopping me like this," Mary-Margaret scolded. "Ye've no lawful reason to be approaching me…jumping out at me, really, like this. And, while I believe we've established that ye are lacking in the reasonable intelligence department, as a police officer, ye must know that this would look very much like stalking to anyone. Particularly anyone in yer criminal prosecution world. Would ye agree, Mr. Gill?"

Detective Sergeant Billy Gilly stood in front of her, completely speechless, her words having knocked any he might have out of him.

"Now," Mary-Margaret said, head held high, shoulders down, "if ye don't mind, I've got, as ye can see, a wee pup in need of running off a lot of energy."

With that, Mary-Margaret turned and began to walk away.

"Mrs. O'Shea," D/S Gill called after her, "next time you interfere, you *will* be arrested."

Mary-Margaret stopped, turned, and looked squarely at him.

"Have ye nothing better to do than threaten pensioners, Mr. Gill? I'd hope ye do. In the meantime, why don't ye get back to whatever it is that occupies yer time and let me get on me way," she said, adding, "And we'll see who solves this murder first."

Mary-Margaret wheeled around and marched toward the park, with Wee

Phil—perhaps for the first time ever—being pulled along by the leash.

Chapter Fifteen

Fortunately, Friday morning was a bit milder than the other day, so there was no frost to scrape off of Daphne. Mary-Margaret hesitated as she slid the key into the ignition, holding her breath before pressing the Start button. She exhaled slowly as the car's engine came to life.

Thank you, St. Christopher, she thought to herself as she drove out of the parking space behind Michael's house.

Anyone else might have thought through the long-term consequences of their actions. Or, at the very least, they might have taken a step back to let things calm down. Or waited more than a day before continuing down a path that they had been clearly warned would lead them to jail.

But Mary-Margaret wasn't just anyone. As a result, she cheerfully drove herself to St. Francis of Assisi's with a clear goal in mind: to get Annette Giancola's home address and pay the widow a visit, having decided for no reason whatsoever that the new widow would, in fact, be alone at her own home this morning. She had also decided that this wasn't going to be a purely social visit. Mary-Margaret was intent on uncovering everything she could about Robert Jensen.

For reasons known only to herself, she also thought she'd see Arthur as Sister Augustine in the church office when she popped her head through the half door. Given that it had just been a day since the offer to take over the role of secretary was offered, it should have been no surprise that she was confronted, instead, by the new New Girl.

"Oh," she said. "Yer still here, then, are ye?"

"Uh, yeah," the new New Girl said, her tone making it clear that she thought Mary-Margaret was an idiot. She chewed her gum as she glanced up from her desk by the door before blowing a bubble and letting it burst. "Where else would I be?"

"Right," Mary-Margaret replied, wanting to break the news to this insolent child that her days were numbered at St. Francis. In a rare moment of self-awareness, however, she held back, realizing that she had probably already pushed her weight around the church as much as she could—for now.

"And Father Miguel isn't in," the new New Girl added, blowing a much bigger bubble that required popping before she glanced at the silent phone on her desk, her expression making it clear she'd rather be talking to anyone other than the woman on the other side of the door.

"Just as well," Mary-Margaret said with feigned cheerfulness, "because 'tis ye I'm here to see. Ye wouldn't happen to have Annette Giancola's home address handy, would ye, luv? That would be the woman whose husband was buried from here yesterday."

"Yeah, I know," the new New Girl said. "And no, I don't have her address."

"A phone number, then? That would do."

"Nope."

"And ye call yerself a secretary, do ye?"

"Listen, lady—"

"Mary-Margaret. Mary-Margaret O'Shea."

"Yeah. Whatever. Listen, I'm not allowed to give out parishioners' personal information, *especially* not to you."

Mary-Margaret stepped back for a moment before approaching the doorway again.

"And is that so, or is it simply because ye just don't know how to access it?"

"Huh?"

"I can appreciate that yer likely out of yer depth here, what with all that goes on at St. Francis, and I don't want to make yer life any more confusing for ye than it already apparently is, so, if ye'll just let me," Mary-Margaret said, reaching around and unlatching the bottom door, "I'll get it meself."

The new New Girl stood up, likely to block Mary-Margaret from entering the office, but the retired secretary was quicker. Mary-Margaret deftly reached around to the desk, tapped a few keys, and within moments, a page containing Annette Giancola's complete contact information began spewing from the printer.

"Ta, luv," Mary-Margaret said, shutting down the computer before snatching up the paper and rushing out of the office, leaving the new New Girl to consider whether or not what had just happened was something she ought to tell Father Miguel about.

"Meh. He probably doesn't care," the new New Girl muttered to herself after Mary-Margaret left, then reopened the computer to get back to her game of *Goat Simulator*.

* * *

There were no driveways at all in front of the houses on this roadway, never mind circular ones, and there was nothing similar to a Range Rover in sight. Instead, Mary-Margaret noticed near-identical SUVs lining the streets, which made what she assumed must be Annette Giancola's BMW stand out. She found a spot and, after several attempts to parallel park Daphne before meeting success, got out and walked towards the address she had printed out a few minutes earlier. The brownstone in front of her was identical to all of the others on the street, none of which were anything to sniff at, but they were a far cry from Robert Jensen's house.

Mary-Margaret barely made it up the ten steps to the front door before Annette Giancola opened it, looking much better than she had the last time Mary-Margaret saw her.

"Come in," she said. "Never mind the mess. I just haven't—"

"No need to explain, luv," Mary-Margaret assured her as she followed her inside.

"And I have to apologize about yesterday. I don't know what came over me."

It's as clear as the nose on yer face what came over ye, Mary-Margaret thought to herself.

"And, to make matters worse, apparently a police officer came by Robert's house to check on me. I was asleep, of course, and he took care of it, but how embarrassing. He's been so kind, letting me stay with him, but I thought I ought to get home. Especially after having the police come to his door like that," Annette said, and then took in a deep breath and smiled brightly in a manner that made Mary-Margaret wonder what sort of antidepressant she was on, and if it had been prescribed by a doctor, or came from Robert Jensen's medicine cabinet. "Besides, now that the funeral is over, life goes on, whether I want it to or not."

"Indeed, it does."

"Please. Sit," Annette said, pointing to a chair in a well-appointed living room that looked like it could use a fresh coat of paint and some fluffing. "I'm afraid I have nothing to give you."

"Have ye a kettle, luv?" Mary-Margaret said, looking back at the kitchen they'd just passed through.

Annette nodded.

"Well then, sitchedoon and I'll make us a cuppa. Ye don't happen to have any biscuits, do ye?"

"Thank you," Annette said with a sigh, collapsing into a chair. "And no, I don't think I have anything like that in the house. But you're free to check if you'd like."

"Ye never know how tired ye are until ye stop," Mary-Margaret called back, poking around in the cupboards far more than she needed to, noting the midrange appliances, common pots and pans, and chain store dishes. Nothing to suggest that the occupants of this home were multi-millionaires.

And there were no biscuits.

"When me Jimmy died, God rest his soul," Mary-Margaret said, passing Annette a mug of tea after she came back into the living room, "I was like a whirling dervish. Doing everything for everyone. I had four smallies at the time and had to keep up me end. Wasn't until me friend, Eleanor, took the wee ones for the weekend that I realized how tired I was. Slept the whole time, and it still took me a few weeks after that to get back on me pins. It's to be expected, luv."

"I don't think it's really hit me yet."

"It might take a while. When ye realize they're not coming back. That's when it hits. Ye need to be sure to reach out to yer friends and family," she said, and then, realizing there was no easy way to bring it up, blurted out, "Speaking of which, I didn't notice his children at the funeral."

"No," Annette said, adding nothing more.

"Any reason, if ye don't mind me asking?"

"Their father wasn't very…kind to them."

"I do recall ye mentioning that, sure, but there's unkind and there's attending yer da's funeral. Did they not think they should have been there to support ye?"

"I don't know what they thought," Annette snapped.

"Well," Mary-Margaret said. *Father, forgive me for what I'm about to say but, as ye'll see, I've me reasons for lying through me teeth.* "I'm glad ye've got Robert."

"Yes," Annette said, her voice much softer. "He's always been there for me. Us."

"So he was aware of how things were between ye and yer husband?"

"I don't know how much he knew—I certainly didn't tell him anything. I loved him."

Mary-Margaret nodded and paused, wondering which man she was referring to.

"And was he a good provider, yer husband?" she asked, deciding this was not the time to clarify.

"Well, let's just say that Marco was lucky that Robert came into our lives when he did."

"How so?"

"My husband was always a hard worker. No matter what else he may have been, I can't take that away from him. He had his garage, and he made a steady income, but, honestly, it wasn't enough."

"Says who?" Mary-Margaret blurted out, immediately wishing she hadn't.

"I…I had a bit of a…breakdown…after my second miscarriage. No, it wasn't a breakdown. It was full-on depression. But nobody talks about it, do they? It's just something to get over. Alone."

"And when was that, luv?"

"Twelve years ago. I know that sounds like a long time ago, but that's when I finally had to admit to myself that I'd never have children. My own children."

"I'm sorry, luv. It must have been hard on ye. Both of yiz."

"I don't think Marco really wanted any more children," Annette said quietly, her words tinged with a hint of bitterness.

"I see," Mary-Margaret said, nodding slowly.

"Anyway," Annette said, "I didn't cope very well. For a long time. Marco ended up hiring a nanny to look after his boys because I just…couldn't."

"But that can't be that expensive, surely," Mary-Margaret said. "They'd be in school, so it would just be for a few hours afterwards."

"And I couldn't cook or clean, so we had to hire a housekeeper."

"But still…a woman in once a week…?"

"It was the retail therapy that pushed us into the red. But it was the only thing that made me feel…anything."

"What about actual therapy?" Mary-Margaret said. "Did the two of yiz consider that?"

"I know this sounds crazy, but that never crossed our minds. Not like we were on the same page on much by then anyway. I bought away my depression while Marco's drinking got heavier. I don't know," she said with a sniffle. "I just kept spending, and he just kept drinking and working and…womanizing. And now he's dead. And I'm stuck with a house that's mortgaged to the teeth."

"And Robert Jensen. How did he come into the picture?"

"I don't honestly know," Annette said, taking a sip of the now-tepid tea. "I think he was one of Marco's clients at the garage. I suppose they got to talking at some point, and Robert could see the potential in Marco's business, so they became partners."

"I don't mean to sound unkind, luv, but what makes Marco's Motors any different from the hundreds of other businesses that these types seem to always find to invest in?"

"Nothing that I'm aware of. I think it was just a case of right time, right place. Robert was looking to do something different, and Marco had what I guess you'd call a necessary business, so they got together and expanded it. It all seemed quite serendipitous, really."

"I'd say," Mary-Margaret said, wishing she had a biscuit to go with her tea.

"And, from what I understand, Robert was quite strategic when it came to picking locations for the garages, so the concept just took off."

"Are yiz going to keep them going, do ye think?"

"I hope so."

"Why's that?"

"The partnership was structured so the surviving partner took control of the business. But the profits—that's another matter. The deceased could leave their fifty percent of the annual income to anyone they liked. Marco left his to me." She paused, and Mary-Margaret thought she saw a slight smile come to her lips before adding, "In which case, I should do just fine."

Mary-Margaret's brow furrowed.

"So if Robert sells the business…?"

"Then I'm left without an income."

"Let's hope he doesn't sell, then," Mary-Margaret said.

Chapter Sixteen

ary-Margaret barely remembered the drive back to Michael's house. Something wasn't sitting right about Annette Giancola, and it had distracted her. The Annette she'd just seen didn't match the Annette from the day before. Of course, no one is at their best the day after their husband's funeral. She knew that all too well. But still... something felt off.

The Annette at the funeral had seemed more attached to Robert than to the man whose cold body she followed behind, clinging to Robert rather than placing her hand on the coffin holding her husband's lifeless form. And later, at Robert's house, she'd behaved more like a socialite after one too many glasses of wine than a widow mourning her loss.

But the Annette she'd spoken to today was different. She appeared fragile, vulnerable—almost like what Mary-Margaret thought a widow ought to appear—but there was a cool calculation lurking just beneath the surface, as though it was being held down by the thinnest layer of ice.

Maybe she was being too hard on Annette. After all, she'd just found her husband dead and she'd only just buried him. On top of all of that, she was only now realizing that the police had already bungled the investigation.

No, something wasn't quite right, Mary-Margaret concluded as she squeezed Daphne into the parking space (*God only knows how me Michael ever got his truck back here*). It just didn't add up.

As she opened the back door, Wee Phil ran past her into the laneway to the bush along the fence to relieve himself. She called after him and, after a cursory sniff of Daphne's tires followed by another quick squirt, he ran back into the house.

"MM, you look *awful!*" Arthur exclaimed, a wet sponge in one hand, his iPhone in the other.

"Ach, ye gave me a start!" she said, steadying herself on the doorframe. She was going to ask what he was doing in Michael's kitchen, but, once she'd regained her composure, she resigned herself to turning the flame on under the kettle instead. "It's been quite the morning of revelations. Have ye time for a cuppa, or are ye in the middle of yer show?"

"Oh, this?" Arthur said, turning off the movie he'd been streaming on Netflix. "I can watch it later. Here. Why don't you go sit in the living room? I'll bring in your tea and a biscuit."

"That would be grand, luv," Mary-Margaret said.

She wasn't quite sure what look he was going for today with the polka dot bandana around his head, cat-eye glasses that did actually flatter his face, blue shirt with the sleeves rolled up, and the form-fitting black capri pants. Was it Rosie the Riveter? A heavier Amy Winehouse? Katie Kaden? Whatever it was, she was glad her friend was here, and especially glad that he knew how to make a good cuppa.

"Here you go, MM," Arthur said, placing a tray with two mugs of tea and a plate of McVitie's biscuits on the little table in front of her. "The last thing we need is for something to happen to you."

"I'm fine, luv," Mary-Margaret said while Arthur settled into the chair beside her. "Just a bit surprised by how some people's worlds work, I suppose."

"Don't I know it," Arthur said, taking an unusually refined sip of his tea. "One day you're cleaning toilets in a church basement, the next you're lined up to be the executive assistant to the main guy."

"Is that playing on ye?" she asked, taking on the maternal role she knew so well.

"Kind of. I mean, I know I can make Father Miguel's world rock, but, well, I've never had a nine-to-five before."

"I don't think anyone expects ye to rock anyone's world, luv," she said with a chuckle.

"No, I mean, I'm sure I can patch up a lot of the deficiencies that have begun since you left. It's just…this whole thing of having to actually *be* somewhere every day…"

"Might not be a bad thing for ye," Mary-Margaret replied softly. "Might give ye a bit of grounding, to be honest."

"I don't know if I can do grounded, MM."

"I'm sure ye'll be fine. But keep yer eye on Father Miguel. Forgive me for saying," she said, looking upwards, "but I don't trust the man. Especially when he changes his secretaries like the rest of us change our socks."

Mary-Margaret took a long sip of her tea.

"I don't think that's actually true," Arthur softly suggested. "Ashleigh's on maternity leave, and Lola's just replacing her until—"

"Well, just don't trust him," Mary-Margaret snapped. "Or anyone else, for that matter."

"I take it you found something out about our case this morning?" Arthur asked, not wanting to upset her any further.

"I did. Popped by for a wee chat with Annette Giancola. She's back in her own home, which, I think, is a blessing. The further she stays away from that lad who was partnered with her husband, the better. A nasty piece of work, that one. And get this: now that Marco's gone, the entire business belongs to that git."

"That doesn't seem right."

"No, it doesn't, but that's what the widow Ginacola told me."

"I guess that's why she's snuggling up with that jerk."

"As things stand now, that arse has the whole company, and she may or may not have half the gross income from the operation, depending on who Marco left his shares to. Although she seems pretty sure it's her. So, yer right: she'd best snuggle up to Robert. Otherwise, she might find herself out on the street."

"Oh," Arthur said, taking another sip of his tea. "That's not a good place to be. Trust me on that one."

"And I'm thinking that we can rule her out as a suspect. Unless, of course, the two of them were an item all along, and it was time to get Marco out of the picture. Robert sells the company, the two of them…what was it she said to us? *Sail off into the sunset?* And gross shares be damned."

"That's what I'd be doing," Arthur said.

"In which case, I'm back to wondering why she called me…us…in at all? Billy Gilly and his lot already concluded that it was an accident or a misadventure or whatever they want to call it. She could have just walked away. Why not let sleeping dogs lie?"

Both Mary-Margaret and Arthur looked up when they heard a slight thud, signaling the end of a round of *chase-your-tail*, with Wee Phil suffering yet another defeat.

"Present company excluded," Mary-Margaret said, glancing at Wee Phil. "But still. Why not just leave it as an accident and get on with it?"

"Maybe because she needs to prove that he was murdered?"

"Because…?"

"Insurance? Maybe she gets a bigger payout that way?"

"I've never heard of anything like that, luv, and it certainly doesn't sound like a clause I'd want on my life insurance policy, but ye never know with these kinds of people, do you?"

"Of course, if she kills him, she wouldn't get anything," Arthur continued, as if reading the fine print on the policy itself.

"So we're back to thinking she did it, and now she's trying to pin this on Robert, are we? I know I suggested it before, luv, but I'm more inclined to believe that it would be a bit of a stretch, wouldn't ye agree?"

"Not if you thought you were smarter than the cops."

"Hardly a stretch at all this time, is it? But then why get us involved? Why not—"

"For fun? To muddy the waters? To annoy Billy Gilly? I don't know," Arthur said, taking a couple of biscuits. "Or maybe she actually wants us to find the murderer because it's not her."

"So it *is* that Robert Jensen. I knew it!"

"What about the guy who owns the building? Could he and Robert be in on it together?"

The two paused to consider this.

"Or," Arthur continued, "what if Marco was just drinking in the shop alone, like they said, and someone came in—"

"But there was no sign of a break-in."

"So he either let them in, or they had a key."

"Who would have a key?"

"I don't know. Another mechanic? Robert? Annette? Or the owner of the building, who, as we know, might have a very good reason to want Marco dead?"

"He was a right eejit," Mary-Margaret admitted.

"Didn't you say a developer wanted that land to build a condo? And didn't you say something about Marco not wanting to sell?"

"Yes, but all the owner would have to do is wait for the lease to expire—"

"Which was how many years from now? And didn't you say that a lot of the properties Marco's Motors sits on are now ripe for development? The only stumbling block to cashing out on the entire business was Marco. Which brings us back to Robert. Now that he owns the company, how long do you think it'll be before there is no more Marco's Motors?"

"And, if that's the case, then Annette's only hope of staying above boards financially is for she and him to…and me stomach turns to think of it… snuggle up."

"I'd say we have a super strong motive for either Robert or that building owner guy. All we have to do is figure out which one actually did it, and I've got a plan!"

Chapter Seventeen

After explaining his plan and clearing the dishes, Arthur didn't have time to clean the house, so Mary-Margaret stepped in to take care of it. Again. That left her with very little time to get ready for her weekly catch-up with Eleanor and Angus Corrigan. She was thankful, though, that Max had made his own dinner plans and Michael was at work—one less thing to manage before heading out for the evening.

O'Leary's was always packed on Friday nights, and tonight was no different. Normally, Big John was working behind the bar along with Johnny and Maeve. But when Mary-Margaret walked in this night, she found Johnny behind the bar, with neither Big John nor Maeve in sight, and several tables without drinks.

"Where's the lads?" Mary-Margaret asked as she walked up to the bar.

"Don't get me started," Johnny grumbled.

"That bad, is it?"

"Worse. My Dad's gout is flaring, Nolan's got strep, so Maeve's upstairs with him, and I'm down here and can barely get the food and drinks out fast enough on my own."

"I'm sorry to hear that, lad, and I can't help ye on the first, but I'll give ye a hand with the second. Oi!" Mary-Margaret called out.

The pub grew quiet.

"Good evening, everyone. For those of ye who don't know me, I'm Mary-Margaret O'Shea, and like most of ye, I come from a place where ye come up to the bar to get yer pints. No tabs. Pay as ye go. Credit or debit only. And ye order yer food and wait as long as ye have to for it to get to yer table.

Tonight, we're shaking things up a wee bit at O'Leary's. There'll be no table service at all—not even for the food. If ye want a drink, hoist yerself up here and get Johnny to pour it for ye. For the food, put in yer order, same payment plan, and Johnny here'll give ye a number and call it out when it's ready. Everybody with me? Good. Sláinte!"

Spotting the Corrigans at their usual table, Mary-Margaret moved through the crowd and headed toward the bar to join her friends. The three of them—once there had been four—had all emigrated from Ireland around the same time, settled in the same neighbourhood, and stayed that way until Angus got promoted and he and Eleanor moved to a posher part of the city. And then Jimmy died. Through it all, Mary-Margaret, Eleanor, and Angus had remained the closest thing any of them had to extended family on this side of the pond, and these weekly dinners were never missed.

"That was impressive," Angus said, standing up as she approached. "Did you get yourself a drink while you were up there?"

"I'll wait until the mob clears," Mary-Margaret said. "And I'll order our dinners while I'm at it. Now, enough about that. Look at the two of ye! Cruising clearly agrees with ye."

"Oh, Mary-Margaret, it was glorious," Eleanor said with a huge smile. "I don't think I've ever eaten as much, though."

"That must have set ye back a pretty penny," Mary-Margaret said.

"Well, it doesn't do you much good when you're gone, does it?" Eleanor said.

"Speaking of gone, I hear Marco Giancola died," Angus said, cutting straight to the point, as he was his way. "An accident, was it?"

"So they say," Mary-Margaret replied.

"But you don't agree?" Angus asked.

"Well, it's not whether or not I agree," Mary-Margaret corrected. "It's about whether or not–"

"Are you getting involved in another murder investigation?" Eleanor asked, a slight sparkle in her voice.

"Not by choice, no."

"Unless things have changed, it's your Michael who's the police detective, not you," Angus said.

"And a fine detective he is. But this one might be far too complicated for him and his lads to unravel."

"So you mean to tell me—" Angus began.

"The line-up at the bar seems to have gone down, Angus. Would you mind hopping up and ordering us all our drinks and dinner, please?" Eleanor cut in.

Angus glanced over at his wife, who gave him a look he understood well.

"Everyone's usual?" he asked as he got up from the table.

"Thank you, luv," Eleanor said before turning to her friend. "Is it that nitwit detective who's in charge of this one?"

"Now ye can see why I have to get involved," Mary-Margaret stated.

"I'm sure Angus will want to hear all about it. Let's give him a minute to come back with the drinks before getting into it."

The two women sat together, the silence between them comfortable, neither needing to fill the quiet with words as they simply waited for him to return.

"Ah, here you are," Eleanor said with a smile. "That was quick."

"Did I miss anything?" he said, setting the drinks down on the table.

"Not a thing. We were waiting for you. So, tell us what happened," Eleanor replied.

Mary-Margaret briefly explained how she came to meet Annette Giancola and how it was Annette who suspected the police were downplaying her husband's death. She told her friends about visiting the crime scene and meeting the building owner—whom she instantly disliked. the well-attended funeral—except for the deceased man's own children. and how she found the business partner's closeness to the new widow unsettling.

She kept quiet, however, about how Robert now owned the entire company, the clause in the contract that allowed the first to die to will fifty percent of the gross profits to whomever he wished, Annette's brief stay at Robert Jensen's house, and how Robert had spiked Annette's drink. She also didn't mention how many of Marco's Motors garages appeared to be on land that had become highly desirable, nor did she say anything about

Arthur's plan. While her omissions were intended to keep the discussion focused on Marco's murder rather than get tangled up in the weeds of the investigation, her decision not to mention Arthur's plan was largely because she wasn't entirely convinced of its feasibility.

"Well, it's pretty much common knowledge that the Marco's Motors just around the corner here was slated to be redeveloped," Angus said, taking a sip of wine.

"I didn't know that," Eleanor said.

"Perhaps not common, then, but there had been a lot of discussion about it. I'm wondering," Angus continued, "if Marco knew anything about it."

"Even if he did, it might not have made any difference," Mary-Margaret said. "Especially if they had a long lease."

"Depending on what the developers were prepared to pay for the land, the owner may have offered to buy Marco out of it," Angus countered.

"I can't see that," Mary-Margaret said. "I mean, yes, I can see this Robert lad leaping at a good offer, but not Marco. He loved working in that garage."

"Number fifteen," Johnny called out. "Three Fish & Chip Specials."

"There's your prime suspect, then. Excuse me, ladies," Angus said, getting up to get their dinners from the bar.

Chapter Eighteen

The sun hadn't fully come up yet as Arthur stood by the front door of Marco's Motors along with another man. Both were dressed in mechanic's coveralls.

"Who are you?" the other man asked.

"Rocco?" Arthur offered, looking down through thick-rimmed glasses at the name that had been sewn onto the coverall he'd picked up from the thrift shop yesterday.

"You don't look like a Rocco," the man stated.

Had Arthur been about a third lighter and a third shorter, he might, possibly, have looked more like Buddy Holly than anyone named Rocco. But being the size he was and with his pasty white complexion, Arthur resembled neither Buddy Holly nor someone named Rocco. The coverall said Rocco, however, so Rocco he was.

Before the man could comment further, another man arrived, dressed in chinos and a crisp cotton shirt.

"'Morning, Eddie. Who's your friend?" crisp-cotton-shirt man asked.

"Dunno. Says his name is Rocco," Eddie replied.

"Doesn't look like a Rocco," the man in the crisp cotton shirt said, pulling out a set of keys and unlocking the front door. He took a last drag from his cigarette and tossed it aside before stepping in. "What do you want?"

"I'm the new mechanic," Arthur said, lowering his voice to a growl as he followed both men into the shop.

"We don't have any new mechanics," crisp-cotton-shirt man said, clicking on the lights and turning off the alarm system.

"Mr. Giancola hired me," Arthur stated. Both men froze momentarily.

"Not likely," crisp-cotton-shirt man said flatly. "Mr. Giancola's dead."

"Before he died," Arthur stated, his voice shifting from a growl to a Brooklyn-Italian grunt.

"Hrmph," crisp-cotton-shirt man said. "Well, we got a busy day today, so I guess you're in."

Arthur silently breathed a sigh of relief.

"'Morning!" crisp-cotton-shirt man said to a woman who came into the shop. "Here for tires?"

"And an oil change. And whatever else needs doing," she said, holding out her car keys. "Greta. My name is Greta. I made an appointment—"

"Yep. Okay. Just leave your keys. Got a number we can call you at when we're done or...?"

Greta proceeded to give crisp-cotton-shift man, whom Arthur assumed was the manager, her cell number just as two other people came into the garage. The manager went through the same routine with them and the three people who came in after that. By the time the garage officially opened at eight, more than a dozen sets of car keys were already sitting on the front desk.

"Here," the manager said, tossing the keys that belonged to Gretta's car at Arthur. "Go get it off the street and bring it in. It's the Lexus over there. Drive it through to the front bay and, when you're finished, bring in the BMW."

Arthur awkwardly caught the keys and walked over to the Lexus. Once he was seated behind the steering wheel, he began to sweat. Not only did he not have a driver's licence, Arthur possessed no natural aptitude behind the wheel.

What would Mario Andretti do, Arthur thought as he started the car.

With great concentration, Arthur was able to jerkily maneuver the Lexis into the garage bay.

"Looks like she'll need more than an oil change," Arthur's co-worker said as Arthur got out of the car. "Might be a transmission thing, the way the car lurched. And it looks like there's something up with the steering."

"Ain't that right," Arthur muttered in agreement.

"Boss?" the mechanic called out.

"Yeah. Sure. Check it all out, and I'll give her a call to let her know. After you get the BMW in, get the Audi in," the manager said, tossing another set of keys at Arthur.

"Better check the brakes on this one, too," the manager called out after watching Arthur jerkily bring the BMW in.

The morning passed in a blur, with Arthur somehow managing to move cars in and out without incident between hauling sets of snow tires up from the basement and then taking the summer tires back down to be stored for the season. Remarkably, he'd avoided any real mechanic work. But after a couple of hours spent hauling tires up and down the stairs, Arthur couldn't help but daydream about his upcoming secretarial job at St. Francis of Assisi. Tempting fate every time he got into a customer's car, and the endless cycle of heavy lifting was not something he enjoyed.

Nor was it the reason Arthur had embedded himself in Marco's Motors. What he wanted to do was get a copy of the customer list. Surely, Marco Giancola couldn't be the only mechanic to have a disgruntled client, and what better way to rage against an unreasonable charge or faulty repair than to murder the mechanic?

Between lugging tires and jockeying cars—a task he was getting rather good at—his attention was drawn to the appointment book on the front desk. It was a simple ledger filled with clients' names and phone numbers. He'd expected the process to be automated and had planned to copy the files onto a thumb drive he'd brought, but knowing he was likely to be fired by the end of the day, he had a backup plan. The glasses he wore not only offered a clever disguise—though he didn't exactly travel in grease-monkey circles or expect to be recognized—they also had a built-in camera, a significant upgrade from the ladies' hats he'd used in previous disguises, which he'd ruled out for this job for obvious reasons.

All he needed was a chance to get a look at that book, undisturbed.

Chapter Nineteen

"Michael, can ye not see that Wee Phil needs to go to the jacks?" Mary-Margaret said when she walked into the kitchen to make herself a cup of tea. "He's dancing like yer Uncle Shamus at the end of the night at his local."

"Oh. Right," Michael grumbled, opening the door to let the dog run out.

"Michael! Get out there after him."

"He's fine, Mom," Michael said, putting the mayonnaise back in the fridge before taking a bite out of the sandwich he'd just made for himself.

"If I thought he would be fine, I'd have opened the door meself. Now. Go. Grab his leash and a bag or two and away with ye," she said, practically pushing him out the door. "And where are yer shoes? Honestly, me son, if it weren't for me, I don't know where ye'd be now."

"Not out in the middle of winter picking up dog—"

"'Tis only November and if ye'd spend more time doing and less time talking…" Mary-Margaret let the words hang in the air, which was just as well because Michael had slipped on a pair of old runners he had by the door and was already halfway down the laneway.

"And close the door after ye," Mary-Margaret said as she shut it herself. "'Tis a wonder his heating bills aren't through the roof."

She put on the kettle and got a mug out for herself. There was a knock at the back door.

Don't tell me I locked the bloody door. I'll never hear the end of it if I did.

She opened the door, expecting the wrath of Michael. But instead, she heard a low 'MM,' and saw Arthur standing there instead.

"Come in, yer out," she said, then checked her watch. "They let ye off early, did they? A bit too early for quitting time, I'd be thinking."

"They kind of...let me go," Arthur muttered, his voice carrying more disappointment than Mary-Margaret expected from a lad who couldn't drive but still managed to talk his way into a mechanic's job.

"Ach, they can't fire ye, luv," she said softly as she got another mug from the cupboard. "They never properly hired ye. Ye just showed up and chucked in, didn't ye? But never mind. I'm sure ye did the best ye could."

"Oh, I did better than that," Arthur said, puffing out his chest as he pulled the thick-rimmed glasses out of his coverall pocket.

"Don't leave me hanging on tenterhooks. What have ye got?"

"Only the entire—well, mostly entire—customer list right here," he said, holding the glasses up. "I just need to download the file to my iPhone."

"So ye've obviously not been home, then?"

Arthur shook his head.

"Nor likely eaten since breakfast?"

"Oh, I don't eat breakfast, MM. I do a daily fast—"

"Here. Have this sandwich," she said, handing him the sandwich Michael had left on the counter. "Can't have ye wasting away now, can we. Go on then. Put it on a plate and take it into the dining room, and let's have a look at what ye've got. I'll be right in behind ye once I get our tea ready."

Arthur grabbed the sandwich from the counter and shoved most of it into his mouth in a way that suggested he hadn't eaten in days—though, of course, he had, but barely. When he made no move to grab a plate, Mary-Margaret's suspicions were confirmed: Arthur wasn't fasting. He simply didn't have any food at home.

"And this," Michael began as he came back into the house, Wee Phil in tow, "is why I don't want a dog. Can you grab me a poo bag, please?"

"One not enough or did ye forget to take any out with ye?" Mary-Margaret said, passing him the box before leaning over and unclipping the dog's leash. "Likely forgot, which isn't the dog's fault now, is it? Come on, Wee Phil. Let's get ye a treat."

"Why does he get a treat every time he—"

"Out ye get before ye let all the warm air out," Mary-Margaret said, again almost pushing Michael out. "Honestly, I don't know how the lad manages. Have ye had enough to eat, or shall I get Michael to make ye another sandwich when he gets in?"

"Another one would be great," Arthur said. "Although I am slimming at the moment."

"Hey, where's my sandwich?" Michael said when he came back inside.

"I gave it to Arthur. Poor lad was a mere shadow of his former self."

"Thanks for the sandwich, Michael," Arthur called from the dining room. "Mom...?"

"Ach, away with ye, Michael. In the time it's taking ye to whine about it, ye could have two more sandwiches made. Ye do want another, don't ye, Arthur?"

"Yes, please."

"I'm not making more sandwiches for everyone," Michael said. "I just want *my* sandwich."

"Well, it's gone. Either make yerself another, in which case ye might as well make two, or go hungry and, judging by the girth of ye, that won't happen in me lifetime."

Mary-Margaret turned and took the two mugs of tea and the plate of McVitie's into the dining room, leaving Michael in the kitchen, his mouth hanging open.

"Did ye get yer files downloaded yet?" Mary-Margaret said, sitting down at her usual spot at the end of the table.

"It'll just take a second," Arthur said, fiddling with the glasses. "There. I had a chance to look at the names before I shot the pics, and I think you'll be surprised to find that most of Marco Giancola's clients were women. Here. Have a look."

Arthur passed his iPhone to Mary-Margaret, who struggled to read the names as she held the phone at various distances from her face. Recalling her earlier predicament, Arthur took the phone and pressed a couple of buttons that increased the font size before returning it to her.

"I see what ye mean," she said, scanning the names.

"What are you two doing?" Michael said, leaning against the kitchen doorframe, his mouth almost as full of sandwich as Arthur's had been.

"Did ye only think of yerself, lad?"

"It's okay, MM," Arthur said. "I'm not really that hungry."

"'Tis not okay. Michael, get back into the kitchen and make—"

"No, I'm good with these," Arthur said, stuffing a handful of biscuits into his mouth.

"So what are you up to, Mom?" Michael said, unmoved by her attempt at distracting him.

"We're trying to solve a murder, if ye must know."

"I thought—"

"Well, ye thought wrong."

"Mom—"

"If ye don't mind, this is a private conversation, so could ye kindly take yerself and yer selfishly-made sandwich somewhere else?"

"You almost got yourself killed once—"

"I'm an old woman. Something's going to kill me sooner than later at this stage of the game."

"And you almost got yourself arrested once—"

"Only once? If ye only knew, me son. If ye only knew. Now, if you'll excuse us...?"

Mike stayed put for a moment, then, realizing arguing with his mother was a lost cause, pushed himself off the doorframe with his shoulder and made his way to the front of the house.

"Don't say I never warned you," he called back as he went up the stairs to his room.

"Now," Mary-Margaret said with a sigh, returning her attention to the photos on Arthur's phone. "I am seeing, as ye've mentioned, that most of these names belong to women. More than I would have imagined, to be honest."

"That's what I thought as well. Do you suppose they're all clients, and when it says 'oil change' in the margins, does it really mean an oil change?"

"What else could it mean?"

"Um…" he said, blushingly slightly

"Ach. Got it. The penny's dropped, luv. So are ye thinking that some of these women are his mistresses?"

"If they are, then we've just come up with a whole new list of suspects, wouldn't you say?"

"Ye don't often hear of a mistress murdering her lover, do ye?"

"Why not? Or what about a jealous husband murdering his wife's lover?"

"I'd say we have our work cut out for us, then," Mary-Margaret said, taking the last biscuit from the plate.

Chapter Twenty

Mary-Margaret and Arthur spent the afternoon at Michael's dining room table, poring over the list of Marco's Motors clients Arthur had managed to gather during his short stint as a mechanic. Mary-Margaret tuned out the muttered grumbles and comments that Michael made throughout the day as he passed by them at various times. When Max finally emerged from his room and came downstairs, she sent him around the corner to the store—who'd only just started stocking McVitie's due to the surprising rise in demand over the past few months—to buy another box.

"And take Wee Phil out with ye," Mary-Margaret instructed. "Or, on second thought, leave him. I'll get yer da to take him out for a piddle."

"I can do it, Gran. And I promise I won't leave him tied up outside. I'll take him in the store with me."

"I know ye would, luv, but I'm just afraid that he'll go mental when he gets a whiff of all the rats I'm sure are living in the back of the store. Michael!"

There was no answer.

"Michael!" Mary-Margaret hollered louder.

"Maybe he's asleep," Arthur suggested.

"Asleep? At this hour of the day?"

"Well, he does work shifts…" Arthur offered.

"I'll go check on him, Gran."

"Ta, luv," Mary-Margaret said, returning to their files. "While I shouldn't be surprised, given the garage is just around the corner, a lot of the parishioners from St. Francis went to Marco's Motors."

"Makes sense," Arthur said, taking a gulp of his lukewarm tea.

"I can't believe that daft Laura-Jean McQueen even has a car," Mary-Margaret said, noticing her name on the list. "I would have thought they'd have taken her license after that time she practically ran me off the road. Can't be the first and only."

"Dad said it's time for Wee Phil to go back to Sally-next-door," Max said when he came back downstairs.

"So I take it he's not going to take the wee pup out? Well, get yerself back upstairs and tell yer da—"

"I'll take him for a walk," Arthur offered. "A break from this might do me some good. Not that I can't focus for long periods of time. In fact, I'm—"

"Grand, luv. Don't forget the poo bags," Mary-Margaret said, cutting him off.

While Arthur was out with Wee Phil and Max was off to get the biscuits, Mary-Margaret continued to pore over the names. The ones she recognized from St. Francis were mostly eliminated from the possible suspect list. *Can't imagine Monique straying off the path, let alone bashing a man's head in. And that daft Laura-Jean McQueen... But Irene Ashford. Now there's a live wire. Of the three, my money would be on Irene to murder—*

"What are you doing, Mom?" Michael said as he came down the stairs.

"Ach, ye've startled me. I thought ye were getting some kip."

"I was. Until Max woke me up to walk someone else's dog."

"Wee Phil is not 'someone else's dog'. He's practically family. And, had I known ye were—"

"More importantly, Mom, what are you doing?"

"Well, what does it look like I'm doing, me son? Honestly, I do wonder how ye manage as a Big City Detective."

"It looks to me like you're going over some list...?"

"No flies on ye this afternoon, are there?"

"Why?"

"Just curious to know who went to the Marco's Motors around the corner from me own house."

"How did you get the..." Michael began and then stopped. "Wait a minute.

You and Arthur aren't getting yourselves involved with that Gianco—"

"I just told ye what we were doing, Michael. Did ye not hear me?"

"Is that why Arthur was wearing those coveralls? Was he pretending to be—"

"I have no idea who or what Arthur believes himself to be on any given day, me son, and 'tis not me business."

"He stole that list from Marco's Motors, didn't he?"

"He did no such thing!"

"And you're trying to solve—"

"For a little dog, Wee Phil sure can pee," Arthur said as he came in the back door.

"Be sure to get him a treat," Mary-Margaret said. "Bottom cupboard by the sink."

"Mom," Michael said. "You can't—"

"I can't find them, MM," Arthur said.

"Ach. Just a minute. I'll come have a look," Mary-Margaret said. "And are ye up or down, me son? I'm just now putting on the kettle if yer interested in a cuppa."

Chapter Twenty-One

"Things no better upstairs, Johnny?" Mary-Margaret said as she walked up to the bar at O'Leary's, the place as packed as one would expect on a Saturday night.

"Oh," Frank Malone said, looking over his shoulder. "I didna see ye come in, luv. Here, let me order yer drink and we can go sit at a table. Johnny, the usual for t' lady."

"Credit or debit?" Johnny said, holding the POS terminal up towards him.

"I take it not," Mary-Margaret said, noticing that Big John and Maeve were nowhere to be seen.

"Thanks for this," Johnny said, looking at the machine as Frank slid his credit card along it. "If you hadn't said anything last night, I'd still be trying to run tabs and serve tables. I'm sure I'd have pulled out all of my hair by now. Which reminds me: you wouldn't happen to know anyone who'd like to be a server for a couple of weeks, would you? They've got to be over thirty, though. I'm done with the younger ones."

Though her thoughts immediately turned to Arthur, she was relieved to rule him out as a possibility, given his upcoming full-time job at the church. Knowing he had something coming up made it easier to dismiss him, rather than feeling compelled to suggest him and then worry about what he might wear to try to fit in at her local.

"No one at the top of mind, Johnny, but I'll keep me ear to the ground," Mary-Margaret said as she led Frank to their usual table in the corner.

"Sláinte," Frank said, raising his pint once they were seated.

"Sláinte," Mary-Margaret replied before taking a slow sip from her half-pint of crown float, letting the taste tickle her tongue.

"I take it ye havena heard?" Frank asked, looking like a cat that had just swallowed a mouse.

"Heard what?"

"Maeve is in the family way."

"And how did ye find this out? I'm sure it wasn't from Herself."

"I have me ways," Frank said with a wink, taking a long sip of his Guinness.

"Yer a pathologist's assistant, not an OBGYN's assistant, last time I checked."

"I was in jus' before it got busy, and Johnny told me. Finally. Said they'd gone to one of them fertility specialists."

"Jesus, she'll be having a litter, then."

"Wouldn't tha' be somethin'," Frank said, looking over his shoulder at the tired man behind the bar. "I donna t'ink our Johnny could handle it."

"Johnny? It's Maeve who'd be rearing them, and I think she could manage a pack perfectly fine. Might make Johnny's life a little easier, to be honest."

"Come on, now, luv. She's just a wee bit high-strung, is all," Frank said gently, taking another sip of his pint.

"Hrmph."

"So tell me wha' me girl has been keepin' herself busy at t'is past week," Frank said, eager to change the topic.

"Funny ye should ask, Francis," Mary-Margaret said. "I'm assuming ye lads did the autopsy on that mechanic that was murdered?"

"If it's Marco Giancola's autopsy yer referrin' to, t'en yes. I was in on it. But I'm not sure he was murdered."

"Why is that?"

"T'ere were no bullet wounds or knives in his back."

"Glad to hear that's the new threshold for murder," Mary-Margaret said sullenly, taking a sip of her drink.

"Well, he did have a fair bit of intracranial hemorrhaging, but nothin' inconsistent wi'h havin' had a fall."

"And why would a grown man have a fall, Francis?"

"Likely pie-eyed," Frank said, taking another quick gulp of his pint. "Sure reeked of it when they brought him in, I was told. And information from t'e report said he was a drinker, so…?"

"How was his liver?"

"Rare to medium?" Frank quipped with a half-smile, letting the humor linger as he finished off the last of his pint and set it down on the table with a sigh of satisfaction.

"Jaundiced?"

"No. No more than me own, likely. But a fella doesn't need to be a drunk to have had too much and stumbled."

"Did his clothes reek of it or just him?"

"T'ey usually don't have a stitch on 'em when we pull 'em out of the ice box," Frank said, rubbing the back of his neck. "So I didna see his clothes, let alone give 'em a sniff."

"And this…intracranial hemorrhaging. Any ideas what caused it?"

"As I said, he could have just hit the ground or, considerin' the man was found dead in his garage, it could have been made worse by landin' on any of t'e tools he likely had lyin' about."

"What if he didn't have any tools lying about. Could it have been caused by being hit with one of those tools?"

"Anythin's possible, luv, but I've never been in a garage where t'ere weren't at least one or two wrenches on t'e ground. In fact, t'at's likely what he stumbled on. T'at or anot'er tool of some sort. Lost his footin', head hit somethin' on the ground, and t'at was t'at. He bled out."

"But ye just finished saying it was intracranial. That suggests to me the bleeding was all internal, no? And, if so, how could he have bled out?"

"Well, 'tis possible, particularly if it was a blow to t'e head—"

"Like being whacked with something—"

"Like hittin' the ground, in which case, t'ere could be visible bleedin' on the scalp, face, or ears. And there would be blood on the ground, especially if t'e wound is open and bleedin' profusely."

"And was there an open wound?" Mary-Margaret asked.

"Yes, t'ere was," Frank said, offering nothing further.

"Did ye see any pictures of the garage before ye did yer autopsy?" Mary-

Margaret pressed.

"No. T'ere was nothin' to go on."

"Do ye find that a bit…odd?"

"Don't get me started, Mary-Margaret. T'ere's been more than a few convos about t'e officers not findin' him and, if t'ey had, how he'd still be alive, but I don't believe t'at part. Not for a minute. He may have bled to death, but, in my humble opinion, t'at blow to the head would have left him brain-dead if the loss of blood hadn't actually killed him."

"But ye just said there was no blow—"

"Intracranial hemorrhaging's what killed him," Frank stated firmly.

"Is what I'm hearing ye say that an injury caused by being whacked in the head with a wrench, let's say, or by bashing yer own head in after falling on a cement floor, would look the same when all's said and done?"

"Leave it, Mary-Margaret."

"Francis, what is it, luv?" she asked, her voice softening.

"If ye want me opinion," he said, giving a quick glance around the pub before returning his attention to her, "and t'is is just between ye and me and the fencepost, yeah? 'Twas someone givin' him a blow to the head what killed him."

"Then why—"

"Because I'm just a technician. Me boss seems to t'ink t'at it's six of one, half a dozen of t'e other, and, given t'at t'e investigation indicates—"

"Don't get me started on that, Francis!" Mary-Margaret snorted, her voice rising as she took another sip of her drink, then slammed her glass down with frustration.

"Listen, luv," Frank said as gently as he could, trying to calm the storm before it got going. "I know ye've done well with t'em other two murders ye looked into, and I could be wrong on me opinion here. Not every death is a—"

"But what if this one is?"

"Ye may be right, but at this point, the best me technical findings can offer is t'at he died as a result of some sort of a blunt force trauma to the head t'at caused him to bleed to death. Me own sense is t'at it was done by someone else, but, because it's not obvious, it's up to the investigators to figure out if it was self-inflicted—"

"As in, he bashed in his own head?" Mary-Margaret said with a guffaw, her crown float now nearly empty. "I'm not sure what's in yer Guinness tonight, lad, but—"

"Meanin'," Frank cut in, "t'at he fell. And, given what Detective Sergeant Gill has concluded—"

"Saint Thomas is rolling over in his grave," Mary-Margaret muttered under her breath, swishing the last of her drink around before setting the glass down on the table, still with a little more force than necessary.

"I'm goin' up for another," Frank said, picking up his glass as he stood up. "Can I interest ye in one?"

Mary-Margaret knew this conversation was over. And she knew that this was one investigation she absolutely could not let go. She trusted Frank's instincts far more than Billy Gilly's poor excuse for an investigation, and now she was even more determined than ever to find out who murdered Marco Giancola herself.

Chapter Twenty-Two

I f Mary-Margaret O'Shea was a force of nature, her Sunday dinners were the embodiment of it. Barring one's own death, they were not to be missed. Except, of course, if one was out of the country on business—a rare exception that only applied to Katie and Ahmed, Mary-Margaret's youngest and her partner, so there was little need to mention it to the rest of the family.

The seating was always the same, whether the dinners took place in the O'Shea family home or, as of late, at Michael's house. Mary-Margaret sat at the end of the table nearest the kitchen, while the place at the top of the table, which had been occupied by Jimmy when he was alive, was set and left vacant. To her right sat Max, and to her left sat Paulie. Before moving halfway around the world, her other grandson, Richard, had sat beside Paulie. The boys were smaller then, so Richard's departure just meant that the spot was absorbed into the table seating. Katie sat beside Paulie, with Ahmed sitting across from her. Teaszy, her second-born, sat beside Ahmed, and Allan, Teaszy's husband, sat beside Teaszy, as far from Mary-Margaret as the table would allow. For good reason.

Across from Allan, there was a place currently occupied by Griffin, Paulie's on-again, off-again boyfriend (currently on again), that was otherwise set for the Unexpected Guest. Years ago, it had been where Petey, Mary-Margaret's younger son, had sat, but he had left home abruptly, barely a man, and never returned. The emptiness of the chair was too much for Mary-Margaret, so she decided it should be put to use and was thus allocated to the Unexpected Guest, who, tonight, was Griffin. Beside him, across from Teaszy and with

Katie to the right, was Michael's place. And so it went, every Sunday since anyone could remember, and so it would go, every Sunday forevermore.

"Oh, look. What's this?" Allan said, his voice dripping with sarcasm as Teaszy passed him the plate of corned beef.

"Here we go," Paulie muttered under her breath. "Aren't you glad you're back, Griff?"

Griffin grinned. As an aspiring anarchist shackled by strong socialist ideologies, he found himself quite at home around the often-chaotic O'Shea family dinner table.

"It's corned beef, Old Man," Griffin said. "Honestly, I don't know what you're complaining about. I love this stuff."

"Ah, sure, ye should, lad," Mary-Margaret said from the far end of the table, her voice warm but sharp. "And 'tis lovely to have ye back."

"Here," Teaszy said, poking a small slice onto Allan's plate before passing it across to her son's boyfriend.

Allan shot her a look but said nothing.

"I don't know what you guys are always complaining about," Max said. "It's food. Let's just eat."

""Tis more than just food, luv," Mary-Margaret said, patting his hand while giving Allan a death stare.

"All I was saying—" Allan began.

"Leave it," Teaszy interrupted, giving Allan a slight kick under the table.

"Pass it down here," Max said.

"While we're at it, Michael, could ye pass the bowl of mashed down as well, please?" Mary-Margaret said.

"Hmm?" Michael said, clearly distracted, his thoughts far away.

"The potatoes, lad. Can ye pass them down?" Mary-Margaret said.

"Sure. Yeah," he mumbled.

"Are ye with us tonight, Michael?" she asked, her voice tinged with concern.

"Another big case, Mike?" Ahmed asked, looking up from his plate with mild curiosity. Despite not being married to Katie, Mary-Margaret considered Ahmed to be her favorite son-in-law. Given that Allan was her only other son-in-law, though, that wasn't saying much, and it didn't really reflect the true depth of her affection for him.

"Speaking of work," Katie said before Michael could answer, glancing over at Ahmed, "remind me to book our plane tickets when we get home." The two of them owned a fashion magazine, and like Michael, she often had her mind on business, even during family dinners.

"Yer off again, are yiz?" Mary-Margaret said, raising an eyebrow. "Where to this time?"

"Nothing too exciting. Just Paris," Katie replied, shrugging as she took a long sip of wine.

"Can I carry your suitcases?" Paulie asked.

"Right?" Max said, piling his plate high with mashed potatoes.

"It's not nearly as fun as it sounds," Ahmed said. "We just fly in, go to a couple of meetings, and then fly out."

"Has no one heard of Zoom?" Allan interjected.

"I'm sure they have, Allan," Mary-Margaret said with a tone thick with disdain. "But those of us who have some civility left in us still appreciate face-to-face meetings, don't we, Ahmed?"

"Something like that," Ahmed replied with a chuckle.

There was a sudden yelp from under the table.

"What th—" Michael began as the small figure of Wee Phil darted out, turned and growled at him, and then pranced over to one of the wingback chairs in the living room.

"So ye've taken to kicking dogs, have ye, me son?" Mary-Margaret asked, giving him a pointed look.

"Dad!" Max exclaimed.

"That's enough mash, luv," Mary-Margaret said, taking the bowl from Max. "Leave some for the rest of us."

"I didn't kick him," Michael said quickly, his face flushing. "He was nowhere near—"

"It was me, Gran," Paulie said, his tone apologetic. "I didn't exactly kick him, but I might've stepped on him by accident. Thought it was someone's foot."

"That was *my* foot," Katie said. "I think it might have been me who pushed him away."

"And now it's me Katie who's taken to—" Mary-Margaret began.

"I'm sure the dog will be fine," Michael said with a sigh, rubbing his forehead. "But now that you've brought it up, when will he be going back to Sally-next-door?"

"When I leave," she stated.

"Which will be…?" Michael asked, looking around the table.

"Well, since we're talking about it and all, I'll be telling ye all at once," Mary-Margaret said, pausing until everyone had set their forks down. "I may have a wee kidney issue."

"Oh, Mom," Katie began, her voice full of concern.

"Is it serious?" Teaszy asked.

"Holy crap," Max said under his breath, his eyes wide.

"If there's anything we—" Ahmed started, but was cut off by Mary-Margaret's dismissive wave.

"Is that why you've been so confused lately?" Michael asked, the words leaving his mouth before he could stop them.

All eyes turned on him.

"Sorry," Michael said.

Teaszy raised an eyebrow.

"No. Mike's right," Allan said, his voice taking on an authoritative tone.

Now all eyes turned to Allan.

"If it's a kidney issue, you could be looking at uremia, in which case you'll experience symptoms like confusion, fainting, bloating," he continued. "It's all a part of kidney failure."

"Since when did you become a doctor?" Paulie muttered.

"I said I was having trouble with me kidneys, lads," Mary-Margaret stated. "Not that I was dying. Likely nothing to get yer knickers in a knot over, but something worth keeping an eye on, I'd say."

"It's the big pharma that puts fear in us," Griffin said. "They want us to be dependent on them. Like sheep."

"So it's not serious, right, Gran?" Max asked.

"Well, let's just say ye won't be inheriting me millions just yet," she said and then held out the bowl of mashed potatoes. "Now. Where am I passing this?"

"So does that mean you *are* going home sooner than later?" Michael asked.

"I think it's probably best if she stays here with you a bit longer, don't you?" Teaszy suggested, looking across the table at her older brother. "She can't go home like this."

"She just said she was having some kidney problems, not dying," he said, glancing at Teaszy in exasperation.

"And *she* is right here," Mary-Margaret said. "And *she* will be going back to her own house when *she* is satisfied that Mister Big City Detective over there can manage on his own, which, by the looks of things, won't be any time soon."

"What's that supposed to mean?" Michael said, his voice sharpening as his lips pressed into a thin line.

"Never mind," Mary-Margaret said with a wave of her hand. She then turned her attention to her son-in-law. "Now, Allan. Are ye still on the verge of losing yer job, or have they already shown ye the door?"

"What?" Teaszy exclaimed, her eyes widening with surprise. "No, Mom. Allan's not getting fired. In fact, he just got a promotion."

"Promotion? To what? Chief Dweeb?" Paulie said, his voice dripping with sarcasm.

"No," Teaszy replied, placing her hand on her husband's shoulder in a rare show of tenderness. "Your father is now in charge of corporate—"

"Don't do it, Old Man," Griffin cut in, raising his fist in defiance. "It's just a part of their plot to oppress the oppressed! Conform the conformists! Rise up!"

Griffin's declaration was met with an eyeroll from Michael and a chuckle from Ahmed.

"One day, Griffin," Allan said, not at all amused by the young man's pretensions, "When you have a job, you may find that—"

"Griff has a job," Paulie stated.

"Really?" Allan challenged. "Doing what?"

"Speaking of jobs," Michael said, trying to steer the conversation away from where it seemed intent on going, "I understand that you're getting involved in someone else's job again, Mom."

"Ach, that new New Girl is hopel—"

"That wasn't what I meant," Michael said. "I understand that you're getting yourself involved in a murder investigation. Again. Despite having been told not to at least twice before."

"Oh, that. Well, yes," Mary-Margaret said, looking around the table. "Anyone want any more corned beef before I clear the table?"

"And you thought our lives were exciting," Ahmed said to his nephews with a wink.

"Don't encourage her," Michael said.

"What I do on me own time is me own business, last I checked," Mary-Margaret said. "Now, Katie, pass this bowl over to Paulie's Griffin before he starts licking his plate. I've more in the kitchen, luv. No need to go hungry. And I can wrap up some of the corned beef for ye to take with ye if ye'd like."

"No, I'm good," Griffin replied.

"Detective Sergeant Gill has already called me at work to ask you to keep out of it, Mom," Michael continued.

"Well, he never called me, so that's between the two of yiz, isn't it?"

"And I believe he came by to caution you in person."

"Fasten your seatbelts, kids. It's going to be a bumpy night," Paulie said.

"No, it's not," Michael stated. "Because your grandmother is going to cease and desist any involvement she might have in the Giancola murder."

"If I'm hearing what I think I'm hearing ye say, Michael, then yes, the night might just become a wee bit turbulent, lads, because yer grandmother has no intention of letting a murderer get away with it. And, speaking of yer Mr. Gill, Michael, he was doing nothing short of stalking me, and I'd like ye to take a report."

"Game. On," Paulie said.

"Mom—"

"Or, if yer not willing to do that, then we've nothing further to talk about," she said, shooting Michael a look that would have shattered anyone not accustomed to it. "Now, if yer not taking any home, be sure to eat another few slices while yer here, Griffin. Where's the plate of corned beef?"

"Remember how you almost went to jail a while back, Mom?" Michael persisted.

"How long ago and which time?" she asked as she saw the corned beef in front of her. She slid a piece of it onto Max's plate before passing it up the table. "There ye go, Griffin. Take as much as ye want. There's plenty more where that came from."

"I've missed you guys," Griffin said with a grin.

"I think we need to go now," Katie said, looking across the table at Ahmed.

"Yiz haven't had yer dessert," Mary-Margaret objected.

"I'm sure they'll have way better desserts in Paris," Paulie said.

"Ah, but they'll miss the insanity here," Allan said.

"Allan!" Teaszy said, giving him another kick under the table.

"And besides, Michael," Mary-Margaret said, reverting to their previous conversation. "'Tis not me investigating a murder so much as me responding to the needs of a parishioner."

"Marco Giancola died as a result of—"

"Ooh, now we have a cause of death," Paulie said dramatically, holding his fork up like a microphone. "But is it the *right* cause of death? Stay tuned, podcast family, as we uncover the truth in this week's episode of Mary-Margaret and the—"

"He was murdered," Mary-Margaret stated.

"Cool!" said Max.

"Capitalism kills," said Griffin.

"Mom," Michael said.

"And I'm going to find out who it was," she concluded.

"And there you have it, folks," Paulie concluded. "A man is dead, and any one of us could be...*the murderer.*"

"'Tis true," Mary-Margaret said, and then winked at Paulie. "Except for yer da, luv."

"Thank you?" Allan responded, confused.

"Because...?" Paulie asked, equally confused.

"Because he has neither the passion nor the smarts to do it. Now, who wants tea with their dessert?"

Chapter Twenty-Three

Mary-Margaret jumped at the sudden rap on the back door. She was standing in the kitchen, having just returned from dropping Max off at school, and was in the middle of putting the kettle on for a cuppa. Aside from Wee Phil going on like he hadn't seen her in ages, the house was quiet, and she had no reason to expect anyone to stop by, which is why the sound of someone at the back door caught her completely off guard.

"MM, look what I've found!" Arthur stated, holding up a green garbage bag.

"As long as it's not another head…" Mary-Margaret said, recalling the last time Arthur had brought in a bag he'd found.

"No, better," he said, stepping inside.

"I'm just making meself a cuppa. Might as well bring it into the living room and ye can tell me all about it."

Unable to wait the full seven minutes it took Mary-Margaret to make the tea—two for the kettle to boil and five for the tea to steep—Arthur relayed that he'd gone by Marco's Motors first thing to pick up the pay due to him for his half-day's work. After his request and his person were summarily dismissed, he took the opportunity to go through the trash set out in the laneway behind the garage. And voilà: he'd uncovered a treasure trove of potential evidence.

"Anything good?" Mary-Margaret asked as she passed him a mug of tea.

"Well, I'm not sure," Arthur said with great flourish, dumping the contents on the floor in front of their chairs, "But I know there has to be something here."

"Ach, me floors!" Mary-Margaret sputtered when, along with piles of paper, a few half-empty Tim Hortons coffee cups spilled out.

"I'll go get something to wipe this up with," Arthur said.

"No. You start going through this. I'll wipe it up," Mary-Margaret said with a sigh as she went into the kitchen to retrieve a cloth.

"Will you look at this!" Arthur exclaimed. "These are the itemized bills for the last few months."

"Grand. So we know it was a functioning business," Mary-Margaret said dryly, her mood dampening as she considered the million or so other things she'd rather be doing than sifting through a bag of garbage.

"I'm noticing a pattern here, MM," Arthur said, holding one and then another of the papers up.

"What? That all three bills were for mechanical work?"

"No. That all three, and the five I can see there—I have exceptional spatial abilities. Couple that with my photographic memory—"

"And what have ye found, luv?" Mary-Margaret said, trying not to sigh again.

"All eight customers had major work done on their cars."

"Another lightning bolt of information. The place is a garage."

"In my brief time in the industry, MM, I can say that most of the repairs listed here are, at best, vague and, at worst, nonexistent."

Mary-Margaret tried very hard not to give Arthur the side eye but failed.

"MM, you of all people should know that I would *never* go into a professional environment without researching it thoroughly. I spent the entire night before my limited tenure at Marco's Motors poring over YouTube videos and online manuals to prepare myself, and I can unequivocally say that most of these repairs have been trumped up."

"So what yer saying," Mary-Margaret had to concede, knowing Arthur had, likely, done his research, "is that they were taking advantage of their clients, were they? Well, that's a fine old kettle of fish, isn't it now?"

"Look," Arthur said, passing Mary-Margaret one of the bills. "Brake pads. Catalytic converters. Really?"

"Oh yes, I see," Mary-Margaret said, having no idea what a catalytic converter was.

"MM, replacing brake pads when they still have lots of life left in them is banal. And, honestly, any mechanic who attributes sub-standard performance issues like poor acceleration, engine misfires, or strange noises to a failing catalytic converter clearly hasn't checked for a clogged oil filter or a bad oxygen sensor," Arthur stated, as if it was common knowledge.

"And to think they let ye go after only half a day."

"Well," Arthur conceded. "I don't actually know what any of that means, but I remember reading it somewhere."

"So where does that leave us?"

"What if a disgruntled customer killed Marco Giancola?"

"That's a lot of anger over an inflated bill."

"There are a lot of angry people out there, MM."

Mary-Margaret nodded in agreement, thinking specifically of her Michael as of late.

"I say you go back over the customer list from yesterday and try to match them with these receipts," Arthur said.

"And what will ye be doing in the meantime?"

"Oh, I can't stay. I've got a cosplay event coming up, and I haven't even begun to get my costume together."

"Of course," Mary-Margaret replied.

Just then, her cell phone rang. Max's school. Her heart skipped a beat.

"Mary-Margaret O'Shea speaking," she practically hollered into the phone. "What's happened to me Max?"

"Oh, relax, Mary-Margaret, it's just me—The Old Bird. I wanted to tell you how much fun I had the other night, and what do you say we do it again? This time, you pick the spot."

"Ach, me stars," Mary-Margaret said, her hand on her heart. She nodded consolingly at Arthur. "That would be grand, luv. Any time in mind?"

"How does tonight look? Early dinner? Leona's in tomorrow, and it's always a bit—chaotic when she's around. I can run things with my eyes closed when she's not here, but, well, I'm sure you know what I mean. A drink or two the night before always helps."

"I know exactly what ye mean, luv. How's 5:30 at me local, O'Leary's, look?"

"Perfect! See you then!"

Mary-Margaret clicked off the phone, her mind momentarily drifting back to her days at St. Francis—the filing, the collating, all that time-consuming work. And then, a thought crossed her mind.

"Is everything alright, MM?"

"It is, luv. Do ye have any issue," she said slowly, "with us gathering someone else to help us out?"

"That depends," Arthur said, looking down at his empty mug. "Three is an awkward number. Don't ask me how I learned *that* painful truth."

"I was just thinking it would be good to have someone to keep track of all of," she said as she looked down at the mess that was on Michael's table and his floor. "This."

"I don't think so, MM. I mean, not like I couldn't use my own EA, but, with my superior organiz—"

"Ach, luv," Mary-Margaret said, giving his arm a squeeze. "I'd never leave ye out. And God alone knows I could never replace ye. Come on. Why don't ye take Wee Phil out the back while I wash up."

Chapter Twenty-Four

Johnny O'Leary looked like he hadn't slept in days, maybe even weeks. In reality, it was probably closer to days. Once again, he was the only one working the bar. If Dinesh or anyone else from the kitchen called in sick, Mary-Margaret had no doubt that he would buckle under the weight of exhaustion and stress. And, if he was like this at 5:30 on a Monday evening, she wondered how Johnny would manage on a busy night.

It had crossed her mind to meet The Old Bird somewhere else, but Mary-Margaret couldn't think of a place where she'd feel more at ease. Besides, if she was going to spend money on a meal she could easily make at home, she'd rather it go into Johnny's pocket than line the pockets of some corporate franchisee—even if it meant adding to the strain he was already under.

"Is Nolan no better, then?" Mary-Margaret said as she paid for her half pint of crown float at the bar.

"Oh, he's fine," Johnny said. "It's Maeve now."

"She's not got strep as well, has she? Not in her condition."

"No. Worse…morning sickness. Seems to go on all day."

"Ach, that's a shame," Mary-Margaret said, passing her credit card over the bar to him. "Don't bother passing me yer machine. Just add yer tip and give it a swipe, luv."

"Thanks," he said, turning his back to ring in the order. "When she was pregnant with Nolan, she hardly missed a beat, but this time…"

"Every time's different, luv. I was sick as a dog for the first few months with me Michael. Hardly knew I was pregnant with Katie," she said, taking the credit card back from him. "So I take it Big John's looking after Nolan, then?"

"Barely, but yeah. If this keeps up, I don't know what I'm going to do."

"Hire a waitress is what ye'll do," Mary-Margaret said.

"I'd rather close my pub than go through what we went through with the last one."

"God rest her soul."

"Sure," Johnny said, shifting his focus to another customer.

Mary-Margaret turned and went to the table she and Frank had sat at a couple of nights earlier just as The Old Bird came in the door.

"Order whatever yer drinking at the bar," Mary-Margaret called to her.

"Old school," The Old Bird said with a grin as she detoured towards Johnny. "I like it. I'll have a margarita."

"Sorry. I'm a bit short-staffed tonight. I can get you any beer I've got on draft, or wine."

"I'll have a glass of Pinot," The Old Bird said. "With an ice cube."

The Old Bird paid for her glass of wine and joined Mary-Margaret at her table.

"Cool place, Mary-Margaret. I've never been to Ireland, but I'm assuming this is what the pubs look like there?"

"Almost," Mary-Margaret said, raising her glass. "Sláinte."

The two women raised their glasses just as seven younger women rolled into the pub, their laughter and chatter loud enough to suggest this wasn't their first stop of the evening. One woman wore a hat that read, *Buy Me A Shot, I'm The Friggin' Bride,* while the other six sported ones that said, *Becca's First Marriage.* Clearly, they were in full bachelorette party mode.

"Ach, Johnny's going to have a conniption, I'm afraid," Mary-Margaret said, glancing over at him standing behind the bar looking more like a dog that had just been beaten than the owner of a flourishing pub. "Bet he never thought there'd be a week-night hen party arriving."

"Hang on a minute," The Old Bird said, setting her drink down on the table before striding towards Johnny.

"Mind?" She said as she stepped around the bar. "Show me where your whiskey is and ring in seven shots. Ladies! Which one of you is Ms.

Moneybags this evening? We're selling by the drink, but don't let that hold you back. I'm assuming you're starting with a shot of the best Irish whiskey you've had in the past fifteen minutes?"

"Yesss!" someone or all of them squealed.

"And you, behind the ladies. I've got draft or wine. You look like a draft-drinker. Stop looking at their butts and get your credit card out. Better yet, buy the ladies a round."

Before long, The Old Bird had poured all the drinks the bachelorette party would be having before heading to another pub, along with a few pints for some of the regulars.

"I'm just going to go back to join my friend, John-o," she said, coming around the bar. "I'll keep an eye on things from there, and, if you need me, just whistle. You do know how to whistle, don't you?"

"It's Johnny," he sputtered as she walked away. "My name is Johnny."

"Ha!" cackled The Old Bird when she got back to Mary-Margaret's table. "I haven't had that much fun in years."

"Yer a natural, that's for sure," Mary-Margaret said. "Those girls must have had three shots each. Wouldn't want to be them tomorrow morning."

"Tomorrow morning? That's hopeful. I wouldn't want to be them in about two hours!"

"Those were the days, weren't they?" Mary-Margaret said, looking at her near-empty half-pint glass.

"They were, but I wouldn't want to go back even if I could," The Old Bird said, taking a gulp of her watered-down wine. "So, what have you been up to since I saw you last?"

"I think I'd best get another half-pint before I get into it with ye," Mary-Margaret said, heading to the bar.

"Might as well get me another Pinot," The Old Bird said, upending the glass. "I'll get the next round."

Drink order filled and back at the table, Mary-Margaret updated The Old Bird on Marco Giancola's murder investigation.

"Ha!" The Old Bird cawed. "You've got me beat. All I've got is an angry mother who showed up in the office, threatening to have Leona fired because she told her kid he couldn't set up his pyramid-scheme business on school property. Said it infringed on his 'entrepreneurial spirit'. Called Leona a *leftard*. I was gonna call the cops, but she handled it."

A loud crash near the bar caught both women's attention. Someone had knocked a pint glass, sending its contents splashing onto the floor. Johnny's shoulders slumped in resignation.

"Hey, John-o. Pass me the dustpan, a cloth, and point me in the direction of your wet mop," The Old Bird said, hopping up towards the bar.

Within minutes, the mess was cleaned up, and The Old Bird was back at the table.

"I hope John-o's got staff coming in; otherwise, he'll never manage when this place starts buzzing," The Old Bird commented.

Mary-Margaret explained why Johnny was left handling the bar on his own, then smoothly transitioned into what she really wanted to discuss with The Old Bird: enlisting her help with some of the more mundane tasks of the investigation. Specifically, comparing the client list with the bills that Arthur had retrieved from the trash bins behind Marco's Motors.

"I'm on it like a cat on a laser pointer," The Old Bird said. "It'll keep me busy so Leona doesn't cook up some ridiculous make-work project. Like sending me down to the basement to haul up a load of dusty boxes and scan every last file. Put me in, coach!"

Chapter Twenty-Five

After taking Wee Phil out for his morning walk, Mary-Margaret went upstairs to her bedroom to get ready for yoga. It had been several months since she'd last gone, thanks, in part, to her feigned broken foot as well as the number of murder investigations that seemed to be requiring her attention. She had to admit that it was hard to get to class while chasing down homicidal maniacs.

After struggling to squeeze herself into her yoga pants, she looked at herself in the mirror. She did not like what she saw.

"Well," she sighed, looking down at Wee Phil, "there's nothing for it but to go back to the studio."

She peeled herself out of the tight pants and stuffed them and a matching Lululemon top into a bag and was rooting around for her yoga mat when her cell phone rang. She looked down at the call display.

Fr Miguel

This will be rich, won't it, she thought as she clicked the phone on.

"Is this Mary-Margaret?" Father Miguel asked, his voice tinged with panic.

"Indeed, Father," she replied, though a million far more entertaining responses danced through her mind.

"I'm sorry to bother you, Mary-Margaret, but I'm in a bit of a bind."

"Are ye now," she said as she walked down the stairs, phone in one hand, yoga mat in the other, bag over her shoulder.

"Well, yes. It seems that Lola has walked out."

"The name doesn't ring any bells, Father," she replied, furrowing her brow.

"Ashleigh's replacement," Father Miguel clarified.

"Oh. Ye mean the new New Girl."

"And I don't have a contact number for Sister Augustine," he continued, "and neither does anyone else, or so it seems, and I was wondering if you had her number so I could contact her about possibly starting early."

"Well," Mary-Margaret began, her mind racing. "It's not quite that...simple, Father."

When he did not respond, she continued.

"Ye see, I don't have a *direct* line for Sister Augustine. I contact her through...someone else, who then relays the message. Unless she's on retreat, which I believe she is at the moment, in which case she cannot be contacted. I can, however, try the other person and see if it's possible to contact her—"

"Why don't you just give me the number?"

"It's not possible."

"Okay," Father Miguel said slowly. "Do I want to know why?"

"The logic behind it is far too complicated for me mind to unravel to ye in this moment, Father, and it matters not. Now, if ye've nothing else to say, I'm going to hang up now and give Arth—Sister Augustine's connection a call and see if he can track her down and get her to contact ye. I'd be otherwise happy to stay on the line with ye and chat, Father, but I'm off to me yoga on account of having spent the last few months—"

"That will be fine, Mary-Margaret," Father Miguel said. "Just get Sister Augustine to call me. Thank you."

Before she could reply, he had hung up.

Mary-Margaret looked at her watch and saw that, even if she left at this exact moment, she would not arrive at the yoga studio in time for the start of the class.

"Ach, is it God's will that me body should fall apart?" she asked Wee Phil before setting down her yoga mat and bag to tap in Arthur's phone number.

"MM?"

"Arthur, luv, can ye get yer nun outfit on and make yer way to the church? Father Miguel's just called in a tizz and says he needs ye early."

"No can do, MM," Arthur said with a yawn. "I'm just about to head off to bed."

"Bed? At this hour of the day?"

"I was up all night working on our murder investigation."

"Were ye now?" Mary-Margaret said, walked towards the kitchen to put the kettle on. "And?"

"Marco's Motors really overcharged their clients."

"We knew that, didn't we? Along with billing them for work that wasn't done. Don't tell me that's what's keeping ye from heading over to the church."

"I haven't collated the numbers—"

"Just as well. Me friend, The Old Bird, is going to be doing that for us."

"Oh," Arthur said, the word barely rising above a whisper. He let a long pause hang in the air, then added, "I see."

"Don't worry, luv. Yer not being replaced. That's all she'll be doing."

"This time," Arthur groused and then came back with his usual false bravado. "As if it was possible to replace me."

"Exactly," Mary-Margaret replied with a smile. "Now, what have ye found?"

"Irene Ashford, that woman from St. Francis. Either she liked hanging out with mechanics, or she had a real clunker of a car because I saw a lot of bills with her name on them."

"I'd imagine it could be a little of both," Mary-Margaret said, recalling how she was dressed at Marco Giancola's funeral. *And to think she thought that she'd get away with looking like that! Sure, what was she thinking? But still...* "Yer not suggesting that she could be the murderer, are ye?"

"As we know, MM, anyone is capable of doing anything."

"That's one thing I've learned from ye, luv," Mary-Margaret said. "Which is all the reason for ye to get yerself over to the church as soon as ye can. Ever since Father Miguel arrived, Irene Ashford's been on every committee known to God and man, so she'll likely be hanging about. The sooner ye get yerself in that front office, the sooner ye can start sussing her out."

"Ugh," Arthur said. "I can't do it. But *you* could."

"What are ye saying, lad? That I go back to me old job?"

"Just until my official start date in a couple of weeks. Isn't there a pile of things still to be sorted out from the bazaar?"

"Ach, what a shambles that was this year. Biggest mistake they ever made, not bringing me back to run it. Not like—"

"MM?" Arthur cut in.

"It's clear the New Girl couldn't organize a night out if ye gave her the tickets and the taxi, let alone manage the complexi—"

"MM?" he repeated, his voice tightening as he tried to redirect her.

"As the fall bazaar. I told them it would be a disaster, but nobody listened to me. Said we could work together, but honestly, luv. I don't—"

"Mary-Margaret!" he exclaimed before taking a deep breath.

"Even want to imagine the mess the New Girl left for the *new* New Girl. No wonder she walked out."

For a moment, neither of them spoke.

"Are you finished?" Arthur finally asked.

"Yes," Mary-Margaret replied.

"Good. Now, first of all, the new New Girl didn't walk out. She got fired because I got hired, remember? Maybe she just figured, why stick around? Who knows. And secondly—and most importantly—I say *you* go in, at least until my official start date, and see what you can find out about Irene Ash—"

"I know all about that doxie," Mary-Margaret stated.

"Well, maybe there's more to her than you thought," Arthur said. "Anyway, it would be good to have you there, to keep an eye on everyone, just in case your friend links anyone else to the dead guy. In the meantime, I have to get some sleep. I'll call you when I get up, and we can compare notes."

Mary-Margaret hated to admit it, but Arthur might have been right. Aside from giving her access to the information that would vindicate her claims that she was the only one who could properly run the fall bazaar, she could do some snooping around and rule anyone from St. Francis in or out as suspects.

The only issue was Father Miguel. Did she honestly think she could manage working with that man for two weeks without saying something that would put her on the fast track to Hell? She looked over at her yoga gear. And then to Wee Phil, who was wagging his entire body. And then she considered the mess Billy Gilly had already made of the investigation.

Forty-five minutes later, Mary-Margaret stood at the front doors of the church, Michael's old electric kettle in hand.

Chapter Twenty-Six

The first thing Mary-Margaret did was unplug the Keurig and tuck it away. The next thing she did was wander down the hall to the kitchen by the gymnasium, kettle in hand—the very same one she'd brought from Michael's house—and fill it up with water. The third thing she did was take it back to her office and plug it in before finally heading to Father Miguel's office.

Of course, the door was shut, so she knocked twice and, not waiting for a response, let herself in.

"Mary-Margaret," Father Miguel said, sitting up sharply behind his desk, forcing a smile that made no attempt to be sincere. "I wasn't expecting to see you here this morning."

"Nor was I expecting to be here, being on me way to yoga and all when ye called, but, as I mentioned, Sister Augustine is on retreat and won't be back until—"

"No, you said she *might* be on retreat," he said, slowly getting to his feet. "And you said you'd call—"

"Well, she is, and I did, which is how I know she is," Mary-Margaret shot back. "I've just put the kettle on. Would ye like a cuppa?"

"No," he said, slithering back into his chair. "No, I wouldn't."

"Suit yerself. In the meantime, ye know where I'll be," she said as she walked out of his office.

"Yes, sadly, I do."

* * *

"Mary-Margaret!" Annette Giancola exclaimed. "I didn't know you worked here. I just thought you were—"

"Just wandering about with nothing else to do but pop in at the church? I've always worked here—except until I retired. But yes, I do work here. At least for the next wee while. And what brings ye in? Not that ye need a reason to come into God's house, but yer hardly what we'd call a regular, are ye?" she said, taking a sip of her tea.

"No," she said with a laugh. "I'm here to meet with the detective sergeant in charge of the case."

"Billy Gilly?" Mary-Margaret said, spitting the name out.

"Is that his name? I thought it was—" she began, fumbling in her purse for something.

"Matters not, luv," Mary-Margaret said, regaining her composure. "And why here? Why not at police headquarters? Or at yer own home?"

"It was my idea. He wanted to speak to me at the house, but Robert's there, and I—"

"At yer house? Robert Jensen?"

"Yes. There's a lot of paperwork to sort out now that Marco's—"

"But I thought ye said the business went to Robert."

"It does, but some of the papers he needs are at the house, and I have no idea where they are. Besides, it's nice to have someone there while I'm sorting through Marco's things."

"Already? When me Jimmy died, God rest his soul, he was at least cold in the ground before I started getting rid of what was left of him."

Annette didn't respond.

"But I guess we're not all the same, are we. Ach. Where are me manners? Would ye like a cuppa? I don't think there's a mug here, but there'll be one back in the kitchen."

"No, I'm fine, thanks."

"If ye don't mind me asking, luv, is it this Robert lad who's pushing any memory of Marco out the door?"

"I don't think that's his intention, no. He's just being very helpful...oh, there's the detective sergeant now."

Both women watched as Detective Sergeant Gill entered the church. The smile he had for Annette quickly faded when he saw Mary-Margaret's face poking out of her office doorway.

"Mrs. O'Shea," he said as he came towards them both. "Was retirement not sitting well with you?"

"Whether 'twas for me or not is none of yer concern, Mr. Gill. But it might be something ye'd like to consider," she replied.

"Oh, I'm sure I'm good to solve a few more homicides before I retire, Mrs. O'Shea," he said condescendingly before turning to Annette. "I believe Father Miguel is letting us use his office, Mrs. Giancola. Shall we?"

D/S Gill and Annette Giancola walked towards Father Miguel's office while Mary-Margaret went back to her tea.

"Just stepping out for a bit, Mary-Margaret," Father Miguel said as he passed her open door, slipping through the same one D/S Gill had just entered.

Mary-Margaret turned and made herself another cup of tea before she sat down at her old desk. She needed to find out what Annette was telling that fool, Billy Gilly. She took a sip, and then she remembered the intercom in Father Miguel's office, which linked to the one in her own. Father Miguel had never used it, of course—which was just as well. She and Father Brian, on the other hand, had had a field day with it, acting like a couple of kids with a set of walkie-talkies.

"We had some good times, me and Father Brian," she said with a smile to the wall in front of her. "Ach. No sense in looking back, me girl. Ye've a murder to solve."

Not two minutes later, file-folder in hand, Mary-Margaret marched right up to the closed door of Father Miguel's office and gave it a couple of hard raps before letting herself in.

"Sorry to bother, but Father Miguel told me to have these files ready for him when he gets back, and I'll likely be gone by then," she said, plowing into the office and scanning Father Miguel's desk for the intercom.

Of course, it wasn't there.

"And I've just got to look in these drawers," she said as she frantically opened and closed all of them, "for a…mouse trap. Yes. According to the new New Girl, he'd seen a mouse the other day, and the silly girl decided to put a few traps in the drawers here to catch it. Quite a stink they make if ye leave their dead wee bodies in the trap. Don't mind me."

Where in God's name did he put it?

She breathed a sigh of relief as she felt the hard plastic of the device tucked away in the back of the bottom left drawer. She pulled it out.

"That doesn't look like a mouse trap to me, Mrs. O'Shea," D/S Gill said.

"No, it doesn't, but it is. What's that old expression? *Build a better mousetrap, build a smarter mouse?* Ye see, we've had so many mice running around here over the years that they've become aware of what the standard traps look like, so we've had to find something different. Cost us a pretty penny, too. Don't mind me. I'll just plug it in over here and be out of yer hair before ye know it."

D/S Gill looked dubiously at Mary-Margaret but waited patiently for her to complete the task at hand.

"There we are, lads. Now, I'll just turn it on and press this button," she said. "Ach, it doesn't seem to want to stay on. Let me just put a wee bit of scotch tape over it, and I'll be on me away. Now, do not remove the tape or else the trap won't work, and, as ye know as well as I: where there's one mouse, there's dozens of them."

"I'm not quite sure how this works," D/S Gill said. "Where do they actually go in?"

"Well, that's the beauty of it, isn't it? They don't. Ye see, this device sends out a sound wave…listen. Do ye hear it? Very high. Very quiet?"

They all waited in silence for a moment.

"I think I do," Annette Giancola said.

"Right. So that's what the mice hear, and it drives them mad. Give it a few minutes and, if Father Miguel really did see a mouse, they'll be marching out the front door in no time. Anyway, that's the end of me. I'll leave ye be."

Mary-Margaret closed the door behind her, took a deep breath, and crossed herself.

Ye know I'm doing yer work, don't ye, God? So ye'll forgive me for all I've said, right inside of yer own house, no less.

She then rushed back to her office, found her end of the apparatus (also stuffed in the back of a drawer), set it up, and began to hear what Annette Giancola had to say.

Chapter Twenty-Seven

The reception wasn't as good as Mary-Margaret remembered it being when she and Father Brian used the intercom. Or perhaps the fun they'd had with it had clouded her memory. In any case, she found herself straining to hear what Detective Sergeant Gill and Annette Giancola were saying.

Regardless, pen in hand, cuppa at the ready, there she sat by the contraption, jotting down what she thought were the salient points of the conversation. In fact, so absorbed was she in the garbled sound coming from the speaker that she nearly jumped out of her skin when there was a gentle knock on the open door of her office.

"Me stars!" she exclaimed when she saw Arthur, dressed in full nun's habit, standing in the doorway. "What are ye doing here? I thought ye were—"

Just then, Father Miguel appeared.

"On retreat," Mary-Margaret stated loudly, and then, looking towards the church door, stated even louder: "I thought ye were on retreat, Sister Augustine."

"I...I was," the nun replied, stepping into full Sister Augustine character. "But, given my advanced level of...retreatedness, I was allowed to return to better serve my community."

"So, you're back?" Father Miguel exclaimed, his relief at the thought of avoiding any further dealings with Mary-Margaret palpable.

"I am, Father," Sister Augustine replied, executing a curtsey so deep that even the King of England would have been impressed.

"That's...wonderful!" Father Miguel gushed. His face lit up as if the Pope

Himself was standing before him. "And can you start now?"

"Of course, Father. Just give me a minute to loosen my wimple."

"Excellent. Well," Father Miguel said, shifting his attention and releasing his disdain towards Mary-Margaret. "Thank you for stepping in, and I'm sure I'll see you another time."

Before she could reply, Father Miguel was practically skipping towards his office.

"Father?" Mary-Margaret called after him.

"Hmmm?" he said, looking over his shoulder.

"The interview. In your office?"

"Oh. Right. Yes. Well, I'll just go…into the parlor until they're finished. You will tell me when they're finished, won't you, Sister Augustine?"

"Of course, Father," she said with a reassuring smile, finding amongst her many façades a calm demeanor intended to convey that she had everything well in hand.

"And I'll be sure to gather me things," Mary-Margaret said, realizing she was probably as relieved to be leaving as Father Miguel was to be rid of her.

"That was easy," Sister Augustine said with a shrug as they watched Father Miguel prance down the hall towards the parlor.

"I am glad yer here, luv," Mary-Margaret said, looking back at the intercom. "Perhaps ye can make out what they're saying."

"As you know, MM, I have an exceptionally keen sense of hearing that—"

"Shhh," Mary-Margaret said. "Listen."

The two of them huddled around the intercom, their heads both tilted to one side as they strained to make out the words being spoken. Mary-Margaret grabbed her paper and a pen and continued jotting down what she thought she heard. Sister Augustine, meanwhile, closed her eyes, as if in prayer.

"Thank you for coming in," they heard Detective Sergeant Gill's voice say as he opened the door of Father Miguel's office. "I'll be sure to keep you updated on any progress we make."

"Thank you, Bill," Annette Giancola said, the words clear—and sounding far too intimate for Mary-Margaret's liking—as the two rounded the corner and came into sight. "Just one last thing, if you don't mind?"

"Of course," he replied with a warm smile.

"Robert had said that all the assets in the company will be frozen until this investigation is concluded, and I was wondering—"

"Well, that's not quite true, Annette."

"Aren't the two of them all cozy-wozy?" Mary-Margaret mumbled. "Perhaps 'tis she who is the one to watch, not that Robert lad."

"He *is* investigating her husband's murder, MM," Sister Augustine whispered. "I can't imagine them not being on a first-name basis."

"Well, the assets don't just *freeze* when a partner dies," D/S Gill said, his voice carrying the weight of someone who clearly believed his knowledge was unmatched. "But things can get held up. I'm not a civil lawyer, but there are certain considerations, like the transfer of shares or their stake in the business, dealing with the estate, and any agreements—like a buyout—that come into play."

"That all sounds so—complicated," Annette said. Mary-Margaret swore she could see her batting her eyelashes. "How long might it take to get it all sorted, Bill?"

"Well, as you can imagine," he continued, "all the paperwork involved can slow things down. I'm thinking the partner agreement would be the key to determining how quickly everything gets sorted."

"So the assets…?"

"Given what you've said, Annette, I wouldn't worry. I suspect that Mr. Jensen will want to reorganize the company sooner than later, and, again assuming that your late husband's will directs his shares of the company's gross profits to you, you should be fine."

"Phew," she sighed, placing one hand on her chest and the other on his forearm. "That's *such* a relief. Thank you, Bill."

"When me Jimmy, God rest his soul, died, the last thing on me mind was money," Mary-Margaret said with a sniff as she and Arthur stepped further back into her office. "Or trying to pick up a man."

"I hear you, MM. I don't like this *at all*."

"Shall I make ye a cuppa? I've just finished me own but, after all I've heard,

I could use another. Ye'll have to go down the hallway to the kitchen to get yerself a mug. Clearly, the new New Girl was just as hopeless as a church secretary as the New Girl was. And ye might want to let Father Miguel know his office is available."

Chapter Twenty-Eight

"Max, will ye take Wee Phil out? He's practically bursting at the seams.

"Sure, Gran," Max said. "So I hear you and The Old Bird are buddies."

"Did ye, now. And where did ye hear this and from whom?"

"At school. She told me."

"Then it must be true. Now, out with ye, and, if I order us a pizza for dinner, will ye go pick it up?"

"Yeah. No problem. I'll take Phil for a longer walk and then pick it up on my way home," Max said. Noticing the look on his grandmother's face, he quickly added, "I'll take Phil into the shop with me."

"Alright, then," Mary-Margaret said.

"Afraid someone will *dognap* him, Mom?" Michael said as he came in the front door and then added, "I should be so lucky."

"Michael! Put the thought right out of yer head! Now, are ye home for dinner, and, if so, we'll not be having pizza. I'll make us all up something instead."

"Aww," Max said by way of protest.

"Pizza's fine. Here," Michael said, reaching into his wallet to pull out some bills. "I'll pay."

"Thanks, Dad," Max said.

"Now, go on. I have to talk to your grandmother."

"Uh-oh…" Max said with a grin.

"If it's about—" she began as Max turned to leave.

"Don't even start, Mom," Michael said. "Max? Take the dog?"

"Right," he said, stepping back briefly to put the leash on Wee Phil before heading out the door.

Mary-Margaret went into the kitchen once Max and the dog were on their way. Michael followed her.

"What are you doing, Mom?" he said.

"What do ye mean, what am I doing? I'm clearly getting some plates out for dinner."

Mary-Margaret said, opening a cupboard and reaching for a stack of them. "Honestly, Michael, I do worry—"

"I got a call."

"Did ye now?" she said, turning around to hand him three plates. "Here. Take these out

and put them on the table."

"From Detective Sergeant Gill," Michael said, reluctantly taking the plates from her.

"Silly Billy Gilly?"

"Mom, enough."

"Ach, I'm just having a wee bit of craic, is all," she said with a smile before turning to

another cupboard to get three glasses. "So, what did yer man have to say for himself this time?"

"It's not so much what he had to say for himself as opposed to what he had to say about you."

"Me? Well, aren't I the popular one?" she said, making a playful face at him as she handed him the glasses. "Here. Take these, too. Mind ye don't drop anything."

"You're meddling. Again," Michael said, balancing the glasses on top of the plates.

"I am doing no such thing, me son," she said, motioning him towards the dining room. "Now, are ye going to stand there with yer gob hanging open, or are ye going to set those on the table?"

"He saw you at the church this morning."

"Father Miguel called me in to help," she replied, following him, empty-handed, towards the dining room table.

"Why do I find that hard to believe?" he said, setting the plates down.

"There," Mary-Margaret said, nodding towards the kitchen. "Me phone is just in me

purse at the back. If ye don't believe me, I can pull up his number so ye can see when he called me. Not that I need to prove anything to ye, my son."

"He says you've been talking to Annette Giancola," Michael continued.

"I may have been," she replied, crossing her arms. "Is that a crime?"

"Only when you're talking to her about the death of her husband."

"Ach, what else would ye expect me to talk to a woman whose husband has just been murdered about? Honestly, Michael. Now, are ye going to set those plates around, or are we to grab our own like we're eating at some free-for-all?"

"He says you've been over at Marco's Motors."

"And…?"

"Inside Marco's Motors."

"And…? The plates, Michael. Sort the plates."

"That you went inside Marco's Motors while it was still a crime scene," Michael said, setting

the three plates around the table.

"And he would know this how? And the glasses, luv. Don't forget the glasses."

"Video cameras," he said, slamming the glasses down by the plates.

"Steady, luv. They're called glasses for a reason."

"Mom, I can't keep digging you out of—"

"*Digging me out,* Michael? I'd say ye've got things turned around, me son. 'Tis I who

keeps digging yer lot out, if we're going to be perfectly honest with one another. I don't suppose I need to spell out what a mess yer man was making of the Jane Ann Hill investigation, do I? Or, better yet, would ye like me to go over the highlights of that git's involvement in the Cassandra Lewis case? Ye've got a nerve, ye have, even suggesting that I've done anything but help the cause."

"And now it's time to hang up your magnifying glass, Sherlock. I've been told to tell you that if you meddle—"

"*Ye've* been told to tell me? What, yer man can't stand up for himself to face a retiree, and I'm supposed to put me faith in him? Ach, Michael, 'tis no wonder yer not Police Officer of the Year."

"Mom, I don't want to be—"

"And it would seem that Billy Gilly shares yer lack of motivation when it comes to doing his job. Now, if ye'll excuse me, Max will be home shortly with our pizza, so I'm just going to give me hands a good scrub in the bathroom upstairs."

"Mom," Michael said, following her towards the stairs.

All of a sudden, Mary-Margaret arched her back and let out a yelp before falling to the floor.

"Mom! Are you okay?" Michael said, immediately at her side.

"Help me up, Michael, and into me bed," she gasped, her eyes squeezed shut, her shoulders tensed. Her complexion remained perfectly fine, but if she could have willed it, beads of sweat would have gathered on her forehead. She couldn't, though, so instead, she lay crumpled on the floor, one hand pressed tightly to her side as if clutching at some pain that was not imaginary, her body trembling just enough to make her shallow breaths seem laboured.

"Hang on," Michael said, fumbling for his cell phone.

"Gran!" Max cried, seeing her on the floor as he came in the door, dropping the two pizza boxes.

"'Tis nothing to worry yerself about, luv," she said as Max knelt down beside her.

Wee Phil began running around her, occasionally stopping to lick her face.

"Get that dog out of here!" Michael yelled, cell phone in hand. Max hurriedly grabbed Wee Phil and held the dog close.

"Michael, stop hollering at the dog, put yer phone away, and help me up," she instructed.

"I think we should call an ambulance."

"And I think ye should help me up. There'll be plenty of time for an ambulance once we get things sorted."

Playing it for all it was worth, Mary-Margaret slowly got to her feet, both Michael and Max on either side of her.

"Grand. Now, Max, why don't ye help me up to me bed and ye and yer da can have a quiet dinner together."

"Are you sure—" Max began, eyes wide as he helped her to her feet.

"Mom," Michael interrupted. "I think—"

"Save yer thinking for yer work," Mary-Margaret said.

Michael stood at the bottom of the stairs and let out a sigh of exasperation while Max helped his grandmother up to her bedroom.

"Are you sure you're okay, Gran?" he asked once she was settled on the bed.

"Ach, I'm fine, luv," she said with a little smile. "Just had enough of listening to yer da is all."

Max looked incredulously at his grandmother for a moment before they both erupted into giggles.

"Close the door, lad. The last thing we need is for yer dad to hear us. Now, go on downstairs and have yer pizza. Be sure to bring me up a couple of slices when yer done and, if ye can, luv, a wee dram might be in order."

Max stood staring at his grandmother, grin still on his face.

"Off with ye, luv, before yer da decides to come up and see what's going on. Or, worse yet, calls for an ambulance. Oh, and can ye get me cell phone out of me purse and bring it up before ye sit down to eat? Tell yer da I need it just in case I start feeling worse and need to give him a ring."

"Why wouldn't you just yell down?"

"Are ye playing along with me or are ye not, luv?"

Chapter Twenty-Nine

Mary-Margaret sat on the edge of her bed, Wee Phil curled up on one side of her, an empty plate on the other. The house was quiet, except for the sounds of the game on TV. From what she could hear, Michael and Max were watching together. She suspected Michael might have figured out she'd been faking her illness and was upset with her—evidenced by Max having brought her a cup of tea instead of the requested dram of whiskey. And, aside from a brief check-in, he had done nothing to engage with her—or, more importantly, to apologize for his accusations, which, while they might've had more than just a grain of truth, were completely unacceptable.

But Mary-Margaret couldn't concern herself with that now, although she did wish she had that dram. Instead, she was focused on conducting a homicide investigation. She glanced at the clock on the nightstand, hoping that it wasn't too late, the phone pressed against her ear as she waited for the call to be picked up.

"Old Bird. 'Tis Mary-Margaret. How are ye, luv?"

"Ha!" The Old Bird squawked, her voice crackling slightly through the line. "I was just

about to give you a buzz. Listen, I was working on those files you gave me, and boy, is Marco's Motors ever crooked. No wonder somebody whacked him."

"Ach, I'd heard about the billing for work that wasn't done."

"Work that wasn't done?" The Old Bird parroted back. "That's chicken scratch for these guys. I'm talking seriously illegal activity."

"What do ye mean?"

"Well, we both know about Robert Jensen."

"Sure," Mary-Margaret said, even though she had no idea what her friend meant. She sat up a bit straighter, taking the cup of now-cold tea off of the plate and placing it on the bedside table, careful not to spill. "What about Robert Jensen?"

"Well, you can tell this wasn't his first rodeo. That customer list you gave me...I'm seeing a lot of women on it, and I'm seeing some old names I remember from my days in the clubs."

"When ye were in yer bands and such?"

"You bet. Best time of my life. Especially the 'and such' part. But yeah. And you know, most of those clubs had ties with organized crime."

"I see."

"That customer list had four names I recognized from back in the day."

"Are ye sure they're the same people?" Mary-Margaret asked, now leaning back against the headboard, Wee Phil having adjusted himself so that she could pat his head. "I'm sure those lads weren't young when ye knew them, and now...?"

"Same dudes, Mary-Margaret. Have you got something to write on? I'll even give you their names."

Mary-Margaret glanced around her bedroom before pulling a bookmark from *Blind Spot*, the crime novel she was reading for her upcoming book club meeting. She paused for a moment, thinking about how much she liked the characters in the series, then spotted a pen on the bedside table.

"Well," she said after she'd written down the names her friend had recited, "I don't know a lot about organized crime and the likes, but I'm sure they must retire, too. Is it possible that these lads have hung up their...cement blocks...and just happen to live in the area?"

"Sure. And I've got Glass Tiger on the other line wanting me to do backup vocals on their next tour."

"I take it ye don't?" Mary-Margaret asked, having no idea who or what Glass Tiger was.

"I wouldn't be talking to you right now if anyone wanted me to do backup vocals, Mary-Margaret."

"So what are ye thinking?"

"I'm thinking that your dead dude, or, more likely, this other dude is involved in organized crime. Who knows how? Guns? Drugs? I don't know."

"And these organized lads yer speaking of—could they be involved in real estate, then?" Mary-Margaret asked, her mind drifting back to Peter Jensen's apparent knack for picking prime locations for Marco's Motors, all of which seemed to have excellent resale potential. Was it luck, instinct, or information that could only come from inside sources, the sharing of which would likely be highly illegal?

"They're involved in anything that'll make them money, if you ask me. Why?"

"Just expanding me knowledge of the criminal element," Mary-Margaret said, her tone casual, not about to give up any more information than necessary. This was, after all, her investigation. And Arthur's. She cleared her throat. "Listen, luv, I hate to cut ye off, but I've got to go on account of young Max feeling a bit under the weather and me being here on me own taking care of him."

"Max? He was fine today."

"Ach, well, ye know how it is with the lads at his age. Anything can go wrong at any time. Anyway, I've got to go. Bye-bye bye bye-bye bye."

Mary-Margaret clicked off the phone with a sigh and placed it on the bed beside her. She glanced at the clock again before picking up the phone and tapping in a familiar number.

"Hey, MM. What's up?"

"Arthur. What do ye know about organized crime?"

"Personally, or...?"

"Listen. The Old—me sources tell me that Marco Giancola and that Robert lad might be involved in organized crime."

"I wouldn't put it past them," Arthur said more casually than Mary-Margaret would have expected.

"So ye knew about this as well? And ye didn't think to say—"

"No, but I'm just thinking that, if they were able to expand Marco's Motors as quickly as they did, they'd need a lot of money up front."

"They were sold as franchises, weren't they? I'm assuming the lads buying the places would have their own garages already."

"No. They were turn-key operations, with the locations strategically placed throughout the city at first, and then the province."

"And ye knew this how?"

"I googled the company."

"Right," Mary-Margaret said with a grimace, feeling quite outsmarted. "Well, in that case, I suppose they would need a lot of money to start, wouldn't they?"

"And now, *quelle surprise*, most of those locations are primed to be redeveloped. Sounds like classic organized crime to me."

"And did ye find out that on yer Google as well?"

"No. A guy in one of my cosplay groups works high up in the part of the government that monitors land development projects, and he said they were noticing an unusually high number of redevelopment plans going in on properties where fairly successful garages were located."

"Why would garages be a factor in that?"

"Because of the risk of contamination, MM. Unreported oil spills, gas leaks, or dodgy refills by tanker trucks can leave a real mess. Garages usually have to do a fair bit of soil testing—or at least they should—before they get cleared for redevelopment, and the guy in my group is noticing this isn't always happening before plans are submitted and, sometimes, approved."

"Right. And ye knew about these redevelopment plans when?" Mary-Margaret said, feeling her blood pressure rising.

"Well, I kind of didn't tell you the whole truth the other morning when you called—and I'm super sorry for that, MM—when I said I'd been working all night on the case. I mean, I suppose I was, but I was doing it in costume, I guess you could say."

Mary-Margaret was going to get angry, but quickly considered that most of what Arthur did was in costume, so she took a couple of deep breaths instead. This withholding of relevant information part was not at all to her liking, but that would have to wait for another day to be addressed. She had bigger fish to fry now.

"And this is something these organized criminals would be into, then?"

"Absolutely."

"And did yer lad at the playgroup tell ye this or...?"

"Oh, no. I figured the organized crime angle out myself. It's one of my areas of expertise. I've been studying for years. Well, I took a correspondence course on it during the COVID lockdown after—"

There was a knock on Mary-Margaret's door.

"I'm sure ye did, luv, but I've got to go. Someone's at me door. Are ye in at the church tomorrow?"

"Bright and early," Arthur said cheerily.

"I'll be stopping by, and we can sort it out then, right?"

"Gran?" Max said, letting himself in, a whiskey glass in his hand.

"Where's yer da?" Mary-Margaret asked as she quickly clicked off her phone.

"Asleep in front of the TV."

"Just as well. Ta, luv," she said, taking the glass from him and nodding approvingly at the level of its contents.

"I figured you could use it. Who were you talking to?"

"Arthur."

"What's his deal?"

"Ye know what his...deal is. He's pansexual. And polyamorous. And likes to wear...ach, he's Arthur."

"Do you even know what polyamorous means?"

"Luv, 'twas me generation who invented the word. Now, what are yer plans for this evening?"

"Dunno. Likely just go upstairs and stream something."

"Would ye mind doing yer old gran a favor before ye get caught up in yer shows?"

"Sure."

"If I gave ye a couple of names, could ye see what ye could find out about them? I'd do it meself, but I'm kind of bedridden at the moment," she said with a wink and a smirk.

"Yeah. No problem. Why don't I go get my laptop and bring it down here?"

"Are ye sure yer da's asleep? Last thing we need is for him to see us in here having a party."

"No, the last thing we need is for him to see me in here helping you solve a murder."

Chapter Thirty

After coming home from dropping Max off at school, Mary-Margaret had planned to take the streetcar across town to St. Francis of Assisi to have a word with God, but when she glanced out the front window of Michael's house, she noticed it had started to rain. She was used to rain, but November rain had a way of cutting right through you, and she couldn't quite see the point of heading out into it. Except, of course, that Wee Phil needed to take a piddle.

"Michael!" she called out.

No response.

"Michael!?" she called again, and, again, there was no response. She noticed that his brogues were missing from the front door, which led her to believe he'd either gone to work, to court, or had hidden them so he wouldn't have to get out of bed to walk the dog.

She sighed and grabbed an umbrella from the front before going to the back door to take Wee Phil out. She was just about to clip the leash on his collar when her cell phone buzzed. She looked at the call display: *Father Miguel.*

"Ach, what now?" she muttered as she clicked the phone on and put on her best voice. "And a good morning to ye, Father Miguel. How can I be of service to ye?"

"You haven't heard from Sister Augustine, have you?" he asked without exchanging any pleasantries.

"And why would I?"

"I just thought—"

"She's yer employee."

"Yes, but—"

"Have ye not got her paperwork in order, Father?"

"Actually, now that you mention it, no. I suppose, in the absence of a secretary, I would be responsible for doing that, wouldn't I?"

"Funny how that works, isn't it? No secretary, no fairy godmother—just you, doing it all yerself."

"Pardon? I'm sorry. I didn't hear you, Mary-Margaret. I was just looking at—"

"I said I'll pop by where she's staying and see what's happened. If there's a problem, of course, I'll step in until we can get it sorted."

"Let us pray to God that there are no problems," Father Miguel said before abruptly ending the call.

"Well, pup," Mary-Margaret said, looking down at the dancing dog, "yer on yer own."

She opened the back door, and Wee Phil practically flew out and was gone down the laneway.

"And don't be bringing back any bloody gloves while yer at it!" she hollered after him.

* * *

Truth be told, Mary-Margaret had never actually been to Arthur's place. She had an address, of course, but never any reason to pay him a visit. And as she neared the address now, she was oddly relieved that she hadn't. She wasn't quite sure what she had been expecting, but it certainly wasn't this. The street was tucked away in an industrial area, dotted with a few run-down houses that were surrounded by warehouses that looked long abandoned— an uncommon sight in a city like this. Off to the side of the curbless road, she spotted a couple of cars that looked like they'd been left for scrap, along with a camper van that had the unmistakable look of being lived in. She assumed Arthur must be in one of the houses, but the number she had seemed to match one of the warehouses.

When she stepped out of the car, she didn't exactly feel unsafe, but she did feel a bit out of place. As such, she was more than slightly relieved to spot a neatly dressed young woman walking a Labrador coming out of the door of the warehouse that matched the address she'd been given.

"Here," the young woman said, holding the door for Mary-Margaret.

"Ta, luv," Mary-Margaret replied as she entered the building.

Much to her relief, this was not a flophouse, although the appearance of the woman she'd just seen should have put her mind at ease. Still, looks could be deceiving, as Mary-Margaret knew all too well.

"MM!" Sister Augustine called out from down the hall. "What are you doing here?"

"I've come to get ye. Yer late."

"Ugh," Sister Augustine replied, striding towards Mary-Margaret. "Don't I know it. I thought I had another habit, and then I remembered that the second one was just a loaner, so I had to wash this one by hand when I got up this morning. Do I look okay? You can't see where—"

"Ye look fine, luv. I'm just parked outside, so I can give ye a lift," Mary-Margaret said as the two of them hustled out the front door.

"I am *so* sorry, MM. Did Father Miguel call you?"

The rain was coming down heavier now, causing Mary-Margaret to flip the collar of her coat up as she hurriedly unlocked the passenger side of the car, noticing for the first time that her friend wasn't wearing a coat.

"Ye might want to consider giving him yer phone number," Mary-Margaret said as she got into her side of the car and started the engine. "And laying yer clothes out the night before."

"I know. And I meant to. Have my clothes ready, I mean, but then I thought it's like a uniform. How hard can it be to get ready when you're wearing the same thing every day, and then I remembered that I'd dumped almost an entire burrito on myself yesterday, so…ugh."

"Have ye had any breakfast?" Mary-Margaret asked as she whizzed towards the church.

"Oh, I don't eat breakfast, MM. I adhere to a strict fasting routine."

"I'll stop by the drive-thru. Coffee and a bagel work?"

"That'd be great. Thanks."

* * *

Father Miguel had left a message taped to the office door.

Gone for the morning. Be back after lunch. Praying for Sister Augustine.

"Well, that makes our morning that much more pleasant, doesn't it?" Mary-Margaret said, tearing the note from the door before crumpling it up a bit more thoroughly than likely necessary and shooting it into the tiny trash bin beside the desk.

"Thanks again for the bagel," Sister Augustine said, wiping the crumbs off of her lips.

"Ye've got to eat, luv. Now, let's get the kettle on and see what we know."

The two were quickly settled in at the desk, Mary-Margaret behind it, Sister Augustine off to the side. Mary-Margaret pulled out the pad of paper onto which she'd transcribed, more or less, the conversation they'd overheard yesterday, and they set to work rejigging the order of their suspect list along with possible motives. The only difference from their previous understanding was that Annette Giancola now rose to the top. Or so Mary-Margaret thought.

"I don't know, MM," Sister Augustine ventured, carefully stirring the tea Mary-Margaret had just made with a wooden stir-stick. "I don't think it's her."

"After seeing her play Billy Gilly like that, in God's house no less, I think it is," Mary-Margaret replied, mug cradled between both hands. "And as much as I hate to say it, I wouldn't be surprised if she's trying to pin it all on that git, Robert Jensen."

"Framing someone for murder is a lot of work."

"It's not if there's double the insurance payout for a murder," Mary-Margaret said after taking a long sip of her tea.

"True," Sister Augustine said with a nod before taking a sip from her mug. "That would be a good motivator. And what about the names your…friend… gave you?" She added the word 'friend' with a slight pause, the idea of Mary-

153

Margaret becoming too close to The Old Bird not sitting at all right with her.

"Hard to say, but it might prove that Robert and the deceased were organized criminals, in which case—"

"*Involved in organized crime*, MM. Not organized criminals. There's a difference."

"Be that as it may, luv," she said as she set her mug down on the desk she had reclaimed as hers. "But if this organized crime business is behind any of this, then I'm also thinking we should be considering that Danny lad as our murderer. If he's not organized crime, then I don't know who is."

"Why?"

"Ach, luv. If ye took one look at the man, ye'd agree with me. Has it written all over his face, that one does."

"I don't think it works that way, MM," Sister Augustine said, looking down at her mug.

"But our girl. Ach, the gall. She didn't even take a breath before asking Billy Gilly about releasing the funds. Digging for money at a time like this, with her husband not even cold in the ground? Horrible."

"I don't know—"

"Well, I do. She's a right piece of work, that one," Mary-Margaret concluded with a nod.

Sister Augustine wanted to protest, but realized that it was pointless and in her best interest not to.

"And now I'm wondering if she's not more tangled up in this organized crime business than we realized. Which means she's a lot more dangerous than she lets on. On the other hand, if she's not, and it's Robert and Danny who are knee-deep in it, then her stirring the pot means that she—or anyone else who gets in their way—might be next."

"Great," Sister Augustine sighed, swirling her tea around nervously in her mug. "Now we've got to worry about the Mafia chasing us down."

"Ach, why would anybody see us as a threat, luv?" Mary-Margaret said with a chuckle, leaning back in her chair, her arms folded across her chest. "We're just a clueless old wan and a nun poking around, likely to come up with nothing. Hardly the sort to ruffle any feathers. And we've got two police officers—a detective sergeant and a detective no less—who'll vouch for that."

Chapter Thirty-One

No one could ever accuse Mary-Margaret O'Shea of lacking a certain tenacity. In fact, if there were an Olympic event for persistence, she'd be on the podium, probably giving a speech about how the rest of the competition was sadly lacking. After her conversation with Sister Augustine, getting to the heart of the peculiar situation between Annette Giancola and Robert Jensen jumped to the top of her to-do list. Which is why Daphne was, once again, parked in front of the widow Giancola's house.

But not before she popped home to change her clothes. If nothing else, she'd learned the power of presentation from, much to her surprise, Arthur. If she was going to pawn herself off as some helpless old lady—which, if Annette Giancola really was a member of the Mob, making this exactly what Mary-Margaret wanted—then she'd better look the part. So, she slipped into an ancient dress that was, by design—at least today—less "vintage chic" and more "forgotten smock," paired with the most unflattering flats in existence.

Not wanting to leave his partner-in-crime-fighting out on a limb, Arthur insisted on going with her. He, in turn, had swapped his nun's habit for the coveralls he'd worn during his brief stint at Marco's Motors, planning to pose as a gardener.

"I think I've really nailed it this time, MM," Arthur stated. "Rocco the Green-Thumbed Maestro will blend in perfectly. Too bad we couldn't get a van to slap that name on the side of."

She was going to remind him that the season for gardeners had long passed, but, given how pleased he seemed to be with his disguise, did not.

Instead, Mary-Margaret marched up to Annette Giancola's front door, while Arthur settled himself comfortably between the shrubbery beneath the front windows and the house. It was, in a way, a perfect spot for him: tucked away, half-hidden, and, one could argue, slightly absurd.

"Oh," Mary-Margaret said when Robert Jensen opened the door.

"May I help you?"

"I just stopped in to see how Annette is coping."

"She's coping fine," he replied, closing the door.

"Glad to hear it," Mary-Margaret said, sticking her foot between the door and the frame to stop him. "Ye know, when me Jimmy died, God rest his soul, it took me a long time to find me feet. Mind if I come in?"

Before he could object, Mary-Margaret was inside the house.

"And where might Herself be?"

"She's…resting."

"Ach. The poor wee lamb. Of course she is. Never mind. I'll just go into the kitchen and make us all a cuppa. Ye do want one as well, I'm figuring?"

"No, I don't," he replied. "And neither does Annette. She's resting."

"I'm sure she is, but I'll just put the kettle on—"

"No," he said, taking her by the arm rather roughly. "It's time for you to go. I'll tell Annette you stopped by."

Robert more pulled than escorted Mary-Margaret back to the door and pushed her out, slamming the door behind her.

"Well. That was odd," she said out loud.

"Just because he won't let you see her sleeping, MM…" Arthur said as he pulled himself out of the bushes.

"No. That's not it, luv. There's something else going on here," Mary-Margaret replied, looking up at the second-floor window where she assumed the primary bedroom was. She then looked at her friend. "Do ye suppose she's got a ladder in that garage?"

"Maybe, but you're not going to climb up to the window, are you?"

"No, luv. You are. On account of the ivy on the wall here. Doesn't Rocco the Green-Thumbed Maestro have a contract to check it every fall? Once yer up there, ye just have to climb through that window and then—"

"Oh, I can do better than that," Arthur said. "Can you run me back home? I've got a drone with a great camera attached. I'll paint a GTM logo on it, and we can record whatever the drone sees."

"We've no time for that. We've got to get inside."

"But you already tried."

"Well, if yer not going to pop in through the window, I'm going to try again," Mary-Margaret said as she pulled her cell phone out of her purse. "Now, ye are going to cause a distraction so that I can slip in through the front door. Once I'm in, I'll go have a wee word with our girl. If she's fine, well, I'll likely just find meself getting chucked out again. If not, we'll have to rescue her."

"I'm still not following."

"Ach. Have I not just spelled it out to ye, lad? Clearly, the logic behind it is too complicated for me mind to unravel to ye in a simpler manner in this moment, so never mind. Just go on over to the garage, there. And make as much noise as ye can on yer way."

Arthur did as he was told and clattered his way to the garage, making more of a racket than Mary-Margaret thought possible, while she stood beneath the second-floor window and dialed Annette's number.

"Hello?" Annette said, sounding very groggy.

"Hello, luv. 'Tis Mary-Margaret O'Shea. I'm just now out front of yer house and was wondering if I could come in and have a word with ye."

Mary-Margaret saw the dark curtain above inch open and waved up at Annette. For a brief moment, their eyes seemed to lock—and in that instant, Mary-Margaret knew Annette was in trouble

"Sure," she slurred, after a brief hesitation. "Lemme jus' get my shooooos on."

Arthur, meanwhile, had made his way to the garage, where he was now locked in a battle of wills with a metal door that was very clearly winning. He yanked at it with the sort of focus usually reserved for those trying to pull a sack of hundred-dollar bills out of the trunk of a burning car. Within moments of this unwinnable battle's start, Robert Jensen appeared at the front door of the house, shouting something unintelligible. Oddly, he didn't seem to notice Mary-Margaret, who stood on the lawn, gazing up at the window Annette had just vacated. When Arthur, unwilling to admit defeat, continued the fight, Robert stormed out of the house, down the couple of steps to the walkway, and towards him with such focus that he missed noticing Mary-Margaret altogether.

"What are you doing?" Robert screamed at Arthur.

"Ah, *buongiorno*, my friend," he began in a horrible Italian accent, puffing out his chest and pointing at the name embroidered on his coveralls as though it were a royal title. "I am-a *Rocco the Green-Thumbed Maestro*, master of hedges and keeper of tools. And I am-a find myself in urgent need of a…how you say?…ladder, if you be so kind, eh?"

"I don't care who you are or what you need. Get the—"

"Ah, my-a dear frien'…I trust I may call-a you dat, yeah? Or no?" Arthur said, raising an eyebrow as though the question itself were a privilege, noticing Mary-Margaret move quickly towards the open door. He was also wishing he'd paid more attention to the dialogue in all those old Sophia Loren movies he'd watched over the years.

"You can call me whatever you want as long as you get off of my property."

"My-a paperwork, of course, is in-a de van—*parked*…how you say?… *discreetly* around de corner, my frien'," Rocco replied, with a slight, knowing nod. "But I am-a believing dat dis property belongs to a *Marco Giancola*, unless-a I am-a mistaken, which-a es vaaary unlikely because I am-a vary seldom wrong-a. So dat must make you…?"

"No," Robert said with a big sigh.

Arthur arched an eyebrow.

"I mean, yes. You're right—"

"Of-a course I am-a."

"About whose residence this is. But what are you doing here?"

"I am-a Roc—"

"Yes, I heard that."

"If I may-a…?" Arthur said, cocking his head slightly to one side.

Robert nodded.

"I am-a, as I've-a *already* had de pleasure of informing-a you, Rocco the

Green-Thumbed Maestro, and I am-a, of course, contractually bound—*legally*, one-a might say—to-a manage de grounds of Mr. Giancola's *most esteemed-a* property," he said, watching Mary-Margaret at the open door.

"A bit late, isn't it?"

"My-a dear frien', contrary to what-a de *amateurs* may tell-a you, gardening is-a, as any true professional knows-a, a year-round responsibility—*even* in a four-a-season climate such as dis."

"So what does that have to do with you trying to tear the door off the garage?"

"Well, I am-a *delighted* you asked, my frien'," he said, quickly glancing over Robert's shoulder just as Mary-Margaret gave him a quick wave before disappearing into the house. He waited a second until she closed the door behind her before he continued. "You see-a, as I've-a *already* mentioned, my van—which is-a, as you may recall, parked in a *discrete-a location* around the corner—and-a, by extension, so to, exists my-a ladder. Radder dan unnecessarily traversing da grounds to fetch dem, I-a thought et far-a more *practical* to simply borrow Mr. Giancola's ladder, which, as one-a might reasonably expect, would, of course, be right here, I'm assuming, in de garage."

"There is no ladder in this garage, so you'd better get the one from your van," Robert said flatly, turning away. He stopped and turned back. "Why do you even need a ladder?"

"Well, my frien'," he began, with a slight tilt of his head as if acknowledging a lesser intellect, "I am-a looking at de vines on dat brickwork dere, and, quite-a frankly, it's clear they are in dire need of a good-a pruning."

"In November?"

"Oh, yes-a. Contrary to what-a de *amateurs* might suggest, de best time to prune vines, as any true professional would-a know, is when de leaves have long since fallen and de vines are, quite properly, in a state of hibernation."

Robert said nothing as he turned and walked back to the house.

"I take it, my frien-," Rocco called out after him, "in de absence of your-a assistance in checking de garage for a ladder, dat de occupant, Mr. Giancola, will have no objection to me-a traversing his lawn to retrieve my ladder for de sole purpose of trimming his vines, yes? After all, I am-a, as I have-a made clear to you, my frien', *the* expert-a on such matters."

"I don't think he cares," Robert muttered, his hand already on the front door handle. He gave it a pull—and to his surprise, it was locked.

Chapter Thirty-Two

Once inside, Mary-Margaret had locked the door behind her before quickly making her way up the stairs to the front bedroom. To her relief, there was Annette Giancola, sitting on the bed, her back to her, seeming as right as rain. But, when Mary-Margaret called her name, Annette didn't so much as flinch. Instead, she simply slumped to her right side, as if the effort of holding herself upright had finally become too much.

Mary-Margaret rushed over to Annette and checked for a pulse. Slow, but present. *At least it's something.* She quickly scanned the room for a pill bottle or some other telltale object that might reveal why Annette had collapsed. There was nothing. She darted back to the bedroom door and shut it just as she heard who she knew would be Robert Jensen furiously rattling the front door.

If she didn't take them herself, then who...?

Of course, Mary-Margaret knew the answer. It confirmed her initial suspicions about Robert Jensen. And as soon as he found a way in, she knew she'd be trapped in the house with him—and a woman who was likely dying.

Arthur would have no idea what danger she was in. Even if she called 9-1-1, it would take time for the police to arrive. But what other choice did she have?

With no time to waste, Mary-Margaret pushed the dresser across from the bed to block the door. Then, she gently moved Annette into the recovery position on the bed. All she had to do now was make the call and wait for the paramedics and police. Hopefully, it wouldn't be too late.

Mary-Margaret heard glass breaking downstairs.

He was in.

Much to her surprise, her hands were trembling horribly as she pulled her phone from her purse. Having almost dropped it, she now held it tightly as she punched in the numbers.

She could hear heavy footsteps on the stairs, and then on the landing. There was a brief pause, and then she heard his hand on the doorknob. The telephone line had connected and was now ringing. Meanwhile, when Robert realized that he was unable to get in, she heard the sound of his shoulder banging against the door.

"Let me in!" he hollered. "I know you're in there, Mary-Margaret. Open the door!"

There was a click on the other end of the line. Before the emergency operator could speak, Mary-Margaret's voice—barely more than a whisper—cut through:

"'Tis Mary-Margaret O'Shea. Detective Michael O'Shea's mother. I'm needing yer lot to get here as quickly as possible, and bring along the paramedics."

Slowly, and with what felt to Mary-Margaret like all the urgency of a sloth on a coffee break, the call-taker methodically took down the address and informed her—who was nearly at her wits' end, desperately suppressing the urge to scream—that she was to remain on the line until the police arrived.

"Are you safe, Ms. O'Shea?" the call-taker finally asked.

"*Missus* O'Shea," she corrected, her voice growing louder. "And no, I've just told ye I'm not. 'Tis just a matter of time before that madman bashes in me door."

"ETA is four minutes, Mrs. O'Shea. Is there somewhere else you can hide in the event that—"

The dresser came tumbling across the room towards her as Robert Jensen smashed the door off its hinges. And then he was in the room.

"I'll call ye back, luv," Mary-Margaret said. "I've just got something to deal with at the moment."

Before the 9-1-1 call-taker could answer, Mary-Margaret had clicked off her phone. And then she pressed the number one and dropped the phone down on the floor beside her.

"So," Robert said with unnerving calmness, beads of sweat dripping down his face, his hair askew. "I see you found your friend."

"Indeed," she said, scanning the room for a weapon of opportunity.

"And, as I'd told you, she's sleeping."

"Hardly," Mary-Margaret said, noticing Annette's slippers on her feet.

"Don't even think about it," Robert said, pulling one of the drawers out of the dresser with two hands and emptying it. He held it up like a shield. Or something to smash over Mary-Margaret's head.

"Me son is on his way," Mary-Margaret said.

"Your son?"

"Yes. Me Michael. *Detective* Michael O'Shea."

"Really," Robert said, unconvinced.

"Truly," Mary-Margaret said, giving the phone by her foot a slight nudge to push it under the bed.

"And so…?"

"And so he'll arrest ye."

"For…?"

"For what ye've done to Annette, here, and—"

Two sirens could be heard in the distance, getting louder.

"I've done nothing to Annette, Mrs. O'Shea," he said with a crocodile smile. "And, I have to admit, I'm glad you came up to check on her."

"Check on her?" Mary-Margaret said in disbelief.

"Well, as you know," Robert began, his voice disturbingly even as he set down the dresser drawer, "I was downstairs after asking you to leave and, had it not been for the gardener arriving, I would have likely continued on with my afternoon and would never have come upstairs to check on Annette until dinner time. Given the look of her now, I'm thinking that she'd likely be dead by then, wouldn't you?"

"But you—"

"Oh, that?" Robert said, looking back at the smashed door. "I had to break it down to check on Annette, and good thing I did. Except that you happened to be in here with her, even after I walked you out, so actually, Mrs. O'Shea, I don't think I'd be too happy to see my son, given that you've broken into this house."

"Police!" a deep voice yelled from the hallway. "Put your hands up where I can see them."

Robert slowly raised his hands, smiling all the while at Mary-Margaret.

Chapter Thirty-Three

Michael passed the ambulance leaving Annette Giancola's house as he turned onto her street in his unmarked police car. He saw two police cruisers parked haphazardly on the street in front of Annette's house, their roof lights still flashing. He then saw his mother's car parked, albeit more carefully, in front of the house. He parked behind his mother's car and slowly got out.

"Thank goodness you're here," Arthur gasped as he rushed towards Michael.

"Where's my mother?" Michael said flatly, pushing Arthur out of the way.

"She's in the house, but they won't let me go in to see her. I hope—"

"Stay there," Michael ordered.

"Absolutely," Arthur said, stepping back.

Michael walked in the open front door and saw four uniformed officers standing around someone seated in a chair in the living room.

"Hi, Mom," Michael said, spotting her perched on the chair. He gave a brief nod to the officers. As if he needed another clue that she was up to something she shouldn't be, he couldn't help noticing she looked worse than he'd ever seen her—worse even than on the days he'd found her on her hands and knees scrubbing the floors Arthur had been hired to clean.

"Ach, Michael! Thanks be to Saint—"

"Can I speak to you for a minute, Detective?" the oldest-looking officer asked, motioning for Michael to step back outside.

Michael straightened his back, raised his chin, and took a deep breath.

"Sure," he said.

"The homeowner…well, business partner of the homeowner's late husband, doesn't want charges laid."

"For…?"

"Break and enter."

"I see."

"And I would have released her while the paramedics were taking care of the homeowner, but—"

"Don't tell me she beat up the—"

"No. Overdose. Paramedics said she'll probably be okay, but, well… Detective Sergeant Gill is on his way and wants to speak to your mother before we let her go."

"Sounds good to me," Michael said, turning to walk back to his car.

"Don't you want to—"

"Nope," Michael called over his shoulder.

"Well?" Arthur said, rushing up to Michael.

"Whose idea was this?" Michael asked without stopping

"It was, well…your mother's," Arthur said.

"Alright," Michael said, unlocking his car door. "Just so you know, D/S Gill is on his way. Good luck to you both."

"OMG, Michael!" Arthur said, his eyes wide with terror. "You can't leave us here! Do you have any idea how—"

"Good luck to you both," Michael repeated before getting into the car. He started the engine and drove away.

* * *

"That man is a disgrace to his profession," Mary-Margaret said to Arthur as they both climbed into her car. "Ach, I swear, if I'd blinked me eye or cleared me throat just one more time, trying to get him to catch on to the innuendo of what I was getting at, I'd have had a conniption right then and there. Dim as a lightbulb in a brothel, that man."

"Well, that guy was pretty convincing the way he made it sound like you broke in. Because, really, MM, you kind of did."

"Broke in? I saved Annette Giancola's life, is what I did. Said so himself, did that git: if I'd not gone up to her room, he'd likely be watching the telly all afternoon while she lay there dying. Which is why I have no idea why that Silly Billy Gilly was so mad. Saved a woman's life, I did. Does he need the work that badly that he'd rather find a dead body than commend the rescuer? Wait 'til I tell me Mandy about this."

"I think you'd be better just to keep this one to yourself," Arthur suggested. "At least until the dust settles."

"And there's another thing," Mary-Margaret said, wrenching the steering wheel to the left, Arthur practically snapping out of his seatbelt as he slid towards her. "I realize that he's had his share of brain trauma over his career, Arthur, but me Michael wouldn't even give me a moment to explain. No wonder he's never been Police Officer of the Year. Ach. What a sorry lot they are."

"Yeah. About that," Arthur said slowly, righting himself in the car. "He seemed kinda mad—"

"*He* seemed kind of mad? What about *me*? Sitting there being interrogated by those junior officers, watching Robert Jensen—the man who tried to kill Annette Giancola and no doubt killed Marco Giancola—turn the story inside out while he patters about the dead man's home like he owned the place. No, luv. It's me who should be mad. And look, I've forgotten to drop ye off at yers. Might as well come in for a cuppa and I'll drive ye home later."

Wee Phil ran out the back door as soon as Mary-Margaret opened it.

"And there's another thing. Wee Phil. Do ye think me Michael could manage to take care of him? Ach, just when I think everything's settling and I can get on with me own life, I see that I can't. I'll never get back to me own house at this rate."

"But I thought—"

"Save yer thinking and go get Wee Phil before one of Michael's miscreant neighbors calls the dog catcher on him. Or gives him a drink. Honestly, I've about had enough."

Mary-Margaret's cell phone rang. She pulled it out of her purse and looked at the call display.

Max

"And then a wee ray of sunshine breaks through. Go on after Wee Phil, Arthur. Hello, me Max," she said into the receiver, her voice warm and gentle, in sharp contrast to the tone she'd just been using. "Do ye need me to come pick you up, luv?"

Chapter Thirty-Four

It had been two days since Mary-Margaret's encounter with Peter Jensen. And nearly getting arrested for breaking and entering. And being lectured by that fool, Billy Gilly. It had also been two days since she had spoken to Michael. They had passed each other in the hall, sat down for dinner as a family, and even watched something on Netflix side by side.

But Mary-Margaret was too annoyed to utter a word to her son.

Imagine him believing a bunch of rookies over her? Or leaving her to be spoken to like a child by that imbecilic excuse for a murder investigator. Or not commending her for her ingenuity, bravery, and calmness in the face of extraordinary danger.

No, she could not bring herself to utter a word to her son.

That he was equally annoyed with her was beyond her scope of understanding. That she had injected herself, again, into a homicide investigation in such a way that could compromise the entire case never occurred to her. That she could have gotten herself killed never entered her mind. That she could have ruined Michael's reputation by associating him with her reckless behavior was the furthest thing from her thoughts.

No, it was she who had the justifiable grudge. And Michael, who owed her an apology.

At least, that's what she thought as she drove Daphne out of the laneway on her way to check on Annette Giancola.

The cell phone in Mary-Margaret's purse rang. She was going to let the call go to voicemail, but then she considered that it might be Max or Arthur. If it was Michael, of course, she would most certainly let the call go to voicemail. And then delete it. She reached inside her purse and pulled out her phone to check the call display.

Max School

"Mary-Margaret O'Shea speaking. Max's gran," she almost shouted into the phone.

"Hola, Mary-Margaret," The Old Bird chirped. "Did I catch you at a bad time?"

"Not at all," she replied with a deep breath. "Is me Max alright?"

"Max? Yeah, he's doing fine. I just wanted to see if you were up for something this afternoon. Maybe head over to that little pub of yours and check in on John-o, see how he's holding up. I'm off around 2:30, and I thought it might be nice for us to, you know, hang out a bit."

"Ach, I don't think I can, luv," Mary-Margaret said. "I'm just on me way to St. Joseph's hospital to check on Annette Giancola, and, depending on what I find out there, I'll likely have a massive amount of running around to do afterwards."

"Anything I can help you with? Leona's not here today, and I can only twiddle my thumbs for so long, you know what I mean?"

"I can't say as I do know that feeling," Mary-Margaret said, recalling how busy she had always been at the church, particularly after Father Miguel arrived. "And it would save me a trip if ye could follow up on our girl, but I know that wouldn't be possible. In the meantime, I'm just now thinking that I'll be off to the pub this evening with me friends, Angus and Eleanor Corrigan. I don't suppose it would do anyone any harm if the two of us met up there a wee bit earlier, would it? Maybe around 3?"

"Sounds good! I'll see you then."

After chucking the phone back into her purse, Mary-Margaret decided to make a detour and drop by the church to see how Sister Augustine was managing since it was practically on her way.

Poor wee lamb. Likely ready to throttle Father Miguel by now. Ach, maybe I should never have got her involved in this. Poor wee lamb.

* * *

As soon as she'd pulled open the heavy front door of the church, Mary-Margaret noticed that something was different. The floors weren't any cleaner, nor were the windows. And yet, it seemed so much…lighter inside this morning.

"MM!" Sister Augustine gushed, grinning from ear to ear. "How do I look?"

"Ye look like ye always do, Arth—Sister."

"Oh no, I don't, MM. You're just not seeing it. I am radiating! No wonder Julie Andrews sang all the time."

"Julie Andrews was not…" Mary-Margaret began and then stopped herself. No point bursting that bubble.

"What can I do for you?"

"Nothing at all, luv. I just thought I'd drop by and see how ye were doing. On account of ye starting yer first…nine-to-five, did ye say?"

"I am *loving* it!"

"And how is it working with…?" she said, nodding towards Father Miguel's office.

"He's great. We're going out for lunch today to celebrate my first week on the job."

"Week? Ye've barely put in one full day," Mary-Margaret corrected, recalling that, during her entire tenure while he was at St. Francis, he never once took her out for lunch. Unless it was in a group and, even then, she noticed his unease around her.

"I know, but he said he wanted to take me out for lunch, so what's a girl supposed to do?"

"Yer not a girl," Mary-Margaret exclaimed, brows furrowed. "Yer a nun! And he's a priest."

"So? Can't a nun have a priest for a friend?"

"I don't trust him," Mary-Margaret said, still scowling. "He's up to something."

"I think I can take care of myself," Sister Augustine said. "Remember how I wrangled Jane Ann Hill's murderer to the ground?"

"I'd hardly call it wrangling," Mary-Margaret said. "Regardless, I can see yer busy and so am I. Off to the hospital. To have a wee word with Annette Giancola. Some of us are still investigating a murder, don't ye know."

"Of course I know, but I also have a full-time job now, so…"

"Everything alright, Sister Aug—" Father Miguel began as he came around the corner and then stopped abruptly when he saw Mary-Margaret.

Suddenly, the church felt just as it always had. The floors looked old and worn, and the windows looked like they could use a good clean again. Or else the sun had just gone behind a cloud. Either way, Mary-Margaret could feel the muscles in her neck tighten.

"I was just giving Sister Augustine some tips, here, Father," she said.

"I don't think that's necessary," he replied with a smile she'd never seen before. "Sister Augustine seems to be doing just fine. Remarkably fine, actually. Now, if there's nothing more, I've got some matters I wish to discuss with my *executive assistant.*"

"Of course," Mary-Margaret said with a sniff. "I'm meeting me friend at the hospital. Some of us have murderers to catch."

"Please don't tell me you're interfering with another police investigation," Father Miguel said after letting out a long sigh.

"Hardly interfering, Father," Mary-Margaret corrected as she stomped out of the church.

Chapter Thirty-Five

Mary-Margaret sat behind the steering wheel of her car in the church parking lot, the engine still off.

What on earth is that muppet playing at, taking Sister Augustine out for lunch like that? He never once took me out, just the two of us. Never. And look at the two of them, acting like a pair of moony eejits. You can bet she'll be calling him 'Miguel' before long, just like the New Girl did. Ach, I do wonder if he's got some sort of spell over those young ones? No, no, don't be ridiculous. He's a Man of the Cloth, not a man of magic. Though, I wouldn't put it past him...

She started the car and was about to put it in gear when her cell phone rang.

Max School

"Your girl's supposed to go up to the psych ward," The Old Bird stated without offering any sort of salutation. "But they've been swamped up there and don't have a bed for her, so she's still in emerge. Need anything else?"

"How did ye get all of that?"

"I made a phone call. A mother of about six of our students is an emerge nurse at St. Joe's, so I just thought maybe I'd give her a call. She's been involved with the school for about as long as I've been here, and I figured it wouldn't hurt to ask a few questions."

"It does not," Mary-Margaret agreed, nodding her head in approval. "Did ye happen to ask if our girl's had any visitors?"

"Sure did. First thing I asked. She tells me that the guy she lives with has been there with her since shortly after she was brought in on Wednesday."

"She doesn't live with anyone. Her husband's just been murdered," Mary-

Margaret exclaimed.

"I'm just telling you what I was told. If you ask me, it's likely that snake, the partner guy. I'm telling you, it's him."

Mary-Margaret didn't reply. Instead, she was wanting to run into the church to tell Sister Augustine the latest while realizing that Sister Augustine likely wouldn't care, now that she was likely starting to get ready to go for lunch with her new BFF, Father Miguel.

"You still there, Mary-Margaret?"

"I am," Mary-Margaret replied, starting the car. "And that's for yer help, luv. I'll see ye around three at O'Leary's. Bye-bye bye bye-bye bye."

* * *

St. Joseph's Hospital was conveniently situated within the parish of St. Francis of Assisi Catholic Church, just a few blocks away from Mary-Margaret's own house. She knew it well, having carted each one of her children there more than a few times over the years. It was also the hospital where she had been brought after her accident at the dog park, when she was knocked off her pins in a manner that, according to a group of complete strangers, required a doctor's opinion. That suggestion had been moderately reasonable, but Mary-Margaret almost blew a gasket when the paramedics insisted that she be checked out at the hospital simply on account of her age.

She parked her car in one of the spots reserved for police vehicles and then reached into her purse to pull out one of Michael's business cards. She placed it, face up, on the dashboard, so it was visible from the windshield.

The sliding doors opened as she walked into the hospital, and sitting there, right at the door of the security office, was the very same security officer who had been on duty when she was here to have her foot looked at a while back. The very same lad who watched her as she hobbled out a couple of hours later using a pair of crutches that she'd nicked on account of having been found with nothing more than a slight sprain at best, but needing a reason for Michael to let her stay on with him. The exact same lad that caused her to realize that she'd need a good cover story or two, hence the one about the invisible cast, the research group, and a host of others that had her praying for forgiveness constantly. And there he was, now, sitting right as rain.

But surely, he knew the crutches had been stolen. And surely, he'd put two and two together shortly after she'd taken them and had figured out that it was her. And surely, he'd been on the lookout for her ever since. And now, here she was, practically standing in front of him. She shrivelled as he glanced in her direction, positive that he was going to arrest her for Theft of Crutches or some other criminal offence that likely carried a very long incarceration term with it.

There was nothing for it but to turn quickly and walk back outside, so that's exactly what Mary-Margaret did, just as the sky opened up and that cold autumn rain started pelting down. The thought of walking all the way to the front of the hospital to the non-emergency entrance and being soaked to the bone did not appeal to her at all.

She needed a new plan.

And then it presented itself to her.

While she stood outside the ER, the rain coming down harder now, an ambulance pulled up—siren off, lights still flashing. Mary-Margaret stepped aside as it came to a stop in front of her. The paramedic who had been driving entered the sliding doors, only to return moments later with a wheelchair. She watched as he opened the back of the ambulance.

A second paramedic, who had been in the back with the patient, helped him out of the ambulance. The patient's arm was wrapped in a bloodied cloth, another cloth wrapped tight against his side, holding his bloodied arm up. Could even have walked into the hospital, or so Mary-Margaret figured. Instead, the first paramedic guided the patient to the wheelchair, and together, they all disappeared through the sliding doors, leaving the back of the ambulance wide open.

She looked towards the sliding doors and saw two women in scrubs… nurses? doctors?…heading towards her.

"Ye certainly have a knack for giving to those who ask", Mary-Margaret said to herself, looking up quickly before she scurried into the back of the ambulance and crawled onto the gurney. That last patient mustn't have lain down because the blanket hadn't been disturbed. Mary-Margaret quickly pulled it back and tucked herself in, noticing that there was a fair bit of blood on both the sheet and the blanket.

"A wee bit of authenticity," she muttered as she tried not to get any of it on her.

She strapped herself onto the gurney and waited. And waited. And waited. Finally, she heard the sliding doors open.

"Hello?" she called out. "Have ye come to get me?"

A scruffy man who had just gotten discharged peered into the back of the ambulance.

"I take it yer not a doctor, luv?" she said.

"Uh-uh," he said, shaking his head.

"Would ye mind getting me one, then?"

"I guess."

The scruffy man disappeared. Mary-Margaret hoped he'd gone back inside the hospital, though she couldn't be sure. Strapped to the gurney as she was, her options were limited: she could either wait, or come up with a new plan. She decided to wait. And this time, she wouldn't sound quite as perky when he returned with help. No need to give herself away.

Don't overthink it, me girl. If I could convince a judge I was Tara Rafferty, I can surely convince whichever doctor that raggedy little fella drags out here that I need to get into the hospital—provided he actually went back in and asked.

Luckily, the scruffy man didn't let her down.

A few minutes later, one of the two women she'd seen in the hospital approached the back of the ambulance. Mary-Margaret raised her head enough to look down towards her.

"Where did you come from?" the woman said, looking back towards the sliding doors for the paramedics.

"Me house," Mary-Margaret said weakly, lowering her head back down on the pillow. "I was clearing some things off the kitchen table when I felt this terrible pain in me side—almost winded me—so I called 9-1-1. Next thing I know, and I'm not saying it happened this way because I don't recall, exactly, but the next thing I know, here I am."

"Where are the paramedics who brought you in?" the woman asked.

"I haven't the faintest," Mary-Margaret said. "As I said, I was just clearing me kitchen table when—"

"Never mind. A crew just brought someone else in. I'll get them to—"

"No. That would be the end of it," Mary-Margaret exclaimed, straining against the restraints to sit up. Seeing the confused look on the woman by her feet, quickly added: "I mean me. I mean…just…no. That would likely make me condition worse. The waiting, I mean. How about ye get one of those wheelchairs ye've got there and wheel me inside."

"But where are the crew that brought you in? Or at least your chart?"

Mary-Margaret was climbing out of the back of the ambulance, having already freed herself from the gurney.

"Are ye going to get me inside or are ye going to wait until I have a fall and God knows what that might do? Or get another bout of the pneumonia by standing out here in the rain like this? I've already had it at least once, ye know. It'll be the death of me, the pneumonia will."

The woman stepped back into the hospital and quickly returned with a wheelchair.

"And could ye grab me that blanket, luv?" she asked once she was seated. "On account of me having the chills. Don't want to get the pneumonia again."

The woman climbed into the ambulance and grabbed the orange blanket from inside and placed it over Mary-Margaret.

"Never mind that, luv," she said, grabbing it from the woman. "I'll just wrap it around me shoulders. And me head. Ye know, ye lose ninety percent of yer body heat from yer head."

The woman knew this wasn't true, but was not in the mood for an impromptu patient consultation—especially not in the rain. So, Doctor Braddock did what any sensible person would do: she got Mary-Margaret O'Shea into the ER as quickly as possible, the orange ambulance blanket covering more of her head—and, perhaps more importantly, her face—than anything else.

They breezed past the security guard, who barely looked up from his phone, and within a very short time—certainly before anyone could question it—Mary-Margaret was admitted.

Chapter Thirty-Six

The ER at St. Joe's was a blur of movement and noise. Gurneys lined the hallways in tight rows, every available inch of space filled with patients waiting to see a doctor. Only the most critical cases were given a cubicle, but even then, the privacy was minimal, with those patients separated from the commotion with nothing more than flimsy cloth curtains. The air buzzed with the sounds of monitors beeping, nurses managing patients until the doctors could see them, and the low hum of general anxiety. Not being considered critical, Mary-Margaret lay in a gurney along the wall.

"Good afternoon, Mrs. O'Shea," a nurse who looked young enough to be a friend of Max's said loudly, setting an IV pole into the corner of Mary-Margaret's gurney. "You'll just feel a slight prick while I get you set up here. It won't hurt."

"I've never met a slight prick that didn't hurt," Mary-Margaret muttered, and then, in a louder voice, added: "And what are ye setting me up for?"

"We don't want you to get dehydrated and, at your age—"

"Me *age*?" Mary-Margaret exclaimed. "And ye don't have to shout. I'm... I've got...I'm here because...well, I'm not deaf."

"Sorry. Just relax your hand, please," the nurse said, poking the needle into her vein. Mary-Margaret flinched. "Do you know why you're here, Mrs. O'Shea?"

"Well, I...I've had...me kidneys..." Mary-Margaret faltered. She'd come to track down Annette Giancola, not end up poked and prodded in a hospital bed. This situation certainly wasn't going to help her achieve that goal.

"Have you ever been diagnosed with hypertension or any form of dementia, Mrs. O'Shea?" the nurse asked as she stuck a series of electrode pads onto Mary-Margaret's body and then connected the wires to the ECG machine.

"Absolutely not!"

"And let's put this on your index finger for a moment," the nurse said, turning on the ECG machine before clipping the pulse oximeter onto her finger.

Mary-Margaret watched as the nurse hooked her up, feeling increasingly helpless.

"Thanks," the nurse said, glancing at the monitor that displayed Mary-Margaret's vitals. "The doctor will be by when she can. Anything you need right now?"

"Just me purse. Me cell phone is in it," Mary-Margaret said, looking around her for the paper bag she'd been told to put her clothes and purse in before changing into the gown. "And maybe another gown? I'm thinking this one's not likely covering everything it should be."

"I can get you your purse, Mrs. O'Shea, but you're going to have to do the best you can with one gown. We're running a bit low on clean ones today."

The nurse reached underneath Mary-Margaret's bed and pulled out the paper bag. Mary-Margaret rummaged through it, looking for her purse. She wanted to say something biting to the young nurse—something about how hospital resources were being misused, how the entire healthcare system was in disarray, mention the government's insistence on underfunding family doctors, and the lack of viable alternatives that was most certainly at the heart of this current gown shortage. But then she remembered that she'd scammed her way into a spot that someone who truly needed it was now being denied, and opted instead to just smile politely.

"Ta, luv," she said, passing the paper bag back to the nurse.

"If you need anything, the buzzer's right here," the young nurse said, handing Mary-Margaret the device before rushing off to attend to her next patient.

Ye've gone and done it this time, me girl. Ye can't even get out of bed for a stroll without having yer arse hang out for all the world to see. And what if they find something wrong with ye? What if ye've got the dementia and they whisk ye straight off to... Ach, no point playing what ifs. I'll give Arthur a ring. He'll know what to do.

Mary-Margaret dialed his number. It rang four times before going to voicemail. She hung up and immediately called the number again. Again, it rang four times before going to voicemail. Again, she hung up, and then she texted Arthur.

911

She waited, phone in hand. Nothing. She continued to wait. Nothing.

The machine attached to her bed began to beep. The young nurse reappeared.

"Everything alright, Mrs. O'Shea?" she asked, looking at the ECG monitor and then down at Mary-Margaret.

"Right as rain," Mary-Margaret replied. "Ye don't suppose I could get a sandwich or something, do ye?"

"Let's get this sorted first," the nurse said, holding out a blood pressure cuff. "I want to check your blood pressure again. These machines aren't always accurate."

Mary-Margaret's phone rang.

Arthur

"Can ye wait a moment, luv?" Mary-Margaret said, pulling her arm away from the nurse. "I've just got to get this. 'Tis me friend."

Mary-Margaret clicked the phone on before the nurse could object. The nurse glanced at the monitor and then at her patient.

"I'll be back in a minute," she said, stepping away from the bed.

"MM! What's wrong?"

"About time ye got back to me. I've only called ye twice and left an emergency message. Where were ye?"

"I was out for lunch with Father Miguel. We're just finishing up, and I thought I'd check my phone and—"

"I see. Well, don't let me interfere with yer socializing, then. I'll manage."

"No. Wait. What's happened?"

"I've only been admitted into the emergency ward at St. Joseph's, is all. But never ye mind. Carry on with yer lunch. I'll be fine."

"I'll be right there!"

"Well, ye best hurry because me blood pressure has just shot through the roof and the medical team is standing by to begin a procedure," Mary-Margaret said, clicking off her phone before Arthur could respond.

"I'm finished, luv," Mary-Margaret said, calling out to the nurse. "Does it matter which arm ye put the cuff on?"

Chapter Thirty-Seven

Their entrance was nothing short of epic. The sea of people parted as the nun and the priest strode into the ER, only to close in behind them as they passed. The fact that the nun was a paunchy six-foot-four and the priest a thin five-foot-ten mattered little. A nun and a priest, side by side, sweeping into St. Joseph's Hospital emergency room—together—was nothing short of epic.

"MM!" Sister Augustine hollered as soon as she saw her friend. "What have they done to you?"

"Sister," Father Miguel said in a much more muted tone as he gently touched her arm. "Perhaps we can wait until we get closer—"

"Are you okay?" Sister Augustine asked, now several steps ahead of Father Miguel by virtue of having longer legs than he, her voice barely lowered.

"Ach, luv, it's all gone pear-shaped on me."

"What's happened?" Sister Augustine asked, leaning over the bed such that they were face-to-face.

"I was on me way to find Annette Giancola, as ye know—"

"And you got attacked! That madman attacked—"

"No. Well, yes. Well, no. Ye see, I was afraid another madman might attack me, so I had to sneak in and, well, my mode of transportation might not have been the soundest, if ye know what I mean."

"I don't, but carry on," Sister Augustine said.

"Has anyone called your son?" Father Miguel asked, having reached Mary-Margaret's gurney.

"I did," Sister Augustine said.

"Ach, why would ye—"

"She's right over there, Mr. O'Shea," the young nurse said, pointing Michael in her direction.

"Oh, Jesus, Mary, and Joseph," Mary-Margaret said with a sigh.

"Are you…" Michael began, striding towards where his mother lay, closing in on the nun and the priest. It took him a minute, but, once he recognized the priest as Father Miguel and the nun as Sister Augustine, he slowed down a bit and took a breath.

"Ach, I'm fine, me son," Mary-Margaret said, careful not to appear too fine. She had not forgotten that she was inches away from being told to return to her own home, and this latest event could buy her a lot of time.

"What happened?" Michael said, looking at his mother, then to Father Miguel, and finally to Sister Augustine.

"We've just arrived ourselves," Father Miguel said softly.

"They said an ambulance brought you in. Did you fall again?" Michael asked, the genuine concern in his voice erasing any animosity he may have felt towards her over the past couple of days.

"Hardly," Mary-Margaret said. "Although me balance hasn't been what it should be these past few days. Likely the kidneys."

"I'm sorry," the young nurse said, suddenly appearing behind Michael, "but I'm going to have to ask some of you to wait over there. You're crowding the hallway."

"We'll give you a few minutes," Father Miguel said, touching Sister Augustine's arm.

"I'd prefer if Sister Augustine stayed," Mary-Margaret said, looking straight at her, eyes pleading.

"We'll give you a few minutes," Father Miguel repeated, this time gently taking Sister Augustine by the forearm and leading her to a row of chairs several feet away.

"So what happened?" Michael asked.

"I don't know how to explain it to ye, Michael."

"Who called the ambulance?"

"I don't know."

"Mom, this shouldn't be that difficult."

"No, it shouldn't, considering yer a big city detective and I'm sure ye ask people these questions all the time. But wait. I'm not under arrest, am I? I'm yer mam, aren't I? Right. So, the question isn't what happened. The question is: are ye going to sign me out?"

"Has a doctor seen you yet?"

"No."

"Well, shouldn't you wait until one does?"

"Ach, Michael. Look at the lot of them, there. And most of them, very ill. With worse cases coming in. How long do you think it'll take before the doctor will come over to me and tell me to go home?"

"I know, but you're here, so you might as well get checked out." Michael pulled his cell phone out of his suit jacket pocket and looked at the screen. "Listen, I've got to go, and you've got Arthur here with your priest, but give me a call when they find anything out, okay?"

"He is Sister Augustine at the moment, and Father Miguel is *not* my priest," she corrected.

"Sure. Just don't leave before you give me a call, even if they do give you a clean bill of health, okay?"

Michael bent over and kissed his mother on the forehead. She took his hand and gave it a squeeze.

"And, um, I'm thinking that it might be best for you to stay on at my place until we get whatever's going on with you sorted out, even if they can't find anything today, okay?"

"If I must," Mary-Margaret said, suppressing a smile.

Sister Augustine stood up when she saw Michael turning to go.

"Keep an eye on her, okay?" Michael said as the two passed.

"Oh, I will, Michael. If there's one thing I'm good at, it's taking care of the people I love."

Most of what Sister Augustine said was lost on Michael, who continued walking out of the ER.

"MM, you look much better already," Sister Augustine said.

"The Lord works in mysterious ways," she replied. "Where's Father

Miguel?"

"Gone to get a coffee. Oh, shoot. I forgot to ask if you wanted anything."

"I don't think I'm allowed to until after they finish with their tests. In the meantime, ye've got to find Annette Giancola."

"Where?" Sister Augustine said, looking up and down the crowded hallway.

"I don't know, luv, but she's somewhere in this ER. The Old Bird told me they didn't have a free bed up in the psych ward—"

"The Old Bird did, huh? I get it," Sister Augustine said, her shoulders slumped, and the spark momentarily gone from her eye. "Well, I'm glad you're going to be okay. Once Father Miguel gets back, we'll be heading out. Lots of work to be done at the church, as you know."

"Yer joking with me," Mary-Margaret said.

"Not at all, MM. You know as well as I that the work never ends at the—"

"Yer jealous."

"Me? Jealous? Hardly. Why would I be jealous? I've got everything a nun who has taken a vow of poverty could want. And more."

"She's no ye," Mary-Margaret said with a gentle smile.

"Nobody said she was. I certainly didn't, anyway. Oh, look. Is that Father Miguel coming down the hallway? No. It's another priest. My god, they all look alike, don't they?"

"Listen, luv, yer still me best mate. Likely always will be, the way things are going—"

"You were doing fine until that last part, just so's you know."

"And I'm still yer best mate, even if Father Miguel takes ye to fancy restaurants and all."

"And spends the whole time talking about himself."

"Well, what did ye expect? He is a man, even if he's a priest," Mary-Margaret said with a smirk.

Sister Augustine smirked back.

"Michael said I'm not to leave until the doctor sees me. Judging by the looks of things, I'll be here until next week."

"You can leave whenever you want, MM," Sister Augustine stated. "You came in voluntarily, didn't you? In which case, you can leave voluntarily."

"I knew that, didn't I?" Mary-Margaret said with a smile. "Come on, then, grab that bag from under me bed, here, and shield me arse from the world as I walk to the jacks over there."

"Excuse me, sister," an orderly pushing a gurney said.

Both Sister Augustine and Mary-Margaret looked over at the orderly. And then the woman on the gurney.

It was Annette Giancola.

Chapter Thirty-Eight

Mary-Margaret almost leapt from her gurney, but then remembered the hospital gown deficiencies and, fearing a wardrobe malfunction, nodded repeatedly to Sister Augustine. Rather than reacting in the manner Mary-Margaret had hoped for, Sister Augustine called for a nurse.

"I think she's having a stroke!" Sister Augustine called out, seeing her friend twitch on the gurney.

"Excuse me," the closest nurse said, pushing past Sister Augustine to render assistance.

"Ach, I'm not having a stroke," Mary-Margaret said with a wave of her hand. "I'm just seeing something that needs a bit of attention."

"Do you need to use the washroom?" the nurse asked, her tone suggesting she knew exactly what Mary-Margaret wanted.

"Yes," Mary-Margaret said. "Yes, I do, and perhaps this young man can help me." She pointed at the orderly, who had begun to move the gurney carrying Annette Giancola towards the elevators.

The nurse hesitated.

"I'm sure me friend, Sister Augustine, can wait with that poor soul all fainted on the bed there while that lad takes me to the jacks."

The nurse thought for a moment.

"I don't need yer level of expertise, luv," Mary-Margaret continued. "The orderly will be grand for this sort of thing. It won't take much to toddle the likes of me down the hall. Ye, on the other hand, have more important things to be doing than that. I'll not be needing any fuss, just a quick little trip, and that lad will have me back in no time. Ye have enough on yer plate as it is, I'm sure. Not that this nun, here, couldn't help me, but I'm sure she's not had the proper training for such things, have ye, Sister?"

"Well, as a matter of—" Sister Augustine began.

"We can debate the merits of me logic all day," Mary-Margaret cut in with a slight growl, "if ye don't mind wiping the piddle off the floor. Now, are ye going to call that fella over there or am I to just…?"

"Carlos, would you mind helping this woman to the washroom? I'll make sure your patient is okay," the nurse called out to the orderly.

"I can stand there just as easily as you can…" Sister Augustine said as she hunched over and looked at the name on the nurse's tag, "Laney. It doesn't look like she's going anywhere soon."

"Nurse! I need a nurse!" a man a few beds down yelled.

Laney hesitated for a moment.

"I said I need a nurse!" the man yelled again, looking directly at her.

"Fine," Laney stated. "But if she starts to—"

"I'll give a little whistle, Laney," Sister Augustine said with a smile and a nod.

"I'm dying over here!" the man yelled. "Anybody. Help me!"

"Just a minute," Laney said as the orderly helped Mary-Margaret get off the gurney as gracefully as possible while Sister Augustine moved over towards where Annette Giancola lay.

As soon as Sister Augustine had replaced the orderly, Annette whispered, "Get me out of here."

"Huh?" Sister Augustine replied, her heart missing a beat. "I thought you were unconscious."

"Get me out of here. Quickly. Don't ask any questions."

Thanks, in part, to her friendship with Mary-Margaret, Sister Augustine was used to following the orders of strong women, so she grabbed the bottom end of the gurney and began hastily pushing it—and Annette Giancola—back the way she had come. Since gurneys were designed to be operated from the front so the patient could see where they were going, Sister Augustine bumped into more than a few other gurneys and the wall before finally maneuvering it to the sliding doors that would take them out of the ER.

It was still raining, though not as heavily. Sister Augustine moved to the top of the gurney, pulled the sheet up over Annette Giancola's head, and then headed outside.

"You're going the wrong way," the security guard said.

Sister Augustine froze.

"You're going the wrong way," he repeated. "Morgue's downstairs. Back that way."

Noticing a bit of commotion down the hall where they had come from, Sister Augustine figured that Mary-Margaret had been returned and that Carlos had noticed his charge was missing. Sister Augustine, meanwhile, realized she didn't have a plan beyond getting Annette Giancola out of the hospital, so she wheeled the gurney back into the ER and stopped.

"Follow the black stripe on the ceiling to the elevators, then go down to B3. You'll see it at the end of the hall," the security guard said, just as a voice was heard mumbling through the radio microphone clipped to his epaulette.

Sister Augustine pushed the gurney as quickly as she could—this time from the front—glancing up periodically to make sure she was following the black line on the ceiling that would lead them to the elevator.

"Hey," Annette said as she pulled the blanket down. "Slow down!"

"Stay quiet," Sister Augustine ordered, pulling the sheet back up over Annette's head without breaking stride. "And play dead."

Within minutes, Sister Augustine arrived at the elevator bank with the gurney. As they waited, the dozen or so people milling about, all perfectly convinced that a dead body was under the sheet, shuffled away. When the doors finally opened, the few people inside of the elevator, equally convinced of the gurney's grim contents, stepped out with the sort of polite haste usually reserved for awkward social gatherings, leaving Sister Augustine with an empty elevator car to take her and the gurney's occupant down to the morgue.

"Ugh," Sister Augustine said once the elevator doors were closed. "That was close."

"Can I take this off yet?" Annette asked from under the sheet.

"No. Wait until we get to the morgue."

"What?" Annette squealed as she sat up.

"Stay down!" Sister Augustine snapped, pulling her back by the shoulders as she glanced at the cameras in the elevator.

"Sorry," Annette whispered from under the sheet, having spotted the cameras. "Wasn't thinking."

"Well, nothing we can do now. Just lie back down, and we'll hope whoever's monitoring them didn't see anything. Not everyone's a professional, you know."

The elevator doors opened. Sister Augustine looked up.

B3

"This is our stop," she said as she wheeled the gurney out into a dim, narrow corridor, where the air smelled faintly of disinfectant and something else. The fluorescent lights overhead didn't buzz or flicker, thankfully, but the artificial glow on the scratched tiles was still unnerving. The walls were a dull, lifeless gray, their paint chipped in places. Clearly, this part of the hospital was not high on the list of places to maintain. Several unmarked doors lined the corridor, each just a few steps from the next. Unlike the ER, this floor was quiet.

Sister Augustine took a deep breath and looked down the hall. She saw a sign over a metal door at the far end.

Morgue

She shivered as she slowly pushed the gurney towards it.

"Why are we still going to the morgue?" Annette whispered. "I'm not dead."

"Right," Sister Augustine said. She stopped to consider what their next move should be and then almost jumped out of her habit as the metal door popped open.

"Hey ho!" a cheery young man in jeans and a lab coat said, his flaming orange hair looking like it was erupting from his head. "Delivery? Been a long time since we've had nuns delivering the stiffs. Before my time, in fact. Saw you coming down on the elevator cam. Must say, you handled that cadaver spasm rather well. I'm Les, by the way."

He put out his hand. Sister Augustine hesitated.

"Don't worry. I washed my hands," he said with a laugh. "I'll take it from here, if you want."

"N-no," Sister Augustine said. "I'd rather...inter the body myself."

"Wrong place, Sister," he said, the smile on his face replaced by a scowl, only to snap back into a grin. "We don't do that here. We just put them on ice. Need a hand?"

"No, I'm sure I can manage."

"Makes my life easier. In that case, I'm going upstairs to have a smoke. They tell me it'll kill me, but hey, after you've worked here for a while, you'll see that everything does. The code to get in and out is three-three-two-three."

"You need a code to get out?"

"I guess they don't want any of the bodies deciding to take a little stroll. Who knows. Zombies could be real, and we don't want St. Joe's to get blamed for the apocalypse," he said with a grin. "Well, since you've got this, I'll leave you to it. And, nice meeting you, Sister...?"

"Augustine. Sister Augustine."

"Patron saint of brewers. Nice," he said, then, noticing the look on Sister Augustine's face, quickly added, "Crazy Catholic mother. Went to church a dozen times a day until I moved out. Well, got kicked out, actually. She didn't approve of...these."

He pulled a package of cigarettes out of his pocket and offered her one.

"Oh, no thanks," Sister Augustine said.

"Oh. Geez. Right," he said sheepishly, holding the metal door open for her.

"I don't smoke often, but when I do," she said, pushing the gurney past him into the morgue, "I only smoke Gatins." Once inside, she paused, waited for him to let go of the door, for it to click shut, and then for another few seconds, just for good measure. "Okay. Now you can sit up, although...you might not want to."

Annette sat up, and they both looked around them at a sterile and frighteningly organized room.

"That was close, wasn't it?" Annette said as she climbed off the gurney.

Neither of them could help but notice the upright refrigeration unit in the corner of the room, which looked suspiciously like a massive dresser with a dozen drawers, three by four. Each drawer was labeled with a number, presumably to record the name of the body stored inside until it was collected and sent to a funeral home or the city's morgue.

"Gross," Sister Augustine said, her eyes fixed on the rows of stainless-steel trays in front of the drawers. A few trays sat in wait, hospital-issued sheets neatly folded at the foot. On the opposite wall were two autopsy tables, both covered in clean, white plastic sheeting, next to a nearby counter with scattered medical supplies—neatly arranged and ready for the next autopsy.

"Let's get out of here," Sister Augustine said.

"And then what?"

"I don't know," Sister Augustine said, jabbing at the numbers on the door lock, relieved when they were the right ones. She shoved the heavy door open. "We'll figure it out."

As they approached the elevator, a very old woman stepped out from one of the doors. Her lab coat looked like it had been tailored in the 1950s, and she gave off the distinct air of someone who'd spent a few too many hours reading medical journals in windowless rooms.

"Oh!" she said, jumping back into her office. "Sorry. I don't often see anyone down here."

"We were just, uh—" Sister Augustine began, equally shocked, then stopped, noticing the woman staring at Annette, who was wearing a hospital gown. "Lost."

"I'll say. Where were you trying to go?"

"To the chapel," Annette blurted out.

"Yes, the chapel," Sister Augustine confirmed with a smile.

"Then you are lost, aren't you? It's on the first floor. Right by the ER. I'm just heading up now…to the cafeteria on the fourth floor, not the chapel. Science and religion very seldom make good bedfellows. Come with me."

Sister Augustine and Annette glanced over at each other and then followed the woman, no one making any attempt to introduce themselves. They all stood silently by the elevator bank, waiting. Once the elevator arrived, they all got in, remaining silent until Sister Augustine and Annette got off at the first floor, exactly where they'd started.

"Now what?" Annette said.

"I don't know," Sister Augustine said quietly.

The phone in her habit began to vibrate.

"Luv, 'tis me, Mary-Margaret."

"Oh, MM, am I ever glad—"

"I've just got meself discharged and was about to drive off when I thought I'd best give ye a call. Where are ye?"

"We're just down the hall from the ER," Sister Augustine nearly cried into the phone.

"Don't be standing there too long, luv. They've got the whole hospital looking for the two of ye. Father Miguel is leading the charge. I told ye not to trust that one. A real snake in a tree, is he. Anyway, try to find yer way to the main entrance, and I'll meet ye there. But don't dilly dally. The parking attendants are brutal, and I don't want to get a parking ticket. If yer not there in ten minutes, I'll assume ye've been caught."

"What'll they do to us?" Sister Augustine asked, her voice quivering.

"Well, I've no idea what Father Miguel will do to ye, but Annette's going to get locked up on the seventh floor until further notice. Now, get moving. Ten minutes. Front door."

Sister Augustine clicked off the phone and threw it back into her habit pocket.

"Come on," she said, taking Annette by the wrist.

The two of them zigged and zagged through the hospital corridors, ducking into broom closets here and storage rooms there as security guards passed by. Finally, they reached the front door. Sister Augustine quickly spotted Mary-Margaret's car, and she and Annette hopped in.

"Now what?" Annette asked from the back seat.

"Jeez, Annette, I just got you out of a psych ward and a morgue in less than an hour. Do you think you could come up with something this time?"

Arthur snapped as he removed his wimple.

"Come on, lads. Ye've had quite a time of it. Let's go have a pint at O'Leary's and we'll sort it all out," Mary-Margaret said as she turned onto the main road, pulling her hospital wristband off.

"I wouldn't mind picking up some clothes first," Annette said, glancing down at her hospital gown, which, Mary-Margaret couldn't help but notice, seemed to cover her nether regions far better than the one she had worn.

Chapter Thirty-Nine

Mary-Margaret and Arthur quickly convinced Annette Giancola not to go back to her house for clothes. If Robert Jensen was trying to get rid of her by any means necessary, the last thing they wanted was to deliver her straight back into his hands. There was no guarantee he'd be at her house, of course, but neither of them wanted to risk it.

Instead, they went to Arthur's. As a serious cosplayer and a lover of all disguises, he convinced them that he'd have just the right outfit for any occasion. Knowing him as she did, Mary-Margaret couldn't argue that point.

Within the hour, the three of them were back on their way to O'Leary's. Arthur looked something like an old Irish sheep herder, complete with cap, knitted jumper, and mucky boots, while Annette looked every bit the age-appropriate working-class woman. Despite his offer, Mary-Margaret hadn't bothered to change, choosing instead to stick with the outfit she'd put on that morning.

"What can I get everyone?" a raspy voice called out. It took Mary-Margaret a moment to recognize the voice as belonging to The Old Bird, who was perched at the bar.

What would she be doing...?

And then it hit her: Mary-Margaret was supposed to meet her friend here at three. She looked down at her watch and saw that it was just going on four.

"Oh, me stars!" she cried. And then it registered: The Old Bird was on the other side of the bar. "What are ye doing over there?"

"Havin' a ball is what! Now, if memory serves, you're the half pint crown float. And you two? What can I get you?"

Mary-Margaret's jaw dropped. While the face and the clothes looked the same and the voice sounded familiar, it was as if The Old Bird had suddenly become every barmaid that ever was in Ireland, except for the accent.

"Where's Johnny?" Mary-Margaret finally stammered.

"Upstairs checking in on his wife," The Old Bird replied, already having poured a quarter of a pint of Guinness in the glass. "She's a real firecracker, that one. Now, what can I get you?"

"I'll have a water, please."

"Flat or sparkly? And you? You look like you could use a shot of whiskey."

"I think we all could," Mary-Margaret said, sitting down at the bar.

"I don't drink alcohol. Doesn't agree with—" Arthur began.

"Then I'll have his," Annette said to The Old Bird, who had already lined the drinks up on the bar.

"So who are your friends, Mary-Margaret?"

"Ach, me manners. This is Arthur. I've told ye about him, and this is Annette."

"Ah," The Old Bird said as she topped up the half-pint glass with Strongbow. "You're the one whose husband got capped, aren't you?"

Annette looked at The Old Bird for a second before upending the first shot of whiskey in front of her.

"Yes. That's me," she said after banging the empty glass down in front of her. "I'll have that other one now."

"Suit yourself."

"So *this* is The Old Bird," Arthur said, eyeing her up and down.

"Sue Bird, but everyone calls me The Old Bird because I'm...old. Please to meet you, Artie," she said, extending her hand across the bar to him.

For a moment, he wondered if she might place him—remember something from that business at the school—but when there was no flicker of recognition, he bristled, unsure whether to be relieved or irritated, and gave her hand a weak shake.

"I'm so sorry I stood ye up, luv," Mary-Margaret said as she sipped her whiskey, the half pint of crown float sitting on the bar in front of her. "It's been quite the afternoon."

"Ha!" The Old Bird squawked. "No worries. You did me a favour. And John-O. Look. He's got me working behind the bar. Gosh, it's been years since I've been on this side. Best time of my life, except for my time with Sid, that rat, and when the band toured with—"

"There's the woman of the hour," Johnny said as he came into the pub from the back stairs. He then turned his attention to The Old Bird. "Not giving you any trouble, are they?"

"I was just telling Mary-Margaret that this might be one of the best things that's ever happened to me."

"Can I get my water, please?" Arthur said.

"Shoot. Sorry, Artie. Here," The Old Bird said, passing him a glass of water. "I got carried away. Again."

"She is *not* the kind of person you want to be hanging with MM," Arthur whispered. "People like that will—"

"This from the guy who was dressed like a nun who stole a patient on their way to the psych ward and took them to the morgue. Now *that's* rich," Annette muttered, the whiskey having already gone to her head.

"Whoa whoa whoa," The Old Bird said. "Let's press rewind and start again. Did you just say stole a what and went with who to where?"

"Why don't you take a break, Old Bird, and catch up with your friends?" Johnny said. "I can manage it from here for a while," Johnny said.

"If you say so, John-O," The Old Bird said, taking off her apron and coming around to the other side of the bar. "Now, which one of you is going to tell me what the heck's been going on?"

The four of them moved off to a table, Arthur dragging his heels.

"Come on, luv," Mary-Margaret said as she wrapped her arm around his waist and gave him a little squeeze. "Yer still and always me best mate."

"Another, bartender?" Annette said as they all sat down around a table.

"How be I get you a water first?" Johnny suggested. "Another water for you, Arthur?"

"No, I'm good," he replied. "If I have too much water, I start to break out. It's tied into a rare bladder condition I developed when I—"

"So what the heck have you kids been up to?" The Old Bird cut in. "Not that I don't care about your bladder, Artie!"

"Ach, I was just at the hospital to see our girl, here, when things got out of hand and the next thing ye know, I'm lined up against the wall like a common criminal on a gurney, and they're wanting to run some tests on me. Something about hypertension and dementia. Dementia! Me, can ye imagine it? Just because I…well, never mind. The logic behind it is too complicated for me mind to unravel to yiz all in this moment."

"They see a gray hair, and they think old," The Old Bird said, looking at the split ends of her bleached hair.

"The real story is what happened to our girl here," Mary-Margaret said, looking at Annette.

"I don't even know where to begin," Annette said. "The only part I really remember is being at the hospital, Robert telling them something about me wanting to kill myself, and then, Arthur dressed as a nun rescuing me."

Arthur sat up straighter and pushed his shoulders back.

"That was some quick thinking there, Artie," The Old Bird said.

"It's Arthur," he corrected. Mary-Margaret gave him a disappointed look. "But you can call me Artie, I suppose. And," he said, looking over towards the bar, "I'll have that second water now, if you don't mind?"

"Well, did ye try to kill yerself?" Mary-Margaret asked.

"No! Why would I do that?"

"Well, with yer husband—"

"I would never do that to his children, especially after their father's… death," she said. "And can I have that other whiskey now, please?"

"Well, when I saw ye on Wednesday—"

"Wait. You saw me?"

"We saw each other. Ye waved at me from yer bedroom window."

Johnny set the glass of water down in front of Arthur and the shot of whiskey down in front of Annette.

"Not ringing any bells, luv?"

CHAPTER THIRTY-NINE

"None," Annette said, sipping this whiskey very slowly.

"I bet that Bobby guy doped you up," The Old Bird said. "Sorry, Annie, but there's something about him."

"You've never met him," Annette said sharply.

"Don't need to. Seen his type a million times before. A *MILLION* times before. And each time, he was a dangerous operator. Now, I could be wrong, but I think this guy also murdered your husband."

"No," Annette said flatly. "He was a great friend to Marco. And me."

"Sure, and Marco Polo gave him a great business that brought in a whole lotta coin," The Old Bird countered.

"If anything, it was the other way around," Annette said. "Before he met Robert, Marco was just a mechanic barely keeping his shop above water week-to-week. Once Robert came along, Marco's Motors took off. No, Robert did great things for us."

"And still is?" Mary-Margaret asked.

"What do you mean by that?" Annette said, a little sharper than she likely had intended.

"I understand he's got the whole business now, but, if yiz get together, ye stand to gain a lot more than just fifty percent of the gross," Mary-Margaret said.

"How dare you—" Annette spat, jumping to her feet in a burst of fury.

"Whoa, whoa, whoa," The Old Bird said. "Cool your jets, Annie. You wouldn't be the first woman to use a man as a stepping stone for a better life—and more power to you if you can pull it off at your age."

Annette paused, as if deciding whether to let her indignation loose or keep it locked up for the sake of appearances. In the end, she chose the latter, sitting down with the practiced ease of someone who'd learned long ago that appearing calm was the best way to keep everyone on their side.

"We're not here to judge, luv. We're trying to solve a murder. And ye can't deny that yer man, Robert, seems to be unusually close to ye."

"Well, Robert and I always got along very well," Annette replied, her voice calm and controlled. "Even before..."

"I know what I'd have to do to have a friend like that," The Old Bird crowed.

Annette shot The Old Bird a look that could've melted steel, then took a deep breath, softened her eyes, and turned to Arthur.

"Thank you for rescuing me," she said warmly to him before looking down at herself. "And for the clothes. I'll have them dry-cleaned and returned to you by tomorrow afternoon. Now, if you'll all excuse me, I'm going home."

"But ye—" Mary-Margaret began. "Ye've got nowhere to go."

"I have a home, Mary-Margaret," Annette stated as she got up, "and I'm going there now."

They watched her walk to the bar, noticing the moment she realized she had no purse, no money, and no credit cards.

"It's okay," they heard Johnny say. "Sounds like you've had quite a day. Your drinks are on the house. Now, how are you getting home?"

"Good thing Maeve's not here," Mary-Margaret said with a chuckle. "She'd have his hide for that."

They saw her glance back at them before turning to Johnny. A moment later, Johnny was handing her his cell phone.

After she made a brief call, they kept an eye on her as she walked out of O'Leary's.

Chapter Forty

"Arthur!" Mary-Margaret snapped, her voice carrying the familiar urgency that told him there was no time to waste. "Don't just sit there. Go after her!"

"Right," Arthur said, scrambling to his feet, his mind not entirely catching up with his body.

"Hold your horses, there, Artie," The Old Bird interjected. "What exactly do you think you're doing?"

"Doing? He's going to see who picks up our girl," Mary-Margaret stated.

"And then...?"

"Ach, I don't know, luv. Something," Mary-Margaret replied, waving her hand dismissively. "We can't just let her go back to that madman."

"Do you think he's going to kill her?" Arthur asked, looking from one to the other, unsure what he was supposed to do.

"He'll certainly give it his best try, I'm thinking," Mary-Margaret replied.

"Doubtful," The Old Bird said, a glint of smugness in her eyes. "Not right away, anyway. If Bobby's half as smart as you think he is, he knows you're onto him. He'll give it some time—long enough to make him think you've forgotten all about him."

"Has he met us?" Arthur said, glancing back and forth between them, unsure whether to stay or go.

"Ach, sitcheedoon, luv," Mary-Margaret said with a sigh, motioning towards his chair. "She's right. We need a plan."

"I think you should call Michael," Arthur said.

"And say what? That I've left the hospital without being properly checked out and am now day-drinking, for all intents and purposes, at O'Leary's? Oh, that would be grand, wouldn't it?"

"I see what you mean," Arthur said.

"And, if anyone still cares, she is now getting into a Range Rover," The Old Bird said, glancing out a window that faced the street.

"Ach, that'll be him."

"Do you want me to follow them, MM?" Arthur asked, all of them knowing that the car was long gone. "I'm particularly adept at locating—"

"I think we know where they're going, luv," Mary-Margaret said, a sense of dread washing over her.

"Let's stay focused," The Old Bird said, leaning in. "This Annie chick. What's her deal? I mean, c'mon—from what you've said, there was no love lost between her and old Marco Polo there. See how she's stomping around like she's grieving, but something's off. Real off. By the looks of her, there's a little too much mascara and not enough tears."

Mary-Margaret considered what The Old Bird was saying while Arthur looked increasingly put-out, his arms folded tightly across his chest as he leaned back in his chair.

"And then there's the partner," she continued. "The business one. Her late husband's right-hand guy. Except I'm guessing his hands were a little more *hands-on*, if you catch my drift. Something was brewing there—emotional espresso with a side of betrayal. Might still be. Now hubby's dead, the partner's everywhere she is, with her at centre stage in the murder musical. Not a good look for her. Not good at all."

"But that partner wants to kill her," Mary-Margaret said. Surprised by the looks she was receiving, she pressed on. "Come on, lads! It's as obvious as the full moon on a cloudless night. He's already killed Marco, would have gotten away with it if Annette hadn't contacted us—"

"We don't know that," Arthur said.

Mary-Margaret looked at him in shock.

"Any of that, really," Arthur continued, sitting back up at the table. "I mean, all we know for sure is that Marco Giancola is dead."

"Are ye going over to Billy Gilly's side then, are ye?"

"No, I'm just saying—"

"Focus, people," The Old Bird said, snapping her fingers like she was conducting a crime scene orchestra. "We know Annie's in a bind. That much is clear. Bobby's a snake in a suit—slick, spineless, and probably hiding more than just offshore accounts. And Marco Polo? Well, he's not exploring anything anymore, is he? He's dead. So let's connect the dots sooner rather than later, especially if we're thinking someone else is liable to end up horizontal."

"Well, if it's motive we're looking for, we need not expand our list beyond Robert," Mary-Margaret stated. "Although I still don't like the looks of that Danny lad."

"Danny?" The Old Bird asked.

"Organized crime," Arthur said dismissively.

"*Hold up*," The Old Bird cawed, throwing up her hands like she was calling off a con job. "That's the kind of detail you *lead* with, Artie. 'Organized crime'? What is this, a Godfather reboot? Somebody wanna tell me why I'm just now finding out that somebody's got Mob ties? This isn't just gossip, this is red-alert-lock-your-doors-and-check-the-shadows kind of stuff. What's up with that?"

"Marco was a grand mechanic," Mary-Margaret began. "But he wasn't exactly the brightest candle in the chapel when it came to business matters—at least that's what Annette's telling us. Then along comes Robert—one of his customers, apparently—with some notion of a business plan. Next thing ye know, they're after buying up a rake of properties to expand Marco's Motors. And wouldn't ye know it, those very properties are now worth a small fortune."

"Okay," The Old Bird said, tilting her head. "So where does organized crime waltz in?"

"Where else would Robert get that kind of money?" Arthur said flatly.

"And ye'd only have to take one look at Danny—"

"Once again, I have to ask...*Danny...?*" The Old Bird said, eyebrows practically hitting her hairline. "I swear, every time I blink, someone's pulling another twist out of nowhere."

"The lad who owns the only bit of land with a Marco's Motors location on it that the company doesn't actually own. And honest to God, luv, one look at the fella and you'd swear he was lifted straight out of *The Sopranos*. While he wasn't wearing a suit when I met him, I've no doubt he's got a closet full of them. Never mind, he's got the hair, the way he talks—he's pure Mob. No doubt in me mind about it."

"Okay," The Old Bird said slowly, dragging the word like it owed her rent. "I'll bite. Danny's Mob-adjacent, fine. But even so—why whack Marco Polo? What's the angle? We've already established that the guy barely knew how to fill out a tax form, let alone hide offshore funds, so how's he enough of a threat to warrant a Mob hit?"

"Well, maybe that's just it. Didn't want any part of it," Mary-Margaret suggested.

"So what does any of that have to do with someone wanting to whack Annie?" The Old Bird countered, voice low and skeptical. "Not that anyone's going to, but that seems to be the biggest question parked in our driveway right now."

"I'm thinking it's because she knows too much," Mary-Margaret said, lowering her voice just a touch. "And sure, she might have a few too many connections for their liking, if you catch my drift."

"Robert couldn't have had enough money to purchase all of those properties. Danny and the Mob did. Maybe Robert was a part of the Mob before, but, if not, he's certainly in deep now," Arthur concluded. "And, if Annette's the one that brought them together, then...?"

"I still think *she's* the one who offed her old man," The Old Bird cut in. "All roads lead back to Annie. The motive's there, the timing's convenient, and don't even get me started on her just happening to find the body. Girl's lying like it's her second job."

"I don't see it meself," Mary-Margaret said with a slow shake of her head. "But I'll tell ye this—if we don't step in, Robert's going to do something terrible to Annette. I know it, sure as I know me own name."

"What if he needs her to stay alive?" The Old Bird mused, eyes narrowing.

Mary-Margaret and Arthur both turned to stare at her.

"No, seriously," she continued, tapping a finger on the side of her nose. "What if this *does* have something to do with organized crime? What if Annie *does* know too much—and what she knows is the only thing keeping Bobby breathing?"

"I'm not following, luv," Mary-Margaret admitted.

The Old Bird leaned in, hands now slicing through the air with each point she made. "Okay, look—Marco Polo. Good mechanic, lousy businessman. We've established that. Bobby? Who knows what he's good at, aside from juggling properties and probably cooking the books."

"I've said all of this already," Arthur muttered, his lips pressed into a thin line as he folded his arms, looking at The Old Bird like she was a piece of furniture that just suddenly started speaking. His gaze flickered to Mary-Margaret, then back to her, clearly not appreciating the competition.

"But Annie—Annie's the wildcard," The Old Bird went on, unfazed, her eyes gleaming like she was assembling a puzzle. "We *know* she's good at manipulating men; she practically wrote the manual. But what else? What's she *really* got up her sleeve?"

Mary-Margaret blinked slowly, as if she could absorb the words through sheer will.

"Nothing," Arthur said, shifting uncomfortably in his chair, rubbing the side of his neck, clearly wishing he'd said something first.

"Marco's Motors was already set up at the spot where he was killed—the flagship, right? And this Danny character just so happens to own that building. So, I'm asking: does Annie know Danny? And if she's cozy with Bobby, is it really that far-fetched to think maybe she got a little snuggly with Danny too?"

"Pfff," Arthur said.

"Stay with me," The Old Bird said, her tone sharp but focused. "What if she didn't have a thing with him, but she knew him? How did she say Marco Polo and Bobby met?"

"He was a customer," Arthur said, leaning forward slightly, more curious than disagreeing.

"Sure," The Old Bird said skeptically. "A customer with a deep pocket. But whatever. From what we know of Marco Polo, he liked being a mechanic. Liked working. Sure didn't have to work at the time of his death. Truth, he should have been rolling in money, given the success of Marco's Motors. And he probably was—"

"Except his house was mortgaged to the teeth, according to Annette," Mary-Margaret stated.

"Really? Given the success of the company, I'd bet Marco Polo had a stash of dough tucked away somewhere, but Annie didn't know about it. Or maybe she does and isn't telling you. Either way, there's money there. And up until he got capped, Marco Polo was still working. Why? Because he loved it. So why would a guy who was doing just fine risk it all and partner with someone else if all he cared about was fixing cars?"

"Well, Annette did say they were in financial difficulties at the ti—" Arthur started, trying to stay neutral.

"And whose fault was that?" The Old Bird asked, raising an eyebrow but not looking directly at him, as if she'd already formed her conclusion.

"'Fault' might be too strong a word," Mary-Margaret said, tilting her head. "She was battling with the depression, poor wee thing, and the spending just got away from her. Happens easier than folks like to admit."

"And Bobby just happened to come along? In shining armour, no less?" The Old Bird asked, her voice dripping with irony. "Call me cynical, but I don't buy it. I'm starting to think Annie played matchmaker, knowing Danny had access to quick cash—mob money, mind you—and Bobby had the business savvy. All they needed was someone to make the introduction. Enter Make-Me-A-Match Annie."

Arthur considered this for a moment, nodding slowly, trying to keep the pieces together.

"So why kill Marco?" he asked.

"Because he was in the way," Mary-Margaret answered quietly, her voice carrying a certain sadness.

"Whose way?" Arthur asked.

"Annie's. Bobby's. Could be both, Artie," The Old Bird said, leaning back in her chair and giving a thoughtful tilt of her head. "But I'll put my money on Annie."

"What about Danny?" Mary-Margaret suggested. "He's got the hired-killer background."

"Too obvious," The Old Bird said dismissively.

"So why not just leave it as an accident?" Arthur asked, leaning back in his chair.

"Because whoever did it was afraid they'd eventually get found out," The Old Bird said slowly. "And they wanted to control the narrative. Shift the blame so far from themselves that they were home free. Or maybe get arrested on their own terms."

"That makes sense," Arthur said, and then added. "In a twisted sort of way."

"Always does with these things," The Old Bird agreed, her eyes flashing with the satisfaction of a theory coming together.

"Or maybe they've had a bit of a pang of conscience and are just waiting to be caught," Mary-Margaret said.

The three of them sat quietly for a few minutes, each lost in their own thoughts. The pub, meanwhile, was filling up with the after-work crowd, with the majority of patrons flocking around the bar.

"Sorry, kids," The Old Bird announced. "Looks like John-o could use some help. Gotta go. Keep me in the loop."

"I don't suppose we should call Michael," Arthur said after she'd left the table.

"Starting without us?" Angus Corrigan said as he and Eleanor approached the table. "Good to see you again, Arthur. No need to get up."

Arthur had no intention of getting up, but being of that generation, Angus had anticipated that he would.

"I see Johnny's got someone new behind the bar," Eleanor said as she sat down. "Let's hope she doesn't end up like that other one."

"I take it that the pregnancy is taking its toll on Maeve?" Angus said, looking over his shoulder. "Are we back to table service, or still going up to the bar these days?"

"Why don't you just go up and get us our drinks, Angus?" Eleanor suggested.

"As you wish," he said. "What are you having, Arthur?"

"Oh, nothing," he said. "I've got to go. I have an epic showdown tonight with my online gaming group."

"Well, that sounds like fun," Eleanor said. "I hope you win."

"I usually do," he replied. "I'll call you later tonight, MM."

Chapter Forty-One

"Dare I ask?" Angus said before they'd even had a chance to catch up on the week's news.

"Ach, I don't know where to begin, lads," Mary-Margaret said, the excitement of the day starting to catch up with her.

"Do we know who did it yet?" Eleanor asked.

"I think so, but I've yet to prove it."

"Always something, isn't there?" Angus remarked glibly.

"But I'm sure we'll have it sorted by next week."

"Oh? And why's that?" Angus asked, wishing he'd ordered them their fish and chips while he was up at the bar.

"Well, if nothing else, I think we can prove Robert Jensen tried to poison Annette Giancola," Mary-Margaret said, her voice steady. "And that should be enough to light a fire under Billy Gilly's behind and get Robert in for questioning. Then, though knowing Billy Gilly as I do, it's unlikely, but, on the off-chance that the man does his job, he might be able to get a confession out of Robert for the murder."

"Poison her? How's that now?" Angus said, his tone light and almost dismissive, focusing on the poison bit because this whole murder investigation business was a bit of a stretch for him. But he knew it mattered to Mary-Margaret—and Eleanor—so he played along.

"Well, I think the legal term is 'administer noxious substance' or the like, but what he did was give her sleeping medication without her knowledge."

"That's hardly poisoning," Angus remarked.

"I believe it is, dear," Eleanor said. When Angus gave her a disbelieving look, she smiled faintly and added, "We've seen it on those shows we watch on Acorn."

"And then he managed to convince the paramedics that she'd tried to overdose."

"That's dreadful," said Eleanor.

"And we know this…how?" Angus said, still unconvinced.

"She told us."

"Told you? When?"

"It matters not, but she ended up at St. Joseph's."

"That could be for any number of reasons, really," Angus said. "Perhaps it was something as simple as feeling overwhelmed with the death of her husband…?"

Mary-Margaret stared at him for a good two minutes before saying: "Luv, ye know what a shock it was when Jimmy, God rest his soul, died."

They all paused to cross themselves.

"And ye all know what a time I had of it with four smallies on me own."

"That was a horrible time," Eleanor confirmed.

"And, truth to be told that I'll tell anyone who asks, if it wasn't for ye, Angus Corrigan, there's no way the company Jimmy, God rest his soul, worked for would have paid out a dime, much less a pension. And, if it weren't for ye talking to Father Richard, Eleanor, I'd never have got that job as the secretary at the church and would likely have gone stark raving mad, but, be that as it may, at no time did I think of taking meself down to the hospital."

"Not everyone's as strong as you are, Mary-Margaret," Eleanor said with a warm smile.

"No, they're not," Mary-Margaret said, raising her glass. "Sláinte. Now, did I tell ye about a clause in the contract between Marco and this Robert lad that states that, if one of them dies, the other gets the lot."

"What?" Angus said, his face scrunched up like a prune. "That's idiotic. Who would agree to that?"

"Marco Giancola, apparently."

"Well, if that's so, then I'm sure the police are taking that into account in their investigation."

"I've no idea, but I also know that Annette and this lad have been having a fling on the side."

"How do you know that?" Eleanor asked. "Did she tell you?"

"Ach, no. 'Tis as plain as day."

"If it is, then why aren't the police arresting him?" Angus remarked. "He's taking on the business, but they're having an affair. Sounds like a classic murder mystery plot."

"Well, and I'm only telling ye this because it's true, 'tis because the lead investigator is that Billy Gilly lad."

"Surely, he can't be that inept," Eleanor said, rolling her eyes.

"He can, and he is," Mary-Margaret declared.

"I hardly think that's why—" Angus began.

"Sorry to interrupt, folks, but I need to borrow Mary-Margaret for a minute," The Old Bird said from behind Angus.

"Is everything alright, luv?" Mary-Margaret said once she'd excused herself from the table.

"Tickity boo, but I didn't want to say this in front of your friends there, especially the guy. He seems a little excitable."

They both looked back at the table and saw Angus gesticulating wildly while Eleanor nodded politely.

"Look," The Old Bird said, holding out a piece of paper. "It's the number Annie dialed from John-o's phone. I got him to show me his call history, and this is what popped up. Any idea whose it is?"

"No, but I'm sure Arthur would know."

"He's an interesting little man, that Artie. But I like him," The Old Bird chortled. "Anyway, for what it's worth."

She handed the paper to Mary-Margaret.

"Keep me posted and," she said, glancing back again, "keep an eye on your friend. I've known more than a few guys his age that just dropped dead. Heart attack. Too tightly wound. I gotta get back to work. Oh, and thanks, eh? I'm having a ball back there."

Mary-Margaret looked at the phone number on the paper and went back to the table.

"It makes no sense to me whatsoever that a murderer would be allowed to—" Angus was saying.

"Excuse me again, but I've got to go to the jacks," Mary-Margaret said, grabbing her purse. "And just forget what I said, luv. I'm sure the police have things well in hand."

"That's what I've been trying to say," Angus said.

Mary-Margaret ducked into the ladies' room and pulled her cell phone out of her purse.

"Arthur. 'Tis me, Mary-Margaret."

"Oh, hi, MM," he said casually.

"Wait a minute. Weren't ye going to be busy—"

"Later tonight, yeah, but what's up?"

"If I give ye a phone number, can ye find out who it belongs to?"

"No problemo. Go ahead."

Mary-Margaret read the number to Arthur.

"Give me a second," he said. "I'm just going to try a couple of different…got it. Belongs to Robert Jensen."

"And yer sure, luv?"

"One hundred percent."

"So 'twas his Range Rover we saw."

"Yup. I think we should go in and get her as soon as we can."

"I agree, luv," Mary-Margaret replied, annoyed with herself for not realizing that the only person Annette could have called was Robert.

"You still at O'Leary's?"

"Yes, but I can—"

"No. Stay there. I'll come up with a plan and call you at…ten o'clock. Will you still be there or will you be back at Michael's?"

Michael. She hadn't called Michael.

She'd meant to–she really had–but that thought had rather got away from her.

Now, how exactly was she going to explain all of this?

And, even if she somehow managed to get past that, how was she going to convince him that she had some disease of the kidney—serious enough to justify her staying at his place, but not so serious that it would sound like she was dying and then he'd likely hire a nurse or something, which would ruin everything?

Ach, me girl. Ye've really gone and done it this time.

"MM? You still there?" Arthur asked.

"Yes, luv, but I've got to go. I'll give ye a ring at ten, and we'll go from there."

Chapter Forty-Two

"Well, my darling," Angus said, looking down at his watch. "Time for us to go. Do you need a lift home, Mary-Margaret?"

"Ta, luv, but I've got me car, so no thanks."

"Suit yourself," he said, getting up from the table. He pulled his wife's chair out and helped her with her coat. "I'll pick up the tab at the bar. Even with your friend there, poor Johnny seems swamped."

"Don't forget to tip, even if it wasn't table service," Eleanor said with a wink. "Want to walk out with us?"

"I'm going to pop into the jacks before I head out. As you know, I'm not just around the corner anymore, and it's a bit of a drive to Michael's."

"See you next week, then."

Mary-Margaret took her purse and coat and went to the ladies.

Not quite ten, but I'm sure he'll have a plan.

"And so…?" she said when Arthur picked up the phone.

"We've got to go in tonight, MM," he stated.

"I know. And I was afraid ye'd say that." The day, the whiskey, the evening…it was all catching up with her. "But I don't know that I've got it in me, luv."

"Mary-Margaret O'Shea! What kind of attitude is that? We've got a killer on the loose, a woman whose life is on the line, and *you're* sitting here telling me you don't think you've got it in you?! Hold. Up. Am I really talking to Mary-Margaret O'Shea? *The* Mary-Margaret O'Shea who's faced down killers and conmen and liars before and always comes out on top?!"

"Ach, yer right, lad," she said with just a hint of pride. "Let's hear the plan, then."

"I haven't quite worked out all the kinks yet—it's not quite ten o'clock, and I did say I'd have a plan by ten o'clock, remember—but here's what I've got. You and I are going to drive over to Annette's place. We'll park Daphne around the corner so no one knows we're there. We'll wait until all the lights go out, then we'll break in. You're going to go upstairs and lead Annette out, and, if he's there, I'll wrestle Robert to the ground. After that, you call the police, and they'll arrest him."

The line was quiet.

"MM? Are you still there?"

"I am, luv," she said with a sigh.

"And...?"

"And I'm thinking ye clearly needed until ten to come up with a plan, didn't ye?"

"Well," he replied, "to be honest, I kind of got busy with other stuff and... forgot about it until you called."

"I see."

Arthur could hear the disappointment in Mary-Margaret's voice.

"I did have my alarm set for nine-thirty, so I didn't actually forget, but... yeah, well...no, I don't have a plan. Except that one, which—kind of—really isn't very good, is it?"

"Not one of yer best, luv, no," Mary-Margaret said, leaning against the sink. "But no matter. Let's talk it through. We can agree that nasty piece of work will be there, which means Annette's in danger. So, we get her out, and we'll hold Robert for the police because we both know Billy Gilly will let him get away if we don't."

"Correct."

"But we know we've got limited resources."

"Well, not exactly. I mean, there's you and me."

"Yes. Limited resources. And we know we've got even less time."

"Correct."

"So, given what we've got—or what little we've got—what's stopping us from just having a quick look-in at Annette, and if she's in danger, calling the police right then and there without involving ourselves with Robert and letting them take over?"

"M.M., I am *aghast*! This is *not* how we operate! Nor is this *not* how we've operated in the past—and let me tell you, we've had a *one hundred percent success rate*! If we left it up to the police–"

"Ach, I suppose yer right, luv. I'm just tired and don't want to muck it up."

"I understand. So, let's go back to the look-in part. Once we're inside, what if we tricked Robert into going into the basement and then—"

"Talking to a secret side-guy, Mary-Margaret?" The Old Bird said as she walked into the washroom.

Arthur, Mary-Margaret mouthed.

"Oh. Hey, Artie," she cawed.

"Who was that?" Arthur asked suspiciously.

"The Old Bird," Mary-Margaret said. "I'm in the jacks at O'Leary's."

"I hope you're not—"

"No, luv. I'm standing by the sink, not having a wee."

"Oh. That's okay, then."

"You two planning on going in tonight?" The Old Bird asked from one of the two cubicles.

"If we had a plan, we would be," Mary-Margaret answered, her tone heavy with disappointment.

"We *do* have a plan," Arthur objected, his voice crackling through the phone line.

"Can I join you? I'm done for the night, and," she said, emerging from the cubicle after flushing the toilet, "let's just say, I'm a bit *wound up*…slinging drinks behind the bar makes me feel twenty years younger. What do you say?"

Mary-Margaret stepped aside so The Old Bird could get to the sink.

"The Old Bird was just this minute wondering if—" she began.

"No, she can't join us," Arthur hissed through the phone. "This is *our* thing. She's just—"

"Here," Mary-Margaret said, cutting Arthur off. "Why don't I put ye on speaker."

"So. What's the plan, Stan?" The Old Bird said.

"Mary-Margaret and I were—"

"We've not got one at the moment," Mary-Margaret cut in.

"No sweat. We'll sort it out as we go. Heck, the best gigs back in the day were the ones where we didn't even have a playlist sorted before we hit the stage."

"*We* don't operate that way," Arthur said curtly. "And catching murderers is a little more dangerous than playing a gig in a two-bit bar."

"Ha!" The Old Bird squawked. "You've clearly never played in the kinds of dives we did. Some of 'em had fencing in front of the stage just to keep the band from getting pelted with beer bottles. Now that…that's some real danger!"

"And besides, Mary-Margaret and I have a rhythm and are able to play off of each other without—"

"If you want to see what it means to play off each other without missing a beat, you should've been at The Music Hall. April 27th, 1985. *New Order* was doing their Low-Life album tour and needed some backup singers. I was in like stink. No rehearsal, no nothing—just walked right up and nailed it."

"Ugh," Arthur groaned dramatically over the phone.

"All right, ye lot," Mary-Margaret cut in, loud enough to command the call. "Since no one else has a plan, I say The Old Bird and I pick ye up in half an hour and we'll head over to Annette's. We'll park on the street, out of the way like ye suggested, Arthur, and then figure out how to get in and check on our girl. If Rob—"

"Wait—The Old Bird is coming?" Arthur said, his voice climbing an octave. "We never agreed—"

"What's the matter, Artie?" The Old Bird said, bone-dry. "Afraid I'll solve your murder?"

"Can I finish?" Mary-Margaret said, like she was settling a squabble at her dinner table on any given Sunday evening.

"Sorry," The Old Bird said unapologetically. "I told you I was a bit wound up."

"Right then," Mary-Margaret continued. "If Robert's there and she's off her pins, we get out and call the police. If he's there and she seems sane and sober, we convince her to leave and go from there. And if he's not there—well, we go home and have a cuppa."

Another pause.

"Sound good?"

"Still not loving the part where *she* comes with us," Arthur muttered.

"We'll see ye in half an hour, luv," Mary-Margaret replied. "Be ready."

"Oh, I will be," Arthur said with a huff before ending the call.

Chapter Forty-Three

"Oh, I'm sorry!" Eleanor Corrigan said as she came into the ladies room. "Mary-Margaret, you're still here. Hello, Old Bird."

"What are ye doing here?" Mary-Margaret asked, taken aback.

"Angus forgot his umbrella," Eleanor said with a sigh. "We were almost home, and I suggested he call Johnny to put it aside until next week, but no—he said he might need it this week. So, we turned back. And then, of course, I realized I wouldn't be making it home comfortably unless I popped into the ladies. Gone are the days of holding it for hours—at least for me."

"So what are you doing now? After you go pee, I mean?" The Old Bird asked.

"Going home, I suppose," Eleanor said. She went into the stall and shut the door behind her. "Unless you have something better in mind."

Mary-Margaret looked at The Old Bird. The two of them shrugged.

"It's up to you, Mary-Margaret," The Old Bird said. "Your gig."

"I say the more the merrier. Can't have too many hands if yer arresting a murderer, I wouldn't imagine."

The two women nodded in agreement.

"Eleanor," Mary-Margaret called to her friend. "Do ye fancy rescuing Annette Giancola and arresting Robert Jensen for murder with us?"

"Sorry, I didn't quite catch that," Eleanor said over the sound of the flushing toilet, slipping between the two women to reach the sink.

"I was just wondering if ye wanted to rescue—"

"Oh. Then I did hear what you said. I just thought…never mind. Yes, I think that would be fun! But—" Eleanor paused, giving the slightest shrug.

"But I don't think Angus would want to come along."

"I've room in me car for ye if he doesn't," Mary-Margaret offered.

"And I don't think Angus would like me going without him, sadly," Eleanor said with a note of regret. "In fact, I'm sure he'd say no."

"So you're going to let some man tell you what to do, is what I'm hearing," The Old Bird interjected, her voice sharp as a knife and just as pointed.

"Well, he's not exactly *some* man. He is, after all, my husband."

"All the more reason for standing up for yourself."

"Let me have a word with him," Eleanor said as she opened the bathroom door. "And it might be best if I do it without the two of you."

"Gotcha," The Old Bird said, tapping the side of her nose.

Mary-Margaret and The Old Bird remained in the washroom for what seemed like an eternity before Eleanor returned with a smile on her face.

"Should we follow you or meet you there?"

* * *

It was just as well that Angus had decided to return to O'Leary's for his umbrella, if for no other reason than that the rain had resumed at a ferocious rate. If someone was going to have to stand outside the house, at least they'd have something to keep them dry, more or less. The heavy rainfall made driving difficult, however, and between that and their running into Eleanor in the washroom, Mary-Margaret and The Old Bird were quite delayed in getting to Arthur's. This, in turn, sent Arthur into an even deeper funk, worsened by the fact that he had to sit in the cramped back seat of Mary-Margaret's car, only to be told that their crew was being expanded yet again.

"I don't like it, MM," Arthur stated for the umpteenth time. "Too many people in the mix. Too many hands on deck. More hands, more mess."

"Got it, luv," Mary-Margaret said, giving him a quick yet stern look through her rearview mirror.

"I disagree," The Old Bird said as she glanced back over her shoulder at Arthur. "I don't think you can *ever* have too much help when you're dealing with a slippery one like this Bobby dude. And are you sure you don't want to switch up and sit up here? You look awfully uncomfortable back there."

"Discomfort is my constant companion."

"I see you're getting yer money's worth out of that jumpsuit," Mary-Margaret commented, hoping a remark about Arthur's clothes might lift his mood.

"It's very comfortable," he replied, pleased that Mary-Margaret had noticed. "No wonder astronauts wear them in space."

"Pretty sure they wear space suits, Artie," The Old Bird said with a laugh. "But yeah, they're comfy. Remember those in the '70s, Mary-Margaret—or are you too young for that?" She grinned. "I was just starting out in the biz back then. First time I ever wore one of those jumpsuits, I was doing backup for Cher. Didn't think the colour worked, but who was I to argue with Cher?"

"Nobody argues with Cher," Arthur said, recoiling slightly as if The Old Bird's comment had struck him in the chest. "She's a deity. The blueprint. I have a Pinterest board and a spreadsheet dedicated to her Bob Mackie era."

"What is yer plan for the evening, luv?" Mary-Margaret interrupted, suppressing her fermenting annoyance with Arthur, choosing to keep her attention fixed firmly on the road instead.

"Well, I don't have one, now that we've got two *more* people involved," Arthur muttered, crossing his arms and jutting out his bottom lip in clear displeasure, even though neither Mary-Margaret nor The Old Bird were looking back at him.

"Ye best get one, Arthur, or I'll turn back and drop ye home," Mary-Margaret said, allowing her displeasure to surface just enough to call forth a tone of voice she hadn't needed since her children were small.

"Fine."

The three of them drove on in silence, the only sound being the rain hammering against the car and the windshield wipers working furiously, struggling to offer even a hint of visibility.

"Okay. I've got it," he finally said, his voice dripping with the smugness of someone who'd just cracked the code to life itself.

"I am on tenterhooks," Mary-Margaret said as she looked back at him through the rearview.

Chapter Forty-Four

"Here's the plan," Arthur said. "It's dark. It's pouring rain. And I'm wearing this oh-so-versatile jumpsuit—"

"I think that's actually a coverall you've got on there, Artie," The Old Bird corrected.

"Whatever. Anyway, we can't just do a door knock. That's an announced entrance, just to keep you up to speed," Arthur said patronizingly to The Old Bird.

"Gotcha," she replied as she turned back to give him a nod.

"But we still have to get in," Arthur continued.

"We'll be there in a few minutes, luv, so get to the point," Mary-Margaret said.

"Right. So, I'm going to knock on the door—"

"I thought you just said a door knock was out," The Old Bird said.

"It's back in. And being done by me. I tell them that there's a power outage in the area and that I need to come in and check their fuse box."

"But there isn't a power outage. Their lights will be on," The Old Bird countered.

"Will you let me finish?" Arthur stated. "So, I go downstairs and check the fuse box. While I'm there, I pull the lever and…*voilà*…a power outage is born. Then, you go upstairs to check on Annette, MM, since you know the lay of the place. Eleanor can go with you. Angus will engage with Robert until I get back up the stairs, and then he and I will tackle Robert to the ground, and I'll restrain him with these slip ties that I just happen to have here in my pocket, and then we call the police."

"What do I do while all of this is happening?" The Old Bird asked.

"You wait in the car."

"I see."

"So? Sound good?" Arthur asked.

"Sounds…reasonable, but what if they won't let ye in?"

"Oh, they will. I can be *very* persuasive. When I was in grade five, I once convinced—"

"What if I go in with Angus and help you guys wrestle Robert to the ground?" The Old Bird offered.

"Really?" Arthur said, his eyebrows practically shooting up off of his forehead.

"Let me tell you a little story, my friend," The Old Bird said, her voice dropping low as she turned around in her seat to look right at him. "It was February 4th, 1985. I was at the ElMo doing a gig. Not my usual jam, mind you, but times were tough, so I had to push beyond my comfort zone with my musical chops. I was doing backup for *The Replacements*, and believe you me, those boys were something else. So right in the middle of a set, Paul and Johnny—God bless 'em—decide to have a little…altercation. You wanna talk about a barfight of mythical proportions, Artie? I'm talkin' fists flying, instruments getting smashed, and the crowd? They were eating it up. Heck, people are still talking about it today. *Today*, Artie. It's the stuff legends are made of. So yeah, I think I should go in with Angus."

Once again, the only sound was the rain drumming on the roof and the steady sweep of the wipers.

"*Wait*—you were *there*?" Arthur finally gasped, eyes wide. "And played at *that* gig?"

"Yepper," The Old Bird said, entirely unfazed, as she turned back and settled into her seat.

Arthur stared at the back of her head, stunned. "That's…insane. I read that half the club ended up in hospital!"

"Likely," she said, checking her nails. "And who knows what happened to the other half."

"Well, that changes everything," Arthur replied, still reeling from the news.

"Okay then. You and Angus are going in together. Someone's got to keep an eye on that old guy."

* * *

Mary-Margaret spotted Angus and Eleanor's car parked by the side of the road, a block away from Annette Giancola's house. She pulled Daphne over alongside it, lining herself up with Angus, and put the four-ways on. She waited for Angus to roll down his window before she rolled down hers.

"What are you doing, Mary-Margaret?" Angus asked, glancing anxiously at the empty street for any sign of oncoming traffic.

"A little trick I learned from me Michael. They do it all the time at his work, so he tells me."

"But you're on the wrong side of the road," Angus objected. "You could get hit."

"And who's coming up behind me that I need to worry about?" she asked, peering into the rearview mirror.

"Yes, but—"

"Or would ye rather I pull over ahead of ye, and ye can get out and stand in the rain outside me window?"

"Angus, I don't think we have anything to worry about at this time of night, do you?" Eleanor commented from the passenger seat, shooting him a reassuring smile.

"I suppose not, but I still don't like it. You never know when some crazy teenager or drunken fool might come racing down the—"

"Agreed, luv, so let's get discussing our plan, then, and get this part over with, shall we?" Mary-Margaret said.

"What is the plan, Arthur?" Eleanor asked, leaning across Angus, her face scrunching

slightly as she struggled to make him out in the darkness of the back of Mary-Margaret's car.

"Well," Arthur began dramatically.

"He knocks on the door, gets in, ye and I follow and head upstairs, Eleanor, while Angus and The Old Bird keep Robert distracted. Then Arthur cuts the power, and the three of ye wrestle him to the ground. After that, we call the police," Mary-Margaret stated.

"Oh, I love it!" Eleanor gushed.

"Hurmph. That's a horrible plan," Angus stated.

"It's a lot more complicated than that," Arthur stated. "MM left out a lot of the details."

"No need to overcomplicate things, luv," Mary-Margaret said.

"It'll be fun, Angus," The Old Bird said with a wink. "You and me and Artie rolling around on the ground. A little hand-to-hand with that jerk. Come on, what could possibly go wrong?"

"I hate to consider," Angus said with a sniff.

"Well, let's not waste time flapping our gums," Mary-Margaret said. "Given the rain, I vote we just drive up to the house. I'm not too fussy on getting meself soaked to the bone if I don't have to and, unless anyone else is in the mood for a swim…?"

"But the plan states—" Arthur began.

"Suit yerself, luv," Mary-Margaret said, with a shrug. "But ye'll be the only one walking the distance." She looked over at The Old Bird. "Sorry, but yer going to have to get out to let Arthur out of the back."

"Never mind," Arthur grumbled.

"Grand. I'll lead the way, then. See ye out front of Annette's," Mary-Margaret said, winding up her window before doing a three-point turn and heading towards the house.

Chapter Forty-Five

"This couldn't have waited until tomorrow morning, could it?" Angus grumbled as he got out of the car, the rain coming down in buckets.

"A woman's life is at risk, Angus," Eleanor said. "A little rain won't hurt you."

"Wait until you see me go in," Arthur instructed.

"Obviously," Angus muttered.

"I'll make sure the door stays unlocked, and then all of you come in."

"All of us? Isn't that a bit much, Artie? Why not have Angus go in with you as your supervisor, and then I can follow behind with El and Mary-Margaret?" The Old Bird said.

"Because that's not how the plan goes," Arthur said childishly.

"Come on. Let's get on with it before we all turn into drowned rats," Mary-Margaret said, giving Arthur a little nudge.

While the four others waited behind the hedges that surrounded the porch, Arthur rang the doorbell.

No answer.

He rang it again, this time leaving his finger on it for longer than any ordinary person would. He saw the curtains move in the front room, and then…nothing.

He rang the doorbell again. Again, he saw the curtain move, only this time, he pointed wildly at the name embroidered on his coverall, as if that would change anything.

Surprisingly, it did.

"Yes?" Robert Jensen said, a sliver of his face visible behind the chain-locked door.

"Electric," Arthur stated. "There's been a power outage."

Robert looked up, as if to confirm that the lights were, in fact, still on.

"Not here. Must have the wrong house."

"Soon," Arthur confirmed. "There's going to be a power outage soon. May I come in to prevent the pending cut from doing irreparable and extraordinarily expensive damage to your electrical infrastructure?" he asked, and then added. "Sir?"

"I don't—"

"Not going to solve anything from the front porch, Sir. The longer we stand here, the greater chance that your wires will be toast after the power outage hits."

Robert's lips parted, then closed again, his head tilting to one side.

"Doesn't matter to me, Sir. I'm just here to make this as painless for you, the customer, as possible. Ultimately, it's your call."

"Do you have any identification?" Robert asked, eyeing Arthur.

Arthur pointed to the name on his coverall.

"Anything more official than that…Rocco?"

"Sir, do you honestly think I'd be standing out here on your front porch on a night like this—the cold rain soaking me in places that I didn't even know I had—if I wasn't here on official electrical business?"

Robert looked closer at Arthur, a glimmer of recognition in his eye.

"And it's a Friday night, sir. While that may not mean anything to a man of your age, Friday night is the beginning of a person my age's binge-drinking time. And yet, here I stand, wearing a coverall that has the name Rocco—which is not my real name, just in case you had some negative experiences with someone whose real name *was* Rocco who might also have been wearing coveralls like this—stitched over my heart, already almost soaked to the skin, hypothermia pending, trying to convince you to let me in to stop a disaster in your home from occurring. You do the math, sir."

Robert closed the door, unlocked the chain lock, and opened it wide for Arthur.

"On behalf of the city, sir, I thank you for your cooperation. Now, where is your fuse box, sir?"

Before Arthur could get in the door, Angus was up on the porch.

"Wait a minute," Robert said, eyeing Angus suspiciously. "Who's this?"

"This is the regional supervisor who is responsible for ensuring that the work of the team runs smoothly. As such, he performs spot checks on his employees. Sir. How'd I do, Boss?"

"Excellent," Angus said, trying to get into character, although which character he couldn't be sure. "Now, if you don't mind...?"

"Certainly," Robert said with a shrug as he showed them in.

"Leave it unlocked," Angus said a bit harsher than he intended. "In the event that the power outage occurs sooner than anticipated and we require additional...electrical people...to enter to assist us."

"Sure," Robert said. "Right this way."

"Shoes on or off?" Angus asked, noticing the shiny floors.

"On is fine," Robert said.

Before the three men could get to the basement door, the front door opened.

"Knock knock," The Old Bird said. "Anybody home?"

"Who is—"

"That's my supervisor," Angus said. "Making a...spot check."

"Everything in order, gentlemen?" she asked.

"We haven't even got downstairs yet," Arthur grimaced. "Couldn't you just wait a few minutes?"

"Well, you better pick up the pace, Rocky. Rain isn't letting up, and nobody's getting any drier out there," The Old Bird said. "Which is to say, that power cut's coming. You fellas go on downstairs to check on that fuse box, and I'll be on my way."

Rather than leave, however, The Old Bird waited by the door until the three of them went down the stairs.

"Coast is clear. Come on in," she said.

Mary-Margaret and Eleanor walked into the house, dripping wet.

"Might want to dry yourselves off before you go traipsing through the place," The Old Bird suggested.

"Good thinking," Eleanor said. "Any idea where the towels might be?"

"We don't have time for that!" Mary-Margaret exclaimed. "How long do ye think they're going to be able to keep Robert downstairs?"

Suddenly, the lights went out.

"Quick. Turn on yer flashlights," Mary-Margaret said.

"I don't have a flashlight," Eleanor replied.

"On yer phone. There's one on yer phone," Mary-Margaret said.

"I don't have my phone with me. You didn't say we'd need our phones," Eleanor said.

"Just follow Mary-Margaret," The Old Bird said. "I can hear them coming up the stairs."

"What if she's not upstairs?" Eleanor said as she followed her friend.

"It's after eleven, luv," Mary-Margaret whispered back. "Where else would she be? Come on. Stay close."

The Old Bird saw the glow of Arthur's phone light before she saw the three men emerge from the basement.

"Now what do we do?" Robert asked, squinting as Arthur swung the light toward him. "Would you mind shining that over here? I can't see—"

"Now!" Arthur shouted, turning the beam full into Robert's eyes and launching himself at him.

The Old Bird piled on, while Angus stood by.

"I thought we were going to wait to see if Annette was okay," Angus said as Arthur and The Old Bird rolled around on the ground with Robert.

"Roles were clear a couple of minutes ago, but I guess you missed the memo," The Old Bird said between gasps. "Hop on. Geez, you're a feisty one."

"Alright, then," Angus said with a grunt, nervously looking over the wrestling bodies as he tried to figure out how to get involved without getting hurt.

"Get. Off. Of. Me," Robert bellowed, continuing to flail about on the floor.

"Not until you tell us what you've done with Annette Giancola," Arthur said, his legs wrapped around Robert's neck.

"She's...not...here..." he said between gasps.

"She's not there!" Mary-Margaret yelled from the top of the stairs.

"What have you done with her, you jerkface?" The Old Bird said, giving him a punch in the head.

"I don't think name-calling is quite necessary," Angus said, still standing beside the melee.

"Get...off...of...me..." Robert demanded, his face turning a deep red.

"Not until you tell us where she is," Arthur said between gulps of air, sweat pouring down his face.

"She...went...to...a...hotel," Robert gasped, and then rolled violently enough to throw Arthur off of him. "Now get off of me, you goon."

Robert struggled to his feet and was about to take a swing at Arthur when there was a buzzing sound, and he collapsed to the floor like a sack of potatoes. He twitched for a few seconds until the buzzing sound ended.

"What was that?" Arthur asked, completely winded.

"Next level," The Old Bird said. "Don't move or I'll taze you again."

"Whoa," Arthur exclaimed, his eyes wide with admiration.

"Not my first rodeo, Artie. Now, everyone just step back and let's hear what Jerkface has to say. Go ahead. You've got the floor."

Arthur, The Old Bird, Angus, Eleanor, and Mary-Margaret stood around Robert in a circle, the beams from two iPhone flashlights shining on him, as he lay moaning on the floor.

"Well?" The Old Bird said.

"I think I've soiled myself," Robert whimpered.

Chapter Forty-Six

After Arthur had turned the electricity back on, Robert Jensen had cleaned himself up, and everyone had dried off as best they could, they all took a seat on the stools around the kitchen island. Robert suggested they move into the living room, but Eleanor didn't think it would be right to sit on such nice furniture with their damp clothes, so they stayed put.

"Can I offer anyone a drink?" Robert asked.

"How about a cuppa, MM?" Arthur suggested.

"I was thinking something a little stronger," Robert said, "but, if that's what you'd like, I'm sure—"

"I'll have a whiskey, if ye have any," Mary-Margaret said.

"I'm sure she's got some somewhere," Robert said as he opened one of the upper cupboards.

"Make that two more…doubles," Angus said.

"Oh, I don't think I could manage a—" Eleanor began.

Robert looked questioningly over his shoulder.

"Perhaps just bring the bottle down, luv," Mary-Margaret suggested.

"And a glass of milk. Warmed up, please," Arthur said.

Everyone stopped and stared at him.

"I know," Arthur said with a shrug. "I'm usually lactose intolerant, but, in cases of extreme physical activity and/or duress, warm milk is my go-to."

Once everyone had their drinks, the atmosphere changed again as the gang began firing questions at their host.

"Ye said she was at a hotel. Which one?"

"I don't know."

"The only reason a gal would leave a nice place like this is if she didn't feel safe," The Old Bird said, looking him over. "So, what's the deal? Why did you try to OD her the other night?"

"I didn't."

"If I were hiding out in a hotel," Eleanor considered, ignoring Robert's mild protest, "I wouldn't use my real name, so how are we going to figure out where she is if he doesn't know?"

"You stand to make an awful lot of money if you're the…sole survivor, if you will…of this tragedy, don't you?" Angus asked, his tone sharp with implication.

"I stand to make an awful lot of money as a result of Marco's untimely death, yes. But as far as anything to do with Annette—"

"So you and her *are* a thing," The Old Bird said, her eyebrows waggling mischievously.

"Do we still need to keep our flashlights on?" Arthur asked.

"No, luv. We've got the overheads now," Mary-Margaret said, giving his arm a gentle pat.

"I think it's time to call the police," Angus said.

"They've already spoken to me," Robert said. "Unless you want me to call them and have you all arrested."

"Well, wouldn't that just be the bee's knees," The Old Bird cawed, throwing her hands up. "You off your business partner, drug your lover, and we all end up in jail. Reminds me of Montreal, back in the day, touring with AC/DC—yeah, not my usual crowd, but hey, I needed the cash. Anyway, it was the *Back in Black* tour in '80, and Bon Scott—"

"I don't think—" Angus cut in, his sharp glare meant to silence her.

"Full circle moment, my friends," The Old Bird said with a nod, clearly having finished the rest of the story in her head. "So, if you didn't try to OD your girlfriend, who did?"

"She took those pills herself," Robert blurted out. "Honestly. I have no idea what happened or why, but, as you saw, she was passed out. Which is why I called 9-1-1 and why I was pushing to have her admitted for a full psychiatric evaluation."

"Occam's Razor," Arthur said.

"Wait a minute," The Old Bird said, her eyes narrowing as she looked at everyone around the island. "You don't mean to tell me that you're buying this crap, do you? Come on, people. He's a lying, scheming murderer."

"We don't know any of that for sure," Angus offered.

"We're going to need a bit more from ye to let ye go," Mary-Margaret said.

"Let me go?" Robert said, looking at the five of them sitting in Annette Giancola's kitchen with drinks in their hands.

"Indeed," Mary-Margaret said. "Ye see, me Michael, Detective Michael O'Shea, and his police colleagues have yer place surrounded on account of how ye murdered Marco—"

"That's ridiculous," Robert said.

"Is it?" Mary-Margaret prodded.

"I didn't see any police cars when we were coming over here, so it likely is," Eleanor whispered to Mary-Margaret.

"Not that part," Robert said. "The part about me murdering Marco. Why the heck would I want to murder him?"

"I can think of about a gazillion reasons why," Arthur said accusatorily.

"Not quite. More like seventeen million, if you're using the net value of the company as your reason. And falling fast."

"I would question that," Angus said. "The real estate alone—"

"As much as you might think the company just landed in my lap after Marco fell down for the last time—oh yes, I said that. The man was a fall-down drunk with a low tolerance for alcohol. This wasn't his first time getting found on the floor, but it was the last. Things had gotten so bad, I had him lined up for rehab, hoping to sober him up before he drank himself to death."

"Well, that's very noble of you, but—" Angus began.

"You seem like a smart guy," Robert said to him. "Maybe you can explain to your friends that it takes months—sometimes years—for a company to change hands. And while all that's going on, every creditor is calling in their loans. In the case of a franchise like Marco's Motors, that means the net revenue drops as those loans are paid off. Decreased net revenues, decreased gross revenues, and less money going out to the franchisees. A lot of them are trying to bail out while they still can. Which means Marco's Motors might have to declare bankruptcy before I become the sole owner."

"But the real estate—" Angus said.

"Markets a bit soft at the moment, and there's no indication that it's going to get any better for quite some time, and I can't sell out from under the franchisees, so, unless I'm going to murder them all…" Robert said, letting the words hang as he lifted his glass. "Anyone else care for another?"

"No thanks," Arthur said. "One glass of milk is okay. A second and I'm going to be spending the night sitting on the—"

"So if it wasn't ye, then who?" Mary-Margaret asked.

"Your guess is as good as mine, lady," Robert said, pouring himself another whiskey.

"Well, I suppose it's back to the drawing board, lads," she said with dismay.

"You are kidding, aren't you?" Angus said, his face starting to get red.

"It was an honest mistake, dear," Eleanor said, feeling her husband's anger.

"It's mistakes like this that get people hurt. Or sued," Angus shot back.

"We need to talk to Annette," Mary-Margaret said.

"Good luck," Robert said. "Now, it's been a busy night. Do you mind if I see you out?"

"One last question, Bobby," The Old Bird said, straightening up as they got ready to leave. "If Annette isn't here, what the heck are you doing here? Don't you have a much nicer house somewhere else?"

"I do, and this is where she wanted me to bring her when I picked her up at that bar—"

"Pub," Mary-Margaret interjected sharply. "It's a *pub*, not a bar."

"So why isn't she here, Bobby?" The Old Bird asked, clearly putting him on the spot.

"Like I said, she took off."

They all looked at him incredulously.

"I was just starting to warn her when—"

"Warn her?" Mary-Margaret demanded, her brow furrowing. "About what?"

"That someone is trying to kill her."

"I think we've already established that," Angus said, rubbing the back of his neck while looking Robert up and down.

"It's not me. It's Danny."

"I *told* you it was the owner," Arthur said, his voice dripping with the satisfaction of being right.

Chapter Forty-Seven

ary-Margaret woke up with a start. It had been a long time since she'd woken up in a strange bed, although that wasn't her first concern.

Where are the jacks?

She scanned the room quickly and then recognized it as Eleanor and Angus Corrigan's guest room.

But...?

And then it all came flooding back: she was there because she hadn't been able to go back to Michael's last night. He still thought she was in the ER at St. Joseph's Hospital. And she hadn't had the time or inclination to tell him otherwise. The logic behind *that* would have been far too complicated for her to try to unravel at any point in time, much less at midnight on a rainy Friday night.

So, here she was.

After she pulled on the clothes she had worn yesterday, went to the jacks, returned to the guest bedroom, and made the bed, she went downstairs where Eleanor and Angus were reading the newspaper and having their morning coffee.

"Smells wonderful in here," Mary-Margaret said, taking a deep breath of the fresh-baked muffins. "Ach, that's enough to tempt a saint off their fast."

"Well, if it isn't Sherlock Hopeless," Angus said, barely looking over his paper.

"Angus," Eleanor said quietly but firmly, shooting him a look before turning to Mary-Margaret. "Would you like a cup of coffee? Maybe a muffin to go with it? I hope you slept better than I did last night. All that excitement…I'm just not used to it, I guess."

"Like a lamb, thank ye," she said. "And I'd love a muffin. With a cuppa."

"Here you are," Eleanor said, passing Mary-Margaret the plate. "I've just baked these, and Angus hasn't managed to eat them all yet. Help yourself."

"How long are you going to hole up here?" Angus grumbled. He still did not bother to lower his paper.

"Angus!" Eleanor cried. "That's no way to—"

"Ach, 'tis alright, luv. He's got a right to ask. Honestly, Angus, I don't know."

Angus dropped the paper.

"Which is to say, I've got some running around to do this morning, so I'll likely give Michael a ring later this afternoon."

"Where are you going?" Eleanor asked as she got up to plug the kettle in. "Anywhere interesting?"

"We don't want to know," Angus said, going back to reading his paper.

"Well, maybe you don't, but I do," Eleanor said.

"I'm going to have a wee word with that Danny lad."

"Come on, Mary-Margaret. Let the police do their job," Angus said, pulling the newspaper down so that she could see the annoyance on his face.

"I would, if they could, but they obviously can't, so what else can I do? Let a murderer roam the streets?"

"I think that's a great idea, Mary-Margaret," Eleanor said warmly, placing a teabag in a mug. "Going to see Danny, I mean. Mind if I join you?"

"What?" Angus stated. "No. You're not going."

"Oh, really?" Eleanor said, recalling The Old Bird's words and her own newfound resolve. "And who, exactly, is going to stop me?"

"Come on, Eleanor. Be reasonable."

"There's no need," Mary-Margaret said. "Arthur will come with me."

"Well, there's a recipe for disaster," Angus said.

"I'm coming, too," Eleanor stated. "I don't suppose you have any interest in joining us, Angus?"

"No. I have none," he said, slamming the paper down on the table as he stood up. "I'll stay here and wait for your call from the police station. Let it be known right here and now that I'm only posting bail for one of you, and I think, Mary-Margaret, you can figure out which one it will be."

"I hope I haven't caused any trouble," Mary-Margaret said once Angus had stormed out of the kitchen.

"Oh, don't worry about him. You know how he is…doesn't like surprises, or anything that's different, or trying something new. He'll be fine." Eleanor unplugged the boiling kettle and poured the hot water over the tea bag in the waiting mug as she spoke. "And if push comes to shove—and I'm sure it won't—he'll bail us both out. No questions asked. Or, at least, very few."

"Do ye mind if I call Arthur before we leave and have him get in touch with Danny for us? I haven't a clue how to reach him, and Arthur's good at figuring these sorts of things out. Say what ye will, he's a good lad, is our Arthur."

* * *

Had she not known that Arthur would be waiting outside of his place for them, Mary-Margaret might not have recognized him. Instead of the paunchy man who wore whatever costume struck his fancy, Arthur was dressed in a tailored suit that downplayed his round midriff. And it was hard to tell if it was the pinky ring catching the sunlight or the gold watch on his right wrist. Then there was his hair—Mary-Margaret had never seen it so neat. Nor had she ever seen him stand so straight, except when he was Sister Augustine.

"I do apologize," he said with a smile, opening the passenger door. "But I'm afraid, Eleanor, I'll have to ask you to step out for just a moment. You see, I must take my rightful place in the back seat of the vehicle."

"Oh, no," Eleanor said with a soft, girlish giggle. "You sit in the front. You're much larger than I am."

"Absolutely not," he said, extending his hand out to her with a flourish. "And now, if you'll kindly excuse me, I'll just slip into this back seat."

She stepped aside as he squished himself into the back.

"Ye certainly clean up well," Mary-Margaret said.

"Not bad, eh?" he replied as he put his seatbelt on. "Ouch!"

"Sorry, Arthur," Eleanor said, shifting her seat forward just a touch. "Is that any better?"

"Marginally."

"She did offer to sit in the back, luv," Mary-Margaret said as she pulled away from the curb. "Now, I take it yer dressed like this for a reason?"

"Absolutely. You know," he said, "of all the clothing I own, I have to say that this suit is likely the most uncomfortable."

"Is that so?" Eleanor asked, turning around to give him another look. "Angus wears suits every day to work, and he never complains. Although, considering how *grumpy* he can be…well, maybe he needs to stop wearing suits."

"I don't think that's why. He likely gets his professionally tailored," Mary-Margaret said with a knowing glance. "I don't suppose yers is, is it, luv?"

"I didn't have time, MM. I had to do it myself, mostly with just safety pins, one of which I think has come undone. Ugh."

"So where are we headed?" Mary-Margaret asked.

"We're going to Yorkville," Arthur said, squirming around until he finally got the rogue pin back in line. "I mean, I'm going there. You two can go where you want. I'm going to the restaurant inside the Four Seasons Hotel."

"Oh, I know that restaurant. Angus and I went there once. Very nice. *Very* expensive. I didn't know it opened before—" Eleanor began.

"It doesn't," Arthur cut in. "They're opening specially for us."

"Us?" Mary-Margaret asked.

"Me and Danny. That's where we're going to have our meeting. Mano-a-mano. Hence the look."

"I'm not saying that ye couldn't make it so, lad, but how did ye pull this off and what happens if he—"

"Oh, he won't, MM. As far as he knows, he's meeting with Chad Chandlermeyer."

"Who is that and why is…?" Mary-Margaret asked, her voice trailing off as she began to doubt the viability of this cover.

"Chad Chandlermeyer. Son of Hartmut Chandlermeyer, founder of Chandlermeyer Developments—a German firm with substantial financial resources and holdings across the globe. I'm currently tasked with identifying new opportunities to expand our North American portfolio."

"And he's meeting with ye…?"

"To discuss the potential acquisition of one of his properties—specifically, the one where Marco's Motors is currently situated," he replied, now fully embracing the Chad Chandlermeyer persona, complete with a tone of voice dripping with a stuffy, pseudo-aristocratic accent.

"Oh, that sounds like a wonderful cover story," Eleanor exclaimed.

"That sounds like a cover story too easily proven wrong," Mary-Margaret muttered.

"MM, you underestimate me," Arthur said, passing an embossed business card, complete with contact numbers and a website address, up toward her.

"Luv, I appreciate what yer trying to do, but ye've made this very compli—" Mary-Margaret began, but before she could finish, Eleanor reached over and took the card from Arthur.

"Go ahead, Eleanor," Arthur said. "Call the 1-800 number."

Eleanor pulled out her phone and dialed.

Hallo. Sie haben die Büros von Chandlermeyer Developments erreicht. Für Deutsch, drücken Sie bitte eins. Für Mandarin, drücken Sie bitte zwei. Für Englisch, drücken Sie bitte drei.

"Oh! She sounds very…*German*. And quite *sexy*, if I do say so myself," Eleanor said with a slight smile.

"Press two," Arthur said.

Eleanor pressed two. She listened to the prompts in English and pressed five. A very warm male voice advised her to leave her number and a brief message, stating that Chad Chandlermeyer would get back to her within forty-eight hours.

Eleanor quickly hung up the phone and began to giggle.

"Now," Arthur said. "Check out the web address."

Eleanor typed it into her browser and, sure enough, a very impressive website for Chandlermeyer Developments popped up.

"Oh, this is good!" she said.

"See, MM. Nothing to worry about."

"Except the traffic," Mary-Margaret said, coming to a complete stop. "What time did ye say ye'd meet him at?"

"Ten."

"Well, we'll be lucky if we get there by ten-thirty. Best give him a call to let him know ye'll be late."

"Oh, no, MM," Arthur said, leaning back with all the dignity he could muster in the cramped seat. "He can simply call me to confirm the time. I certainly don't need to be bothered with the details."

They drove on, bantering back and forth about everything *except* Arthur's meeting with Danny. As Mary-Margaret had predicted, Daphne pulled up in front of the Four Seasons just after ten-thirty. A porter approached the car.

"He's in the back, luv. Other side," Mary-Margaret said.

The porter came around and opened the door. He extended his hand to help Eleanor out and then pulled the seat forward and offered his hand to Arthur, who, upon taking it, almost pulled the man into the car.

"I'm here for a private meeting. With Danny Caputo," Arthur advised the porter once they were all safely on the pavement.

"Ah. Yes. Mr. Caputo is waiting for you, sir. Follow me, please."

"I'll see you in an hour," the man who had become Chad Chandlermeyer said over his shoulder as he strode towards the doors, shoulders back, head held high.

"He does look the part, doesn't he?" Eleanor said when she'd gotten back in the car.

Before Mary-Margaret could answer, another porter was at her window.

"Is Madam waiting for the gentleman? Mr. Caputo will pay for parking if so."

"Oh, it would be *such* fun to do a little shopping around here, wouldn't it?" Eleanor exclaimed.

"As long as we don't buy anything," Mary-Margaret said, and then looked over at the porter. "That'd be grand, lad. Where would ye like me to park?"

"Oh, we'll take care of the car, Madam," he said, simultaneously opening her door and offering his hand.

Chapter Forty-Eight

"Mr. Chandlermeyer," Danny Caputo said, rising to his feet, arm outstretched.

"Chad. Just call me Chad, Danny," Arthur declared, his stuffy cadences touched with a hint of a German accent. "No need for such formalities now that we're face to face, hmm? Let's not stand on ceremony. And I do appreciate you making time at such short notice."

"Oh, sure. For a minute there, though, I thought you weren't gonna show," he said, letting out a nervous laugh as he shook Chad's hand vigorously, his sweaty grip a little too firm.

Chad did not crack a smile as he pulled his hand back.

"Which is to say, of course, I knew you were gonna be here. I was just…you know…kinda nervous, so it seemed like—"

"Tell me about the property," Chad interrupted, settling into his seat with exaggerated ease, as though his time were far too valuable for pleasantries.

"Right," Danny said, sitting down with much less flourish. "You want a coffee or something? Maybe a…?"

"Please," Chad said.

Danny waved the waiter over.

"A coffee for Mr. Chandlermeyer and could you bring my friend an apfelstrudel as well, please."

Chad raised an eyebrow.

"I read that it's your favourite," Danny said.

"Indeed," Chad said with a patronizing nod. "I *do* applaud you for your thoroughness. Not everyone is so…particular, you know."

"Well, it's not every day a guy like me sits down across from—"

"No, it's not," he interrupted, his voice flat. "Now, the property. Tell me."

"It's currently zoned as industrial commercial, which means—"

"I know what that means," Chad stated as he flashed a condescending smirk.

"Right. Of course you would. It's approximately forty-five hundred square feet—"

"So approximately four hundred and forty-five square metres," Chad murmured, looking just above Danny's head, as if the answer were written on the wall behind him.

"Yeah. That's it," Danny replied, beads of sweat starting to form on his forehead.

"Any contamination issues?"

"Uh, well, not really."

Chad cocked his head as the waiter set a cup of black coffee and a plate with an apfelstrudel down in front of him.

"Explain," Chad said.

"Well, uh, right now, it's being used as a, uh, mechanic's garage."

"So, there are contamination issues," Chad said, his brow furrowing in mock disbelief.

"How…inconvenient."

"Well, not really," Danny said, sweat rolling down his forehead.

"No matter," Chad said, waving a hand dismissively. "Any…history… involved?"

"Like, is it a designated site? No, not at all. You can do whatever you want—"

"No," Chad said, raising an eyebrow. "History. Like…violent criminal activity, perhaps? You know, something…homicidal."

"Uh…well…I'm not sure."

"You're not sure, or you don't want to tell me?" Chad asked, flashing a knowing smile.

"Well, it's kinda funny you bring that up, y'know, 'cause there's sorta this investigation going on at the garage right now."

"And you've got inside information you're wanting to share with me—information you haven't passed along to the police," Chad said, his voice smooth with a patronizing edge. "I'd expect nothing less, given the company's…interest in acquiring this property. So, Danny," he leaned in slightly, "what do you know?"

"Gee," Danny began, his nervousness palpable as Chad scratched his right ear. "Nothing's been determined, of course—I mean, in terms of it being, y'know, criminal. But the owner of the place was found dead inside a few days ago."

"And you think he was murdered?" Chad asked, raising an eyebrow.

"Well, I don't know—"

"But…?"

"I think his old lady did him in," Danny blurted out.

"Really. Interesting," Chad said, his voice dripping with feigned intrigue. "How…fascinating."

"Not really. Happens all the time over here. I'm sure it's the same in Germany."

"Whether it is or it isn't is immaterial," Chad said sharply. "I'm merely suggesting that it's interesting because the…old lady, did you call her? Yes. Mrs. Giancola seems to think you murdered her husband."

"Me? That's ridiculous. Why would I murder my tenant?"

"Oh, I don't know," Chad said, his voice laced with irritation. "Maybe so you and I could be sitting in this lovely restaurant early on a Saturday morning, discussing the possibility of my purchasing a property you wouldn't be able to sell unless it was about to become available?"

"Come on, Chad. You don't honestly think—"

"I don't think," Chad cut him off, annoyance barely hidden. "I know. I'm a businessman, like you. A good business opportunity like the one I'm offering doesn't come along very often." He paused, scanning the room. "Speaking of which, have you seen our waiter? I'd like another one of these coffees. They're really good."

"Of course," Danny replied, a hint of confusion creeping into his voice as he tried to process the sudden shift in Chad's demeanor. "Waiter?"

"Listen, Danny, let's be honest with each other," Chad said softly, tilting his head slightly to the right. "We've all made mistakes. We've all done things we're not proud of. How else do you think we got ahead? It's a tough world, and sometimes we…push the boundaries. You're not the only one who's, you know, maybe gone a little too far."

"I have no idea what you're talking about."

"You were right when you said a lot of things here are probably the same in Germany," Chad said, smiling almost patronizingly. "I wasn't always at the top of my game. Back in the day, I had some…well, let's just say, less-than-ideal properties. But unlike you, I knew how to turn them around. And now, here I am."

"But your father started the company," Danny said. "I'm sure you didn't have to—"

"*Strenge mit Liebe,*" Chad interrupted with a grin, raising an eyebrow. "It's like your *tough love*. Anyway, we've all had tenants who've driven us mad. So what do we do? We pay them a little visit. Have a little chat. Tell them how things are going to go. Maybe they don't like it. Maybe they start running their mouths. Maybe we've had enough of their lip. And maybe, just maybe, we grab a wrench, for example…and give them a little tap in the—"

"Hey, you got it all wrong there, Chad," Danny interjected, shaking his head. "Marco Giancola was a good guy. If he was murdered, it was the wife that did it. She's psycho."

Chad's brow furrowed, a flicker of disbelief crossing his face.

"Oh, she looks great, sure," Danny added, leaning in with a knowing look. "And now that she's a widow, she's playing the part like a pro. But don't be fooled. She had Marco running scared—scared, I tell ya."

"I heard he was a fall-down drunk," Chad said, leaning in slightly, dropping all pretense of an accent. His voice was now steely, with just a hint of gossipy malice. "Not exactly the kind of guy anyone would want to have around, eh? Especially the guy holding back your business plans."

"He was an ideal tenant. But her—sheesh. No wonder he drank like a fish," Danny said, rubbing his temples. "Poor guy was workin' himself to death while she was spendin' every dime he made. And then some."

"And that scared him?" Chad asked, his tone laced with thinly veiled skepticism.

"No more than it would scare any other guy. Her problem was that she knew too much."

"About...?"

"The business, the partner...I never met the guy. I negotiated the lease on that garage with Marco before this guy showed up. So this place isn't a part of the Marco's Motors franchise, as far as I know. Anyway, this guy—who doesn't know one end of a spark plug from the other—took the business from a small-time owner/operator setup to this massive chain. Where'd he get the cash to do that? You tell me. Not from Marco, that's for sure. I'm thinking he had some, uh, connections, if you know what I mean. And that was before he started with the crazy broad. And trust me, I know there was some pillow talk going on there."

"So why are your prints on the murder weapon?"

"Who told you that?" Danny said, jumping out of his seat, his voice rising. "I told the cops, and I'm tellin' you now—it wasn't me. It was her!"

"So why did she go to the police after they told her his death was an accident?"

"I don't know. Because she's crazy?" Danny said. "Because she wants to frame me? Because she wants to stick it to lover-boy? I don't know! For someone who wants to buy a property, you sure know a lot about what happened there the other day."

"I make it a point to stay informed," he replied, resuming the full Chad Chandlermeyer persona as he leaned forward. "Do you happen to know where this Annette Giancola woman is now?"

"No idea," Danny said, rising from his chair and beginning to pace. "All I know is we're supposed to meet at one today at the property. She said she's going to make me some sort of offer, and me, being the nice guy I am, figured I'd hear her out."

"I'm not liking what I'm hearing, Danny."

"What do you mean?"

"You thought you could play me, and I don't like that. Pitting me against the condo corporation eyeing the property—that I understand. But throwing this unstable woman into the mix? Come on, Danny. We are not amateurs, are we?"

"I—I didn't—" Danny stammered, but Chad cut him off.

"Maybe we can salvage our relationship. What if I come to that meeting with you?"

"I may not have to go if you make me an offer now," Danny countered.

"Ha!" Chad laughed, the sound sharp and mocking. "Chandlermeyer Developments is a massive operation. We don't 'make offers' on a first meet."

"Then I'm going to the meeting. Alone," Danny said, turning and storming away.

Chad took a slow sip of his coffee, savoring the moment, before reaching up to his ear and pressing a button on his Bluetooth earpiece to stop the recording.

"Will there be anything else…?" a waiter asked.

"No, thank you," Chad said, rising smoothly from the table. "Do be sure to tip yourself well when you add this to the junior associate's tab."

Chapter Forty-Nine

"Look what the cat dragged in," Angus said with disdain when he walked into the kitchen and saw Eleanor, Mary-Margaret, and Arthur sitting around the table. "Or should I say, look who my wife is cavorting with now. You clean up well, Arthur. Going corporate, are we?"

"Oh, Angus, you wouldn't believe the morning we've had!" Eleanor gushed, her voice bubbling with excitement.

"You're right there, my darling. And I don't think I want to know. Are they staying for lunch?"

"You haven't had lunch yet, Angus?" Eleanor asked, trying to mask her disappointment with Angus's response. "Well, maybe that's why you're in such a mood. Sugar levels dropping."

"No lunch for me, thanks," Arthur said as he uploaded the audio file he'd recorded on his earpiece to his iPhone files. "I've already had—"

"Hrumph," Angus grumbled as he turned to leave the kitchen.

"Done," Arthur said. "Listen to this."

"Ye might want to stay and have a listen, Angus," Mary-Margaret said. "Arthur tells us it was quite the convo."

"I'm already more involved in this mess than—" Angus began.

Mary-Margaret's cell phone rang. Under normal circumstances, she would have left it, but it might be Max. She did not check the call display.

"Hi, Mom."

"Oh. Hello, Michael."

"Where are you?"

"I'm at…in…the ER at St. Joe's me son. Where else would I be?"

"I don't know, but you're not here."

"Here?" she echoed.

"At St. Joe's."

"And ye know this how?"

"Because I'm here. In the ER. At St. Joe's. And I'm being told that you checked yourself out yesterday. Against the doctor's advice."

"Really?" Mary-Margaret replied. "Well, perhaps they've got me mixed up with another Mary-Marg—"

"Where are you, Mom?"

"Since ye must know," she said, her voice enveloped with a calmness that comes from years of prevarication, "I'm sitting right this moment at Eleanor and Angus Corrigan's kitchen table, aren't I, lads? Say hello to me Michael."

"Hello, Michael!' Eleanor called out and waved at the cell phone. Angus remained silent.

"Mom, this isn't a joke. You were brought into the ER yesterday by ambulance and—"

"Hello? Michael? Are ye there? Hello?" Mary-Margaret said and then tapped the phone several times.

"Mom," Michael replied with all the patience he could muster.

"Ach, yer breaking up, me son. Hello?"

"Mom!"

"I can't hear a word yer saying, me son. Bad connection. Or low battery. Yes, that's it. Forgot to recharge me phone. Going to lose the line soon. I'm alright. Thanks for c—" She clicked the phone off.

"Everything alright, Mary-Margaret?" Angus asked skeptically.

"Right as rain, luv. Just me Michael, checking in to see how we're all doing. Ye know how he is. Such a good lad, is me Michael."

Angus rolled his eyes and walked out of the kitchen.

"All set?" Arthur asked, poised to play the recording.

"I think we should be calling The Old Bird in for this," Mary-Margaret said, cell phone still in hand.

"No!" Arthur stated.

"It might not hurt," Eleanor suggested. "She did seem to have some good insights, and she's certainly invested in this now. Yes, why don't you give her a call, Mary-Margaret, while I put the kettle on and sort us some lunch? I know you said you weren't hungry, Arthur, but honestly, a tiny pastry isn't nearly enough to sustain you, is it? Yes, do give her a call, Mary-Margaret."

Arthur grumbled as Mary-Margaret made the call and Eleanor prepared lunch for four, knowing Angus's curiosity would draw him back into the kitchen sooner rather than later. They ate in an uneasy sort of way while they waited for The Old Bird to arrive. Mary-Margaret and Eleanor chatted about their children and grandchildren, deliberately avoiding any mention of the morning's events—well aware that it would only set Angus off. Arthur, meanwhile, sat in a funk, arms crossed and expression stormy after inhaling the sandwich placed in front of him, still annoyed that The Old Bird had been allowed to get involved at all. It wasn't until she finally arrived and he began playing the recording of his encounter with Danny Caputo that his mood began to lift.

"Oh, you were terrific, Arthur!" Eleanor exclaimed, her eyes twinkling. "If I didn't know better, you would have had me fooled, too."

Arthur beamed.

"One thing troubles me, though, lad," Mary-Margaret said, her lips pursed together. "How do we know his prints were found on the murder weapon?"

"Oh, we don't," Arthur said. "I just made that up. To see where it would go, you know? Maybe get a full confession out of him right then and there."

"You're playing with fire," Angus grumbled.

"Bold move, Artie. I like it," The Old Bird stated. "Would have been better if it had worked. But hey, don't beat yourself up. Even the pros miss a shot now and then. I remember it like it was yesterday. December 10th, 1977. Me and Sid, that rat, were at The Horseshoe, and The Viletones were doing their Christmas gig. Undercover cops everywhere—"

"What does this have to do with—" Angus interrupted

"Give me a sec, Grampa Grumble. Anyway, the place was rocking, and those sneaky pigs stuck out like sore thumbs. Not saying you did, Artie, but you get where I'm going with this—"

"Did he say he was meeting our girl at one?" Mary-Margaret said, looking at her watch. "Sorry, luv, didn't mean to cut ye off, but I think we'd best be on our way if we're wanting to have a wee talk with her as well."

"No worries, Mary-Margaret. I've got a million stories," The Old Bird squawked.

"And I bet we're going to hear every one of them," Angus muttered.

"So are we on our way then?" Eleanor asked. "Just leave the mess. I'll clean it up when—"

"You're not going anywhere, Eleanor," Angus said. "I think you've done quite enough already."

He pushed himself away from the table and walked out of the room.

"I don't like the sounds of that," The Old Bird said, her words cutting through the air like a sharp hiss. "Since when does any man—"

"Well, as I've said before," Eleanor said matter-of-factly, "He's not just any man. He's my husband. And I think I've pushed him as far as he can go for one day. Whye don't the three of you go ahead? I'll stay back, and you can tell me all about it later."

Chapter Fifty

"You get in the front, Artie," The Old Bird said, squeezing into the back seat of Mary-Margaret's car. She let out a little chuckle and shook her head as she settled into the back. "You know, the last time I sat in the back seat of a car was—well, maybe that's a story for after a few bottles of wine. Or, knowing *you*, Mary-Margaret, a few shots of whiskey, eh?"

Arthur gratefully slid into the passenger seat, while Mary-Margaret settled in behind the steering wheel and started the engine.

"What's the plan?" Mary-Margaret asked, glancing over at Arthur.

"I say we just run in and pound on that tricky little lady in mourning," The Old Bird said. "Reminds me of the time when—"

"I don't think that's going to work too well, luv," Mary-Margaret said, looking back at The Old Bird through the rearview mirror. "We need a confession."

"I've got it!" Arthur stated. "What if I, as Chad Chandlermeyer, go in as if I'm crashing the meeting. Maybe I decided that I wanted to acquire the property for the Chandlermeyer Developments portfolio, and so I go in there intending to strong-arm Danny into making a deal with me?"

"Brilliant, luv. But how are ye going to get a confession out of Annette?"

"I…don't know, but I've got my earpiece ready," Arthur offered weakly.

"I'm hearing some great brainstorming up there," The Old Bird said, "but here's the plan. I walk in cold, just some old broad looking to find a good mechanic in the neighborhood."

"But Annette knows you," Arthur said flatly.

"Ok, so I walk in not so cold," The Old Bird shot back. "Whether she knows me or not doesn't mean I can't be just an old broad looking for a decent mechanic, does it?"

"This isn't going to—"

"Sure, it will. No matter what, I'll have interrupted their meeting. Then, I snuggle up to Annie, do a little heart-to-heart, woman-to-woman kind of chatter, and the next thing you know, I've got her spilling her guts. You give me that ear thingy, Artie, and I get it all down on record. Meanwhile, you two stand by, and, when I give the signal, call the cops, and they swoop in and arrest her. Sound like a plan?"

"No," Arthur muttered, crossing his arms in front of himself. "I think we should—"

"It might work," Mary-Margaret offered.

"Well, should we give it a shot? We've got nothing to lose at this point, do we? Pass that ear thing back, Artie."

Mary-Margaret pulled the car around into the back lane behind Marco's Motors, intending on parking there while The Old Bird got a confession out of Annette Giancola. What she hadn't counted on, however, was that a police car was also parked in the back lane. Not an unmarked car that would suggest some sort of covert operation was in effect, but a marked scout car, parking almost exactly where Mary-Margaret had seen one parked when she first came to this laneway.

"No mind," said Mary-Margaret, pulling Daphne up right behind the scout car. "Just goes to show that Billy Gilly's no further along in his investigation than I thought. In fact, I might have actually given him more credit than was due."

"I don't think you can park—" Arthur began.

"I'm not seeing any signs saying ye can't in the laneway, are ye?" Mary-Margaret said, pulling up the parking brake.

"Quick question," The Old Bird said, raising an eyebrow. "How the heck am I supposed to signal if you're parked back here? I mean, no offense, but I don't think you've got a clear shot to the office from these back windows. Or am I wrong?"

"I've got an idea," Arthur said, pulling a couple of things out of his pocket. He passed one of them back to The Old Bird. "Here. Take this. I almost forgot I had it in these pockets. Wait. Is it charged up? Ooo! Yep. Sure is."

"Wait a minute, Artie," The Old Bird said with a smirk as she took it from him. "This isn't the kind of tool I had in mind for this job."

"What is it?" Mary-Margaret asked.

"It's a little…device I use when I'm…oh, never mind," Arthur said, his face reddening. He turned his attention back to The Old Bird. "Just press this when you're ready, and I'll leave the other piece here on the dashboard, and it'll vibrate when you—"

"I'm sure it will. You're an interesting little man, Artie," The Old Bird said. "But whatever. Okay. Let me out, my friend. I'm goin' in."

Chapter Fifty-One

"Hey, what's an old broad gotta do to get some attention over here?" The Old Bird hollered as she banged on the front door of Marco's Motors.

"We're closed," a short, heavy-set man wearing a black pork pie hat yelled through the glass.

"Well, get open!" she yelled back.

"CLOSED!" he repeated, eyes bulging.

"OPEN!" she yelled back.

"Listen, lady," the man said as he opened the door just enough to push his pudgy face out. "We're closed. Can't you read the sign?"

"Yeah, I can read, sweetheart," The Old Bird shot back. "But you're here now, so how about you let me in? I just wanna book a time to get my car looked at. Well, it's not *mine*, but it's a car. You want my business or what?"

"I don't," he said.

He tried to slam the door shut, but The Old Bird's foot was between it and the doorframe.

"What are you?" he said, looking down at her foot. "A cop?"

"Do I look like a frigging cop to you?" The Old Bird shot back. She leaned slightly and placed her hands on her hips. "Come on, you think they'd hire someone like me? But since you're puttin' it out there, you got somethin' to hide?"

"No, I don't. Now, move your foot before I—"

"What, tough guy? Gonna step on my toes now?" The Old Bird said, narrowing her eyes. "Listen, pal, I used to be in the music biz—down in the trenches. I know all about foot pain. So, what's it gonna be? You lettin' me in or not?"

"Let her in," a very bored voice came from the office.

"Oh, I see how it is," The Old Bird said, peeking around him. She gave a nod and a light grin. "You got yourself a woman in here, huh? Nice. Is that the kind of business you're runnin'? Ain't what I heard. I just moved into the neighbourhood, and everyone told me to check out Marco's Motors, but if you're that kinda guy—"

"What do you want?" the woman said, emerging from the office. "Wait— wait. You're the…that friend of Mary-Margaret's, aren't you?"

"Yeah, that's me. And sorry for your loss, Annie," The Old Bird said, not missing a beat. "I was just telling your buddy here, I need a mechanic. Figured now that your old man's, you know, six feet under, you'd be wanting to rake in all the business you can, you know? Gotta cover all of those costs, right? Death isn't cheap, or so they say. Me? I'm divorced. Well, not *exactly*. Me and Sid the Rat weren't legally married. But hey, might as well have been. Until he dumped me. Right after the last song of Bowie's *Serious Moonlight* concert. I still get a lump in my throat every time I hear that track…*I'm just a kid, and I'm lonely…*"

She wiped her nose on the back of her hand.

"Maybe you should come in," the man said with a shrug. "I've been there. I know how that feels."

"Thanks," The Old Bird said, shaking her head. "Holy crap, man. Had no idea how much pain I'm still holding onto." She paused, looking a little dazed. "You mind if I grab a glass of water or somethin'?" She let out a sigh, then shoved her hand out. "Oh, and I'm…well, they call me The Old Bird."

"Pleased to meet you. I'm Danny. And, well, you know Annette, apparently."

"Sorry again, Annie," The Old Bird said, shaking Annette's hand.

"So you want to make an appointment. Let me just get the computer fired up," Danny said. "Annette, you got any idea how this thing works?"

"It's Marco's Motors, not Annette's Autos," she said with a smirk.

"Now that," The Old Bird said, slapping her knee with a grin, "was funny.

And to think your husband just died…how long ago was it…?"

"A little over a week ago."

"And you're already yukkin' it up. Wow. You are one tough broad," The Old Bird said with a whoop. "Either that, or you killed him and couldn't give a crap!"

Danny looked nervously at Annette, who stared blankly at The Old Bird.

"Either way, ha-ha, she's a funny one," Danny quickly added.

"So, what's next, Annie?" The Old Bird asked, leaning in with a grin. "Gonna sell up? Move somewhere warm? Or maybe rebrand as *Annette's Autos*?"

"That's what Danny and I were just discussing."

"Oh. So it's you two who are a thing," The Old Bird said, her eyes widening.

"H-hardly," Danny hastily stated. "I'm the owner of the building."

"Nice," The Old Bird said, eyes scanning the empty bays. "Looks like you've got a buildin', she's got a business, and you're both…available, more or less. Jeez, this is a match made in heaven!"

"In fact," Annette said, "I was just suggesting to Danny that he might like to sell me this building."

"So what's holding you back, my man?" The Old Bird said, leaning in. "Maybe this is your chance to relax. Go somewhere warm. Lie on a beach. Drink those fruity drinks with the little umbrellas in them."

"Naw," he said with a sad smile. "Not quite my thing."

"You might not have an option if you don't act quickly," Annette said, her tone turning sharper, the air between them growing heavier.

"Whoa. That sounded like a threat," The Old Bird said, raising an eyebrow. "Listen, maybe I should just come back tomorrow. You open around nine? I could do nine," she said. She slipped her hand into her pocket to press the device Arthur had given her to activate the vibrator that should be on the dashboard of Mary-Margaret's car.

"Yeah. What do you mean by that?" Danny said to Annette.

Annette smiled, but it was more of a sneer, her eyes cold and dangerous.

"Come on," Danny goaded. "Say it. We got a witness here, so say it. If you've got anything to say."

"You guys are intense," The Old Bird said, taking a step back, her hand finding the device again and giving it another little press. "I think I'll—"

"Okay, I will," Annette said, her jaw tightening, looking over at The Old Bird. "Danny killed my husband."

"You know, every day's full of surprises," The Old Bird said, glancing toward the front of the garage. "My Aunt Zelda used to say that. You wake up, think your day's gonna go one way, and *blamo*—next thing you know, you're in a garage, listenin' to someone accuse someone else of murder. Full of surprises."

"Don't listen to her," Danny said, his voice rising loudly, his face flushing with anger. "I didn't kill nobody."

"Anybody," The Old Bird corrected, wagging her finger for emphasis. "'I didn't kill anybody.' I'm a high school secretary by day, just picked up bartendin' at the pub around the corner at night. You two should drop by sometime. I'll spot you a drink. Once you get your little differences sorted out, of course."

"You had motive and opportunity," Annette said, her tone cold, almost calculating.

"So did you," Danny shot back, his eyes narrowing. "And you found him."

"Wow. That must've been something, eh?" The Old Bird said, holding the button down on the device in her pocket. "I've never found a dead body before, although I did think Greg was dead that time I found him in his apartment in '83." She paused, her brow furrowing slightly. "Turns out it was just a drug overdose, and he lived—though it was a real turning point for him. Got him to reevaluate the role heavy drugs played in his lifestyle. But yeah. He wasn't dead, so…not quite the same thing. Wow."

Chapter Fifty-Two

"You don't happen to have anything to eat with you, do you?" Arthur asked.

"We just ate, luv," Mary-Margaret said, looking over at him. "But check the glove box. I'm sure I've got some McVitie's in there."

Arthur opened the glove box and removed a baggie full of biscuits.

"A cuppa would go well with this," he said as he pulled a handful out. "Want any?"

"No thanks, luv. I'm trying to watch me figure."

"Good for you, MM."

"What? Are ye saying I need to?"

"Oh. No. Not at all," Arthur quickly said. "It's just, you know, I'm glad to hear you're taking care of your health."

"Well, I've got to, don't I, especially given how much me Michael needs me. Speaking of which, I wonder who's been taking care of Wee Phil while I've been gone. I don't suppose it would occur to Michael to take the dog out. Max would do it, though. Never mind."

The two sat in silence, staring at the police car ahead of them.

"You know, come to think of it, I *could* use a cuppa. And one of those biscuits, too, so don't eat them all. Wait right where ye are, luv, while I go and ask one of the lads up there to get us both one."

"Can you ask them to pick me up a bagel, too, please? Only if they're going to Tim's. If they're going anywhere else, never mind."

"Will do," Mary-Margaret said.

She got out of her car and walked the few steps up to the driver's window of the police car parked in front of them.

"Excuse me," she said, tapping on the closed window.

The officer inside jumped and then lowered the window.

"Ach, sorry to startle ye, luv, but I've a favour to ask. I'm Mary-Margaret O'Shea, Michael O'Shea's mother. He's a detective, as ye probably know. Anyway, me and me friend, Arthur, are parked behind ye for a bit, and we were wondering if ye wouldn't mind going to get us both a cup of tea. I take mine with just milk while Arthur—"

"I'm sorry," the officer said. "I can't do that."

"Ye can't, or ye won't?"

"I…can't."

"I see," Mary-Margaret said and thought for a moment. "Well, can ye get on yer radio there and call for someone else to pick us up a cuppa? I wouldn't ask if it wasn't important. Oh, and Arthur's asked me to tell ye that, if yer going to Tim's, to also pick up—"

"Ma'am, I'm guarding a crime scene," the officer said.

"And a fine job yer doing, luv. But, since we're also here, ye could pop away for a few minutes and perhaps pick yerself up something while yer at it."

"Who did you say you were?"

"I'm Mary-Margaret O'Shea."

"So, you're not related to this investigation in any way."

"Well, that's a matter of interpretation. Which is to say, if ye ask the lad in charge of it, then no, but if ye ask anyone who knows me, then yes. Now, are ye going to get us that cuppa or not?"

"Sergeant Tanaka to P.C. De Almeida," a woman's voice came over the radio.

"P.C. De Almeida," the officer said after picking up the microphone, relieved to have a reason to stop engaging with Mary-Margaret.

"I'm just around the corner and wondering if you need a couple of minutes' relief."

"Yes, I do, Sarge," the officer said, looking up at Mary-Margaret.

"Okay. Dispatcher, mark me off at the crime scene for a few."

"Well, isn't that just grand?" Mary-Margaret said with a grin. She stuffed a ten-dollar bill in the breast pocket of the officer's uniform. "This should cover things. And be sure to pick yerself up something while yer at it."

"I can't—" the officer began, but it was too late. Mary-Margaret was already almost back at her car.

"Well?" Arthur said when she got back in the car.

"Lovely lad, that P.C. De Almeida. His sergeant is popping by so he can get us our tea."

"Did you ask about the bagel? But only if he's going to Tim's."

"I started to, luv, but got interupted."

"That's okay, I guess," Arthur said.

"Are ye sure, luv? Ye look a little—"

"No, it's the jacket. It's kind of uncomfortable."

"Why not just take it off, then? No sense being uncomfortable if ye don't have to be."

Arthur began to get the jacket off, which proved to be more of a performance than he'd anticipated. With a bit of help from Mary-Margaret, however, he was soon much more comfortable.

The two then sat and watched as Sergeant Tanaka pulled up in front of P.C. De Almeida's scout car. They watched P.C. De Almeida get out and walk over to Sergeant Tanaka's car, point back at them, return to his own car, and drive off. They then watched as Sergeant Tanaka backed her car into the spot left by P.C. De Almeida's car, directly in front of their own. What neither of them had noticed was that, likely in the process of removing Arthur's jacket, the vibrator—their only line of communication with The Old Bird—had been knocked off the dashboard, onto the floor, and had rolled beneath Arthur's seat.

Chapter Fifty-Three

"I did find him," Annette said, her jaw clenched. "And he was quite dead."

"Of course he was," Danny shouted. "Because you killed him."

"He was quite stiff when I found him, which tells me he had been dead for a while."

"Did you know that before watching *CSI*, or after?" The Old Bird asked, tapping her chin. "It's wild how much forensic stuff we all seem to know now, isn't it? I can't help but wonder if we would've figured it all out on our own, or if—" She trailed off, trying not to look too obvious as she strained to see if anyone was coming towards the front of the garage.

"Because you killed him earlier," Danny blurted out, his voice getting louder. "That's how you knew when to come looking for him."

"That's ridiculous," Annette snapped, her face tight with anger.

"Oh yeah? I'm sure the cops got you on the security tapes here coming and going the night you reported him missing."

"Really? Do you honestly think—"

"Yikes. He might have you there, Annie."

"If they have me coming and going on the night I reported him missing, then they also have you coming and going after me," Annette replied.

"Pass the popcorn," The Old Bird said with a cackle. "This is better than Netflix."

"But they don't, do they?" she said, leaning in, her eyes cold and unblinking. "And why do you think that is?"

"Because I wasn't here," Danny said, his jaw clenched, a flicker of frustration creeping into his voice. "Why would I just randomly drop by a property I own in the middle of the night?"

"To off the guy who worked here and was stopping you from selling this joint for a gazillion bucks and living your best life?" The Old Bird offered.

"Because the video machine was turned off that night," Annette spat.

"Oh! Good one," The Old Bird said, eyes wide with surprise. "Did not see that coming."

"How do you know?" Danny asked, the colour draining from his face, his voice a little too thin.

"Because otherwise," she replied with a razor-edged smile. "They'd have video of me coming to the shop that night."

"Ho-ly!" The Old Bird exclaimed with a low whistle. "So you *did* kill him. I had my money on Dann-o, no offence."

"None taken," he replied.

"I didn't mean to. Or," she said, flashing a tight, almost amused smile, "Maybe I did. Doesn't really matter now, does it? The end result is the same."

"I knew you were a psycho," Danny spat, his eyes narrowing. "I always said, never trust a woman with perfectly plucked eyebrows."

"Oh yeah," The Old Bird said, looking closely at Annette's face. "They are perfect. Good call, Danny. But why did you kill him, Annie? There is such a thing as divorce, you know."

"I gave him a push."

"And that did him in?" The Old Bird asked, not convinced. "One little push and then—lights out?"

"And then I gave him a kick."

"Getting there," The Old Bird said with a slow nod.

"And then I picked up one of those wrenches that he kept just over there."

"Ouch. That's gotta hurt."

"And then—"

"Okay. We get it. You killed him," The Old Bird said with a shudder. "Sheesh."

"Why are you telling us all of this, Annette?" Danny asked.

"Because I'm…what did you call me…psycho?"

"Yeah, but—" he began.

Annette pulled a small handgun from her coat pocket.

"A gun. Great. She's got a gun," The Old Bird said, staring out the front windows of the garage before letting out a long, exasperated sigh and turning back to face Annette. "Haven't seen one of those since Iggy Pop, Sid the Rat, and I went out for drinks after the show in 1980. Scared the crap outta me when he whipped it out. Kinda like you're scaring the crap outta me right now. What, exactly, are you planning to do with it, Annie?"

"I'm going to kill you both."

"Wait a minute, Annette," Danny said, his voice trembling. "Let's be reasonable."

"I can't be, can I, because I'm a…psycho."

"But you never explained why," The Old Bird said, her voice surprisingly calm. "If I'm gonna die, I'd at least like to know why you offed your husband. For real. None of that 'because I'm a psycho' crap."

"Alright," she began.

"Mind if I sit down somewhere?" The Old Bird said, looking around the shop.

"Here," Danny said, pulling a chair out of the office for The Old Bird.

"Thanks, Dann-o. You're a real gentleman," she said, wincing as she lowered herself onto a chair. "I got a bad knee on account of Iggy. Nothing to do with the gun. It was those darned mosh pits. He loved 'em. Every show. Anyway, let's just say I got dropped a few times, and ever since then…well, I can tell you when it's gonna rain before you even get your phone unlocked to check the app. Okay, Annie, spill."

"Marco was a drunk.'

"That's half the guys I ever dated," The Old Bird said with a shrug.

"He owed a lot of money."

"See above comment."

"And he didn't make any secret about his…philandering ways."

"Geez, maybe I dated him at some point. You don't have any pictures of him hanging around, do you?"

Annette gave The Old Bird a cold stare.

"I'm not helping myself any, am I?" The Old Bird said.

"No. Not at all," Annette said.

"Okay, so," The Old Bird continued, looking unimpressed. "Your old man's a dog. So what?"

"And then I met Robert."

"So all the more reason to leave that good-for-nothing," The Old Bird said with a nod. "If it was me rather than Sid the Rat who had a side piece—"

"And he made Marco and I very rich."

"I'm not following."

"Let her speak," Danny exclaimed.

"The longer we stall, the longer we live," The Old Bird whispered to him, giving him a pointed look. "Not the brightest bulb in the box, are you?"

"But he was a dog, too," Annette continued.

"Listen, Annie," The Old Bird said with a slight laugh. "You seem like a clever girl, and I would have thought that you would have figured out that all men are dogs…no offence, Dann-o."

"None taken."

"And I also found out a few things about how this business was run. For example," she said, looking directly at Danny, "I understand that, if Marco died, you could take immediate possession of this building."

"Not could—do," Danny replied. "And it's not an unusual clause."

"Except that this Marco's Motors, in this garage, is the only one I had any claim to. And what good is a business without a building?"

"What's the point of murdering a guy if the kill doesn't stand to profit, you mean?" The Old Bird chirped. "Sounds to me like your dearly departed was worth a whole lot more to you alive than dead, Annie. So, offing him? Probably not your most strategic financial move."

"You don't know the half of it," Annette lamented.

"I'm all ears, doll," The Old Bird said.

"I was supposed to get half of the profits of the entire business if anything happened to Marco."

"Well done," The Old Bird said. "So why kill the two of us?"

"Do you have to remind her?" Danny asked, shooting The Old Bird a terrified look.

"And then I was supposed to get double the insurance money if Marco's death was a murder."

"I'm hearing a lot of 'supposed tos' here, Annie, so I'm taking it that there's a problem."

"Robert's not going to give me anything," Annette said.

"But a deal's a deal. He signed over—" Danny began.

"He's going to sell Marco's Motors," Annette said with a sigh. "And it's just a matter of time before the insurance company thinks I killed Marco."

"But you did," Danny said. Now it was The Old Bird's turn to glare at Danny. "What? She just told us she—"

"Hang on, let's see if we can figure this out," The Old Bird said, holding up a hand. "You were supposed to get half the profits from the whole business if Marco died, unless it got sold, in which case there aren't any profits. And then, you were supposed to get double the insurance payout if Marco was murdered—unless, of course, you're the one who did the murdering. Is that about right?"

"In a nutshell, yes," Annette said.

"And now you think offing me and Dann-o here is gonna...what? Convince the guy to keep the business? Change the insurance company's mind about you killing your husband? Which, by the way, is gonna make no big-picture difference when it'll be pretty darn obvious that you killed us. Come on, Annie. Work with me here."

"I have, as you've suggested, nothing to lose. So why wouldn't I?" she asked.

"That's all you've got?"

"Yes."

"Well, since you've been so honest with me and Dann-o, I'll be honest with you," The Old Bird said, raising her hands slightly. "You're not gonna kill me, because here's the thing: I am a cop. And if you kill a cop, Annie, you go to jail for life. So, how about we put the gun down and talk this through?"

"I knew it!" Danny said, clapping his hands together.

"Settle down over there, Dann-o. We're not out of the woods yet," The Old Bird said, leaning back and crossing her arms. "See, I've got your whole confession on tape, so you're toast as far as getting done for killing Marco. And threatening to kill me and Dann-o over here. But here's the thing: my backup seems to be sleeping at the wheel, and I'm running out of ways to keep you talking—and frankly, I really have to use the washroom. Which reminds me—those exercises they tell you to do when you're younger? Do them. You, too, Dann-o. Trust me. I even think about laughing, and I'm peeing my pants. So, what's it gonna be, Annie? And don't even think about turning that gun on yourself, because with your luck, you'll probably just end up hurting yourself enough to spend the rest of your life blinking to spell things out."

"I knew you were a cop," Danny exclaimed, clapping his hands again.

"Is that like a nervous twitch thing for you, Dann-o?"

"I'm a very excitable guy," he said, pulling his hands down to his side.

"So, Annie, give me your gun," The Old Bird said.

Annette didn't move.

"Just give me your gun, and we're done, here, Annie," The Old Bird said, slowly getting up from her chair. "Otherwise, somebody's going to be wiping pee up off the floor, and it's not going to be pleasant for anyone. Let's wrap this up. It's almost home time."

The Old Bird reached out and, to everyone's surprise, took the gun from Annette.

"Dann-o, how about you make yourself useful and call 9-1-1," The Old Bird said. "Now, Annie, aside from being a cold-blooded killer and probably as crazy as a bag of hammers, you seem like a fairly dignified person. So, how about you take my seat over here and just relax until the cops show up. Or I could grab some of that duct tape over there and tape you to the chair. Your choice."

"I'll…sit," she said.

"Good choice. While you don't exactly light up the night," The Old Bird said, giving her a once-over, "You might not actually be the dimmest streetlight on the block."

"Thank you."

"Cops said they're on their way," Danny said, putting his cell phone back in his pocket.

"Good. You might want to unlock the front door," The Old Bird said. "Otherwise, they'll just smash it in. Reminds me of the time Neil Young was in town. Sure, the cops got the wrong address, but when we were talking about it later, I said, 'Neil, just unlock the door so they can get in next time.' Anyway, hurry up because I have to go pee, and we can't just leave Annie here alone."

Chapter Fifty-Four

"Ta, luv, and did ye get something for yerself?" Mary-Margaret asked as P.C. De Almeida handed two cups of tea through the car window, along with the ten-dollar bill she'd pressed into his pocket. "Ach, no. Ye picked it up—least I can do is pay for it."

"They give it to us for free," P.C. De Almeida said.

"As they should," Mary-Margaret said with a nod. "Now, do ye think ye'll be parked here long?"

P.C. De Almeida looked a little closer at her.

"Not that it matters much to us, does it, Arthur?" Mary-Margaret quickly continued. "We're just here 'til our friend's done with what she's doing. But I'd wager it's not much fun for the likes of ye, eh? Young lad like yerself, probably rather be out there wrestling criminals to the ground, I'd imagine, no?"

"I…I have to get back to my car, Ma'am," the young officer said. He turned quickly and scurried away.

"No bagel for me," Arthur said, snapping the lid off the cup.

"I suppose not. Sorry about that, luv," Mary-Margaret said, taking the lid off her cup and having a sip. "Oh my, that's hot—though, as me mam would say, 'Ye'd be hot, too, if ye were just off the boil.'"

The two sat in silence, sipping their tea, watching P.C. De Almeida's head bobbing as he talked on his phone, waiting for The Old Bird to give them the signal.

"How's Teaszy?" Arthur asked.

"Fine, as far as I know. Why do ye ask, luv?"

"I don't know. Haven't heard you talk about her for a while."

"Not much to say. She's doing well, boys are well. Paulie's back with that lad—"

"Griffin?"

"Yes. That's the one. Nice lad. I'm not too fussy on all the tattoos and whatnot, but it's none of me business. Seems like a good match for Paulie. Better match than Allan is for Teaszy."

"But they've been married forever, haven't they?"

"Sure, but that doesn't mean anything. Ye can be married and miserable, ye know."

"Are they?"

"Likely. Though who knows, really. Allan's probably unemployed and sleeping on the couch for all they tell me."

"Ugh. Sleeping on the couch. That's rough."

"I take it ye've done yer share of sleeping on couches, then?"

"Oh yes. But those days are behind me now, thanks to you getting me in as Father Miguel's executive assistant."

"About that, luv—"

"You don't think he'll fire me just because I ran off with the gurney Annette Giancola was on and helped her escape, do you?"

"Well, when ye put it like that, it sounds likely, but, if ye put it another way—"

"I sure hope he doesn't. I kind of like him."

Mary-Margaret glared at her friend.

"Seriously, MM. He's not half bad."

"Father, forgive me for what I'm about to say—" she muttered.

"I think maybe you two just got off on the wrong foot."

"Wrong something, that's for sure."

"Okay. So he can be a bit condescending, and a bit pompous, and a bit self-centred, but, aside from that, he's just a guy doing his job."

"Well, I'm glad you see it like that," Mary-Margaret said.

They were silent again, both lost in their own worlds, oblivious to the faint humming coming from underneath Arthur's seat.

"Does Michael know you checked yourself out of the hospital yesterday?"

"It's hard to say what Michael knows and doesn't know, really."

"He knows, doesn't he?"

"Yes."

"Mad?"

"Likely," Mary-Margaret said with a nod.

"What are you going to do? I mean, he's still a little annoyed because of the last few things—"

"Annoyed?" Mary-Margaret scoffed. "He should be thanking his lucky stars that I…we…got involved in those other murders. Speaking of which," Mary-Margaret said, glancing at her watch, "It's been a while. I wonder what's taking The Old Bird so long. That device of yers not vibrated yet?"

"Nope," Arthur said, his voice flat. He glanced absently at the empty dashboard—then froze, his eyes widening as a surge of panic ran through him.

"What is it, luv?"

Arthur reached under the seat, his fingers fumbling around until they brushed against something vibrating wildly.

"MM! The Old Bird needs us," he said, holding the vibrator up. "And it's warm, so that means she's been buzzing us for a while."

"Jesus, Mary, and Joseph, Arthur. I'll go get P.C. De Al—"

"No. It'd take too long to explain, and we don't have the time. We need to go in alone."

Chapter Fifty-Five

It could be argued that emptying her bladder was a perfectly reasonable course of action. It could equally be argued, however, that The Old Bird had made what could have been an unfortunate, if not fatal, decision. Regardless, she was certainly startled when she returned from the washroom to find Annette and Danny standing side by side, staring at her. And she was even more startled to see that one of them was now holding the gun she'd carelessly left behind—and was aiming it directly at her.

"Holy crap!" The Old Bird screeched, her eyes wide. "You two are just *full* of surprises, aren't you? Reminds me of that time back—"

"Enough with the war stories already!" Danny shouted.

"Sheesh," The Old Bird muttered, shaking her head. "I was just trying to let you know that I don't scare easily, especially by guys like you. If I'd been that way inclined, hanging out with Marianne Faithfull would've been the death of me."

Annette and Danny looked at one another.

"Poor choice of words?" The Old Bird asked, raising an eyebrow. "Anyway, I take it all back. All that stuff about you—*both* of you—not being the brightest—"

"You know we're going to kill you, don't you?" Annette asked.

"Yeah. I kinda figured that was where we were headed," The Old Bird said with a slow nod.

Bam! Bam! Bam!

"What was that?" Annette asked, looking over at Danny.

"Someone's at the front door."

"Guess I'm not the only one who can't read the sign," The Old Bird said with a laugh.

"Well, answer it. And get rid of them," Annette ordered. "Whoever it is can likely see us in here. Hopefully, they didn't see the gun."

"Oh no," Danny mumbled as he approached. "It's Chad Chandlermeyer."

"Who?"

"The guy—never mind. Just get her into the office and close the door."

"Chad," Danny said brightly as he opened the door. "I wasn't expecting to see you—"

"Well, seems I've been called back to Germany for…matters of *considerable importance*," he said, his hand waving dismissively through the air as he breezed past Danny. "I've had a change of heart, as is my only flaw, and thought it best to wrap things up before my departure."

"Yes, but I'm not—" Danny began. He tried not to look at the closed office door as he tried to figure out what to do next.

"Is anything wrong, Danny?" Chad asked, raising an eyebrow.

"No. Nothing. I…I just wasn't expecting to see you here. So soon. Right now."

"That's Chandlermeyer Developments, Danny," Chad said. "We always do the unexpected. It's what sets us apart from the rest." He gave a small, self-satisfied smile, then turned his gaze pointedly to the closed office door. "Now, where may we sit?"

"Uh…"

"Unless, of course, you no longer wish to sell the property?"

"No. I mean…sure. Come in."

Chad pushed past Danny towards the office.

"Uh. Wait," Danny said, a catch of panic in his voice.

Chad paused for a moment.

"It's, uh…occupied."

"Then get it…*un-occupied*," Chad stated. He glanced at his watch. "I must get back to Germany as quickly as possible, and don't wish to delay the take-off of my private jet."

"Yeah. Of course not. It's just that—"

Without waiting, Chad opened the door to the office. Annette's back was to him, hiding the gun she was holding to The Old Bird.

"Ah," Chad said, his eyes narrowing with feigned amusement. "I see you're entertaining some ladies. How…charming." He gave a smug smile and then addressed the women with an exaggerated politeness. "Perhaps, ladies, you could *excuse* us, so that we can finish up some…*important* business."

"Sure," The Old Bird said, stepping past Annette. "I'm good to go."

Annette fumbled, having nowhere to hide the gun.

"A very…serious…meeting," Chad said, his eyes glancing quickly at the gun in Annette's hand as The Old Bird rushed out of the office. "Is this the way business is usually done in this country, or am I missing something?"

"You look very familiar," Annette said, eyes narrowing. "Your face…I've seen it before."

"I have a very generic look, sadly," Chad said with a slight smile. He glanced at the gun in Annette's hand, his expression unbothered but his tone sharp. "Now, are you planning to hold on to that gun, or are you going to put it away?"

"Sorry, Chad," Danny said as he came into the office and grabbed the gun from Annette. "My…friend, here, is uh—"

"Wait a minute. Do you know this guy?" Annette asked.

"My…other friend," Danny stammered, shoving the gun in a desk drawer as he looked towards Chad, "is, uh—"

"I've come to buy this building, *mein dummes Mädchen*," Chad said with a slow smile. "Oh, my mistake," he added with a feigned, charming laugh. "Perhaps I shouldn't be discussing business with this…*friend* of yours, Danny."

"Purchase the building? That wasn't in our plan," Annette said, looking over at Danny.

"Well, we didn't exactly *have* a plan—"

"Oh yes, we did, you idiot."

"I am seeing some disagreement fermenting. Perhaps you aren't as certain as you thought you were, Danny?" Chad said. "Although why you feel the need to confer with this *Schlampe* is beyond me, so, if you'll excuse us, madam…?"

"Danny?" Annette said, looking expectantly at him.

"Uh, hang on a minute. May I speak with you out there, Annette?" Danny said, grabbing her arm as he led her out of the office.

"Well, fancy meeting the two of yiz here," Mary-Margaret said as Danny and Annette stepped back into the garage.

"You!" Danny said.

"You," Annette said.

"And…you?" Danny said, seeing The Old Bird beside Mary-Margaret.

"Where did you say that duct tape was, Dann-o?" The Old Bird said, as Arthur stepped out of the office, gun in hand. "Careful where you point that thing, Artie. Don't want to shoot either of us by accident. Reminds me of that time with Ozzy at the Royal York in 1982. It got written up as a misfire, but still…nobody needs that."

"*Arthur?*" Danny said with an unmistakable look of betrayal on his face. "You mean you're not Chad Chandlermeyer from Chandlermeyer—"

"See, MM? Once again, I have gone undetected. Until…now."

"You mean Chandlermeyer Developments isn't going to buy this dump?"

"You were going to sell up from under me?" Annette said, disbelief and hatred flashing in her eyes.

"Under you? Come on, Annie," The Old Bird said as she rummaged around for the duct tape. "He already told you he had the rights to the place. What part did you miss?"

"Ach, luv," Mary-Margaret said. "It's always about the money, isn't it?"

"Can you help a girl out here, Dann-o, and give me a clue about the tape?"

"You can only shoot one of us at a time," Annette said to Arthur. "Pick one because the other one's going to get away."

Before anyone could move, Annette shoved Danny towards Arthur and pushed past Mary-Margaret. She rushed through the front door of Marco's Motors, right into the arms of P.C. De Almeida, who quickly handcuffed her and led her away.

Left on their own, Mary-Margaret hit Danny in the back of the head with her purse, the contents of which were weighty enough to cause him to fall to the ground.

"Good move, Mary-Margaret," The Old Bird said. "Not that I don't think you could have held him at bay, Artie."

"I absolutely could have," Arthur said, pointing the gun down at Danny.

"Please don't shoot me!" Danny cried.

"I've never held a gun before," Arthur remarked, his finger gently resting on the trigger. "There's something…oddly empowering about it."

They could hear sirens getting louder in the background.

"Pass it to me, luv," Mary-Margaret said. "There's no need for anyone to go to jail who shouldn't be. Danny, luv. Hold up yer right hand and no horsing around."

Danny held up his right hand as Mary-Margaret took the gun from Arthur. She took Danny's hand and wrapped it around the handle of the gun.

"Now, hold on to this."

Danny held the gun, arm still raised.

"Grand. Now, don't move."

Mary-Margaret, Arthur, and The Old Bird stood over Danny while the sound of the siren got louder.

"Just relax yer arm, luv," Mary-Margaret said, holding his arm up, gun still in his hand. "If I knew it was going to take them this long to get here, I would have waited."

"Everyone! Put your hands up!" a male voice yelled into the garage.

"'Tis alright, lad," Mary-Margaret said. "No need to get yer knickers in a knot. Everything's under control."

No sooner had Mary-Margaret got the words out than five uniformed officers stormed the garage, guns drawn.

When they saw the well-dressed man and two older women—one of whom was holding the wrist of the man on the floor, who had a gun—they stopped.

"Well, now that yer all here," Mary-Margaret said, and then directed her voice to Danny, "ye can give me the gun now, luv." She took the gun from him and held it up from one of the police officers to take. "Here ye go, lads. Mind yerselves. No one wants to get shot."

The more senior of the uniformed officers quickly stepped forward and snatched the gun from Mary-Margaret's hand and passed it off to another officer who was behind him. Another officer quickly handcuffed Danny.

"All in order," the more senior officer said into his radio. "One under arrest."

"They're over there, Detective," P.C. De Almeida could be heard from outside.

"What have you got...*Mom?*" Michael said, his voice tight with disbelief. His eyes narrowed as he took in the sight of her—his mother—standing in the middle of a gun take-down.

"Ach, it's good to see ye, luv," Mary-Margaret said casually, well aware that he was struggling to suppress a mix of shock and frustration that, if not properly managed, could easily make things much worse for her. "I was just wondering if ye'd been remembering to take Wee Phil out since I've been—"

"In the ER at St. Joe's, waiting to get some tests done?" Michael enquired.

"Well, clearly I'm not, but the wee pup still needs taking care of."

"I could have done that," Arthur offered.

"No ye couldn't, luv," Mary-Margaret said. "Ye were with me, remember?"

"Right. Sorry. It's been...a big day," Arthur said, slinking past Michael.

"Don't go too far," Michael said. "You'll need to give a statement."

"Well, that's me, then," The Old Bird said with a nod. "Can I hitch a ride home with you, Mary-Margaret?"

"Actually, all three of you will have to come to the station to do a video statement," Michael said.

"Oh, I don't do videos," Arthur said, arching his back. "I'm not at all photogenic, and videos make me look—"

"Bob said the same thing when music videos first came out. But he looked okay on *Jokerman*," The Old Bird said with a shrug. "Come on, Artie. Let's give 'em what they wanna see."

Chapter Fifty-Six

"It 'ought ye had forgotten me," Frank said, brightening when he saw Mary-Margaret walk through the door at O'Leary's.

"Ach, Francis," she replied. "I could never forget ye!"

His face dropped when he saw Arthur and The Old Bird follow her inside.

"Don't mind me, Frankie," The Old Bird said with a wink. "I'm just going to borrow your gal for a quick debrief, and then I'm behind the bar. Notice I said 'behind the bar,' not behind bars. Last thing I need. Leona would have my head if that happened. Although, now that I think about it, I'm not sure what she'd think of me moonlighting in a pub."

"Make it quick, if you don't mind, Old Bird," Johnny called out from the bar. "I'd like to get upstairs to say goodnight to Nolan before it gets too late."

"I've got your back, John-o!"

"Come on, lads, let's find a table," Mary-Margaret said.

"What can I get everyone?" Frank asked after a moment's hesitation. "I know what ye want, Mary-Margaret, but what about t' rest of yiz?"

"A quick shot of whiskey'll do me if I'm on bar duty," The Old Bird said.

"Oh, alcohol doesn't agree with me," Arthur began. "I break out in hives and then—"

"A ginger ale, then?" Frank said, cutting him off.

"Sure," Arthur muttered, shoulders slumping as he followed Mary-Margaret and The Old Bird to a table.

A few moments later, Frank joined them at the table, drinks in hand.

"Now," he said, passing them around, "Here's to yiz and all t'ems what wish t'ey were!"

"Sláinte," Mary-Margaret said, raising her glass and taking a sip of her crown float.

"The lot o' ye look like a clowder o' cats t'at swallowed a flock o' birds," Frank said. "So tell me what mischief have yiz have been up to."

"It was The Old Bird that carried the day today," Mary-Margaret said, glancing at her friend.

"Hardly," Arthur muttered.

"Well, I'm not going to lie," The Old Bird said, her eyes flicking down to her empty shot glass as she dove right into the story. "I was starting to wonder what took you two so long to come in after me."

"Oh, that was my fault," Arthur said. "As you know, I did a quick tailoring job on that jacket I wore earlier for that crucial piece of investigative work that led us to the actual murderer. And it was a perfect alteration—so long as I was standing. Or, at least, not cramped up in a car. But sitting in that car—front seat or not, nothing against Daphne, of course—for any length of time isn't exactly comfortable for a guy of my size, especially when I'm wearing a jacket like that."

"Arthur, yer a fine lad and all, but I'm not getting any younger," Frank said. "Can ye cut to t' chase?"

Everyone smiled, except Arthur.

"What he's trying to say is that he knocked—" Mary-Margaret began.

"*We* knocked," Arthur corrected.

"We knocked the vibrator—"

"T' what?"

"The vibrator, Francis. We knocked the vibrator under the seat, so we didn't get yer signal, luv."

"Yikes!" The Old Bird said. "So how'd you know things were going seriously south?"

"Well, we figured something must be up since ye were gone so long," Mary-Margaret said.

"I'm glad you got there when you did," The Old Bird said, shaking her head. "I thought Annie was going to cap me. She's got more than a few broken toys rattling around in her attic, that one."

"She had a gun?" Frank exclaimed.

"Ach, it was just a small one," Mary-Margaret replied, as if the whole thing was hardly worth a second thought.

"But still—"

"'Twas nothing," Mary-Margaret said.

"And yet ye thought she was innocent from the get-go, luv. That's not like ye," Frank said.

"I let me guard down, lads," she said, looking around the table. "It felt personal to me. Seeing her in there with Father Miguel, arranging her husband's funeral. I sat in that very chair across from Father Richard, arranging me Jimmy's funeral, God rest his soul."

Both she and Frank crossed themselves while Arthur and The Old Bird briefly bowed their heads.

"It brought it all back," she concluded.

"First rule of being a PI, MM: don't let it get personal," Arthur said.

"But we're not PIs, are we? We're just following up on these murders that seem to be happening wherever we go. It's not like we go out looking for them, is it?"

They all nodded in agreement.

"So if she did it," Frank asked, "Why didn't she just leave well enough alone? Why call yiz in?"

"God only knows," Mary-Margaret said.

"Almost done?" Johnny called from the bar.

"Just a sec, John-o," The Old Bird called back, holding up a finger before turning back to her friends. "The part I don't get is why she ended up back in the shop. It doesn't add up."

"Well, duh," Arthur muttered, flicking a dismissive glance toward The Old Bird. "Danny wanted to sell the building. Marco didn't. With Marco dead, the building was his to sell."

"And," Mary-Margaret added, her tone a little softer, "if he sold it, Annette would have no business."

"So she thought that by arranging a meeting and then showing up with a gun, she could…what?" The Old Bird said, arching an eyebrow. "Scare

Dann-o into not selling the building to the highest bidder? As if he was ever going to hold onto the property to run the place with that whack-job."

"Old Bird?" Johnny called again. "Sorry to interrupt, but—"

"I'm on it," she replied. "Okay, kids. Gotta go. Good work, Artie. You too, Mary-Margaret."

"I've got to go, too," Arthur said, standing. "It's been a long day, and I just want to get out of these clothes."

"Alright, luv. Do ye need a lift home?" Mary-Margaret asked.

"No. I'm fine."

Mary-Margaret and Frank watched Arthur leave.

"I know it's not my business, luv," Frank began, his voice low, cautious. "But about t'is gun…"

"Do ye see a gun now, Francis?"

"No."

"Then there's no need to talk about it," Mary-Margaret said firmly.

Her purse began to pulsate.

"Sorry, luv," she muttered, reaching into her bag with a sigh. "It might be Max." She glanced at the screen.

Unknown Number.

"Do ye have to get it?" Frank asked.

"No. Don't worry, luv," she said, shoving the phone back into her purse. "I suspect it's only Michael, and if it's truly important, he'll call again. Now, tell me all about yer week. It seems like forever since we've had a good chin wag."

"Aye, it does, doesn't it," Frank said with a warm smile.

As the two settled into their usual Saturday evening banter, Mary-Margaret let the phone dance away in her purse, ignoring it completely. She was far more interested in listening to Frank ramble on about absolutely nothing, and for a brief moment, everything felt just right. This was about as much excitement as she was willing to take—for now.

About the Author

Desmond P. Ryan spent thirty years as a Toronto Police detective, and now he channels that experience into writing—*amongst other things*—cozy mysteries with heart, humour, and a healthy dose of realism. From routine investigations to high-stakes cases, Desmond's time in policing gave him a front-row seat to the quirks of human nature—and it shows in his stories. His characters are richly drawn, his settings grounded in the rhythms of urban life, and his plots carry just enough grit to keep things interesting. Whether it's a nosy amateur sleuth or a seasoned investigator, Desmond brings compassion, wit, and authenticity to every page, with a touch of humour that keeps readers coming back for more.

AUTHOR WEBSITE:
  http://realdesmondryan.com

SOCIAL MEDIA HANDLES:
  Facebook: https://www.facebook.com/DesmondPRyan/
  Insta: DesmondPRyan
  TikTok: RealDesmondRyan

Also by Desmond P. Ryan

A Pint of Trouble Series

Mary-Margaret and The Case of The Lapsed Parishioner (Book 1)

Mary-Margaret and The Case of The Thieving Barmaid (Book 2)

The Mike O'Shea Series

10-33 Assist PC (Book 1)

Death Before Coffee (Book 2)

Man at the Door (Book 3)

Blind Spot (Book 4)

Dangerous Assumptions (Book 5)